MURDER AT THE BEACH

Bouchercon Anthology 2014

MURDER AT THE BEACH

Bouchercon Anthology 2014

EDITED BY
DANA CAMERON

DOWN&OUT
BOOKS

Down & Out Books
3959 Van Dyke Rd, Ste. 265
Lutz, FL 33558
www.DownAndOutBooks.com

Cover design by Bill Cameron

ISBN: 1937-4958-0-9

ISBN-13: 978-1-937495-80-0

To all librarians, everywhere.
Thanks!

CONTENTS

CONTENTS

Introduction
Dana Cameron

For me, Bouchercon is homecoming for crime writers. Every fall, everyone returns from all over the world to celebrate crime fiction, both the writing and the reading of it. For established authors, it's a chance to reunite with friends, trade ideas, and get recharged about the genre and the work. For new writers, it's about jumping into the deep end of the pool, finding your footing, and becoming a part of the community. For readers—and remember, that's all of us, writers and non-writers, alike—it's an opportunity to go running down the smörgåsbord of crime fiction—from traditional mystery to noir to thriller to cross-genre blends— and sample a little bit of everything. B'con is a giddy long weekend of talking mystery and suspense and partying—and hopefully, no bonfires. And no arrests. Or murders.

What's wonderful about Bouchercon is also what I hope you'll find is wonderful about this collection of stories. *Murder at the Beach* is the theme, and you know there's plenty of scope for murder and various forms of mayhem when roughly half the world's population lives within sixty kilometers of a coastline. Sure, the population density increases the possibilities for crime, but it's more than just statistics. Piracy, smuggling, and the alluring notion of slipping into a boat and making a quick getaway by dark tell us that, throughout history, coastlines, oceans, rivers, and lakes have had their own special brand of lawlessness.

The nifty thing is that the theme of this anthology is broad and no two stories take the same approach: They reflect the big tent that is crime fiction. In the contributions from several of our Bouchercon 2014 Guests of Honor, we have stories that turn their sights on the writing life, and sometimes, not coincidently, Bouchercon itself. Lifetime Achievement Honoree Jeffery Deaver describes the seamier side of conventions—and the amount of study that every student of crime and crime fiction must undertake—in "The Writer's Conference." International Guest of Honor Edward Marston gives us "Murder Weapon," a tale of success, obsession, and an unexpected form of self-defense on the south coast of Devon. Our Fan Guest of Honor, Al Abramson, responds to the common question, "How can you do such terrible things to your characters?" with "My Victim's Killer," where he looks for motives the Long Beach honorees' characters might have for doing away with their authors.

The other stories are as varied as their watery settings. For example, it's always bad news when crooks collide. "Honeymoon Sweet," by Craig Faustus Buck, considers some of the complexities of newly-married life for a pair of honeymooning criminals who haven't made it to the big leagues—yet. And in "Man in the Middle," by Ray Daniel, a hacker/fisher reels in more trouble than he expects at Revere Beach in Massachusetts. Two of the stories that fall into this category feature professional hitmen. Roger Angle's "The Hit-Man" is about a father—with some extraordinary skills—coming to the rescue of his shop-owner daughter in Venice, California. Tanis Mallow's tale of two killers for hire combines danger and sexual obsession on the Florida coast in "Nightshade."

And then there are the ordinary folks, getting tangled up in nasty business. "Marlowe's Wake" and "On Pacific Beach" describe some of the trials of parents living—and perhaps dying—on the fringes of society. Phillip Depoy takes us half a world—and four hundred fifty years—away to the troubled times and Elizabethan intrigues of 16th-century Canterbury, while Patricia Abbott's story is of a woman worrying about her homeless mother while a serial killer stalks southern California. Judith Cutler's "Life's a Beach" is about a proposed beach party at an English country manor—more, it is a moral about getting everything you want in a high-flying lifestyle—and then wanting just a little more.

Portland, Oregon is famous for its characters, and Bill Cameron demonstrates this in "Daisy and the Desperado," where an aspiring police detective has to deal with feuding neighbors with a long history of exchanging accusations and various...projectiles.

The unreliable nature of human observation—what you think you saw, what you could have *sworn* you saw—is a staple of crime fiction. In Sharon Fiffer's "The Sand Fairies," the elderly beach-goer/narrator believes she's observing the ordinary drama of a fractured family—or is it something much, much darker? And "The Haunted Room" by Gigi Pandian features the battle between logic, magic, and mysterious happenings in a storied house in San Francisco.

Two of our contributors address the complexities that arise when cultures come into conflict. The aftermath of a tsunami in Japan washes up evidence from a murder on a Washington state shore, more than complicating life for the police and the rest of the community in "Tsunami Surprise" by Delaney Green. Sacrifices, swamp traditions, and gangsters make for a bad combination in Hugh Wilson's "Rounder Jon."

One traditional element of Bouchercon is the craft and research panels, designed to inspire and inform aspiring and experienced writers. This year, Bouchercon Long Beach, in addition to supporting the Long Beach Public Library Foundation, is also supporting WriteGirl. WriteGirl is a creative writing and mentoring non-profit for teen girls in Los Angeles dedicated to promoting creativity and self-expression. I am delighted to include WriteGirl Krista Nave in this collection, with her story about the complications of identity and the human heart in "The Gum Shoe Actor."

This project could not have occurred without the contributions of many people. Big thanks are due to Ingrid Willis, the 2014 Bouchercon Convention Chair, Janet Reid of FinePrint Literary Management, and Eric Campbell of Down & Out Books. The anonymous first readers took on a most important job as did Janet Rogerson, who handled the incoming mail. And from me, a note of thanks to everyone who submitted a story as well as our final contributors (especially our busy Guests of Honor).

So now, stretch out under the umbrella, dig your toes into the sand, or sit on the storm wall. Listen for the foghorns and buoys that warn of danger as you enjoy these stories.

Murder Weapon
Edward Marston

She knew that he'd find her one day. He always did. It was only a question of time. On the last occasion when she'd made a run for it, he tracked her down within a week. The one person to whom Selina had given the new address was her literary agent, Melanie Fry, a woman with a reputation for protecting her clients at all costs. When Selina's husband had failed to bully the information out of Melanie, he hired someone to break into the agent's home to secure details of his wife's whereabouts. Nothing could be proved, of course. But when Jake turned up unexpectedly on her doorstep with a complacent grin on his face, Selina guessed what must have happened.

Once again, she'd been dragged back home.

It was ironic. Selina Wyman had achieved fame as the author of a string of romantic novels featuring beleaguered heroines who were eventually liberated by the love of a good man. On the fly-leaf of each book was a photograph of Selena with her husband, projecting an image of marital bliss. To the naked eye, it appeared that she'd wed a handsome, wealthy, supportive man who revelled in her success and, during speaking engagements, Selina contributed to the myth by acknowledging the huge debt she owed to Jake for the way he'd encouraged her career.

In fact, he'd taken pains to stifle her urge to write because it was something he couldn't control. Jake Wyman was a leading property developer and his wife was just one more item in his portfolio. During their courtship, he'd been affectionate, obliging and utterly charming. Once they were married, however, he'd dictated her life in every way. Things Selina had desperately wanted—children, friends of her own choice, visits to theatre and opera, the chance to play tennis regularly—were denied her. In their place were endless meetings with potential business associates Jake was cultivating. Selina had nothing whatsoever in common with them, still less with their pampered, acquisitive, braying wives. Jake ruled the roost. He determined what they ate, what they wore, where they took their holidays, when and how they made love.

His domination was complete. She was his.

Writing had been her escape. Enraged to discover that she'd written a novel in secret, his anger cooled when it joined the best-seller list. A celebrity wife was an asset he could exploit. Because Selina gained him valuable publicity, he made sure they were always photographed together at public events. Since her husband handled their joint finances, however, fame brought her no independence. She was a woman with a substantial income she was unable to spend.

Selina had to break free.

'What did you find?' he demanded.

'Mrs Wyman spent three weeks living in Scarborough.'

'What the hell was she doing up in Yorkshire?'

'She rented a cottage in the name of Mary Winchcombe,' said the man. 'That's what put me onto her, you see. Mary Winchcombe is the name of the heroine in her latest novel.'

'Don't mention those damn books to me!' growled Jake Wyman. 'They're at the root of the trouble. I should never have let her write them.'

'My wife enjoys them. Maggie says they're very good.'

'I'm not interested in your wife, Dowling. I just want you to find mine. Where did she go when she left Scarborough?'

George Dowling shifted his feet uneasily. 'I'm working on that, sir.'

He was the third private detective hired to locate Selina and he'd seemed to be more alert and resourceful than his predecessors. Unlike them, he picked up a scent that took him to Yorkshire but the trail had ended there. Jake was disappointed. When his wife fled, he usually recaptured her within a relatively short time. It was annoying to think she'd now been at liberty for several months.

'Her agent is behind this,' he snarled. 'My wife couldn't possibly have done this by herself. She needed help. Melanie Fry planned everything.' He made a graphic gesture with both hands. 'I could strangle that interfering old bat.'

'Have you tried bugging the agent's phone?'

'Yes—but it didn't work. She's too canny to give anything away. I had the place burgled again but there wasn't a single reference to my wife in her files.'

'Women can be clever devils,' said Dowling.

He was a short, slight, deferential man in his thirties with hair combed forward to disguise its dwindling presence on his head. Jake, by contrast, was a big, fleshy man in his fifties with a flowing white mane and an intimidating air of prosperity. Accustomed to get his own way, whatever it took, he was deeply frustrated by the situation he found himself in. His tone was peremptory.

'Find her, Dowling. Get out there now and find her!'

It had taken months to work out the details and Selina had relied heavily on the advice of her agent. Melanie had pointed out that it would be difficult for such a well-known author to fly the coop. Any one of her legion of fans would recognise her at once. A disguise was needed. Selina had therefore dyed her hair and changed the style dramatically. Carefully-applied cosmetics added another level of disguise and thick horn-rimmed eyeglasses transformed her appearance completely. A new wardrobe was also vital. Because he was fifteen years older than her, Jake had always made her wear clothes that aged her, turning her into a rather dowdy, matronly figure. Bright new dresses and smart casual wear took well over a decade off her. By adopting a different posture and a brisker gait, she was able to banish the familiar portrait of Selina Wyman altogether. She'd been reborn.

Money—that was the key to it all. Hitherto, every penny she earned was sent to her husband. Because of his financial acumen, she'd been happy at first to let him take care of her income. Jake had insisted on seeing her contracts so he knew exactly how big her advances were. But he reckoned without the guile of a literary agent. Melanie Fry sent him duplicate contracts for a smaller amount than Selina was actually paid. The real contract was sent to the publisher. When the cheque went to Melanie, she simply subtracted the amount Jake was expecting and held back the rest for her client. The money was paid into a separate account created by Melanie and accessible to her client. For the first time in her life, Selina could spend the fruit of her labours as she chose. She was free, rich and very happy.

But it couldn't last indefinitely. She accepted that. No matter how long it took, Jake would find her in the end and she had to be ready for that eventuality. In the past, he'd browbeaten her into returning home. The last time, he'd resorted to physical violence and punished her even more brutally in the bedroom. It would never happen again. She'd promised herself. Living alone had toughened her to the point where she would do anything to avoid the tortured existence of being Mrs Wyman. If he came for her, she was prepared to fight back. The weaponry was all there. She had a revolver, a shotgun, an axe, a meat cleaver, an array of knives and a series of blunt instruments scattered throughout the cottage. Wherever she went, there was a means of defence. Best of all, she had Rex, a loyal, well-trained Alsatian who provided companionship and reassurance. Anyone who threatened her would have to cope with a dog that wouldn't hesitate to attack.

Selina had threatened him with divorce a number of times but had lacked the will to carry it through. Her husband had an unlikely ally in Melanie Fry. The agent had fostered the image of a contented author in a happy-ever-after marriage and she feared its destruction might affect book sales adversely. Some fans would be sympathetic but others might well feel Selina Wyman was a quintessential hypocrite, pretending for years to be the Woman Who Had It All while, in reality, being under the thumb of a tyrannical husband. There was an even stronger reason why she could not press for divorce. Jake had warned her that, if she did so, he'd have her killed. His threats were never idle.

Her absence was easily explained. Since they'd lived in a mansion set in an estate, they had no immediate neighbours. Nor did she have any real family. Her parents had both died and there were no siblings to whom Selina could turn. Anyone who enquired after her could be told she was on one of her extended book tours abroad or was resting at their holiday hideaway in Mustique. While she was being hunted by private detectives, Selina felt confident of keeping one step ahead of them. If news of her disappearance had been splashed across the national media, however, the whole country would be on the lookout for her and she'd be doomed. As it was, she could please herself for once. Confident in her disguise, she didn't have to live in splendid isolation. She could watch a film, see a play, visit a museum, linger in the library or indulge herself with a shopping spree. Nobody would have the slightest clue that she was a famous author with guaranteed best-seller status.

Selina was in paradise—for the time being.

On his previous visit to the Wyman mansion, George Dowling had come back more or less empty-handed. He was in a buoyant mood now. There was a spring in his step and he had the smirk of a man expecting thanks and congratulation. Jake sensed the breakthrough had at last come. He showed the detective into the library, a large, well-proportioned room in which the great masters of literature took second place to the accumulated novels of Selina Wyman, Queen of Romance.

'You found her?' asked Jake.

'I think so.'

'Where is she?'

'Don't rush me, sir. Let me tell you how I went about it.'

'I just want the result.'

'Then you'll have to be patient,' said Dowling, determined not to be robbed of his moment in the spotlight. 'I've worked long and hard on your behalf, Mr Wyman.'

'That's what I pay you for.'

'Well, I'm ready to claim the bonus you promised.'

'I'll be the judge of that,' snapped Jake. 'If this turns out to be another blind alley, I'll kick you out of here without another penny and find someone better.'

Dowling was indignant. 'There is nobody better.'

'Prove it.'

'You had to sack the people you employed before me. They never even got a whiff of your wife. I was on to her at once.' Seeing the look in Jake's eyes, he went on quickly. 'The agent gave her away,' he said. 'I reasoned that sooner or later she'd meet Mrs Wyman face to face. All I had to do was to wait and watch. Melanie Fry is a cunning old bag. In case she was being followed, she changed trains three times to shake off pursuit. But she was no match for me. I stuck to her like a limpet—except she didn't see or feel me, of course. I was Melanie Fry's shadow.'

'Where did she go?'

'She went to Exeter.'

'Did she meet my wife?'

'No, sir,' replied Dowling. 'First of all, she called on another of her clients, a woman who writes mysteries under the pseudonym of A.J. Hillier. Her real name is quite different. According to her neighbour, the books are crap but they're the kind of crap that sells. Anyway,' he added with a sniff, 'most people would have thought they'd reached the end of the line. Literary agent visits client—nothing suspicious there. But I've got a second sense where these things are concerned, you see. It felt like a deliberate ruse to me. So I bought a cup of coffee in the bar opposite and bided my time. Eventually, out she came. After a good look round to make sure nobody was watching her, she walked back to the railway station to fulfil the real purpose of her visit. I caught the same train.'

'Where did it take you?'

'There's a little coastal village, thirty miles south. Melanie Fry walked to a cottage near the shore. A woman let her in and they talked for hours.' He thrust out his chest. 'I've reason to believe the woman in question was Mrs Wyman.'

'What's she calling herself this time?'

'Enid Goodband—that's what they told me in the pub,

anyway.

Jake was livid. 'My mother's maiden name was Enid Goodband,' he said, eyes ablaze. 'How dare she? That's a terrible thing to do.'

'At least, it proves it must be her,' said Dowling. 'Nobody else could have come up with a name like that. On the other hand, Mrs Wyman—or Goodband, as they all know her— doesn't look anything like the photos you showed me. That's what put doubts in my mind at first. Maybe I'd got the wrong person. Then I saw the way she said goodbye to her agent. They were like conspirators, hugging each other and grinning stupidly because they believed they'd got away with it. That's when I knew for certain I'd hit the jackpot. It was Mrs Wyman, as large as life.' He took out his mobile phone and clicked it a few times. A gallery of photographs came into view. 'There she is, sir.'

Taking the phone from him, Jake studied the woman embracing Melanie Fry. At first glance, she didn't look anything like his wife. Closer examination, however, revealed a clear resemblance. The woman was younger, slimmer and more attractive than Selina but it was undoubtedly her. Jake felt a sudden lurch. He now had to ask a question that had tormented him ever since she'd fled. In running away from him, had his wife been running towards another man?

'Does she live alone?' he asked.

'No, sir.'

Jake's heart sank. 'There's someone else in the cottage?'

'Yes,' said Dowling, 'there's this bleeding great Alsatian.'

Freedom had had a remarkable effect on Selina. She felt younger and fitter than she'd ever been. She ran along the beach every morning and swam daily in the sea. She exuded a sense of good health. Deprived by Jake of her chance to play tennis, she atoned by inventing her own variation of the game, using her racquet to hit the ball hard along the wet sand so that Rex could charge off to retrieve it. They spent hours playing together. It made Selina feel truly alive. Her new-found vitality was reflected in her work. Her novels had always been well written, beautifully crafted and filled with the surging passion that had become her trademark. But there was something else now. After reading the first draft of the latest romance, her agent had remarked on it. There was an added zest, a profounder depth and an increased resonance. Selina was pushing out the boundaries of her talent with impressive results.

That day followed the usual sequence. Before breakfast, she had a run along the beach, played a tennis match against Rex, had a bracing swim with the dog beside her in the water then returned to her cottage for a shower. During the meal, Selina considered the improvements she could make to what she believed would be her best ever novel. It was not long before she was sitting at her desk, immersed in her work and letting the hours drift gently by. Nobody came, rang or contacted her by email. Cocooned from the outside world, she was able to work at her own pace. Nothing else mattered. As far as Selina was concerned, her husband was a million miles away.

Jake Wyman had caught a train to take him to south Devon. He, too, had contrived a disguise. Instead of his customary impeccable suit, he was now wearing the sort of anonymous casual clothing that allowed him to pass for a holidaymaker. Nobody gave him a second look. By the time he reached the village, light was fading. Set apart from the rest of the housing, Selina's cottage was exactly where George Dowling had told him it would be. Jake was at once thrilled and sobered, delighted he'd found the runaway at last but stung by the thought that his wife preferred to live alone in such a tiny house when she could have enjoyed the luxury of their mansion.

His immediate problem was the dog. Dowling had forewarned him so Jake had come prepared. He studied the cottage through a pair of binoculars and saw the animal pacing the garden before settling down on a patch of grass. After waiting until shadows had lengthened, Jake moved stealthily in.

* * *

Selina was so engrossed in her revision that she lost all track of time. When she saw how late it was, she scolded herself for leaving Rex outside and was surprised he hadn't been barking to be let in. Unlocking the back door, she expected the dog to come bounding up to her but there was no sign of him. When she stepped into the garden, she was grabbed from behind and pushed roughly back into the cottage by her husband. Jake slammed the door shut behind him.

'Hello, Selina,' he said, icily calm. 'How are you?'

She was aghast. 'What are you doing here?'

'I came to reclaim some lost property—my wife.' As Selina glanced towards the back door, he grinned. 'Don't worry. The dog won't interrupt us. I gave him a tasty meal laced with a sedative. He'll sleep for a long time.'

'Leave me alone.'

'I'm sorry, my love, but I can't do that.'

'I don't want to live with you, Jake.'

'That's a decision only I can make.'

Selina's blood froze. She'd known that the confrontation would eventually come but she was unequal to it. Until now, she'd drawn great strength from Rex. He was her friend and protector. She relied on him totally. But he was no help to her now. Making an effort to regain her composure, she reminded herself she was not defenceless. Since they were in the kitchen, she had several weapons within easy reach. What she lacked was the courage to reach out for one of them.

'You used my mother's name,' he said, clicking his tongue. 'That was very naughty of you, Selina.'

'It was the first thing that came into my mind.'

'Don't lie to me. You chose it deliberately. I daresay you had a good laugh when you passed yourself off as Enid Goodband. Well, I don't think it was funny and neither would my mother, if she were still alive. You'll have to be punished.'

'Get out of here, Jake.'

'I'll be happy to do so and I'll take you with me.'

Selina stiffened. 'No, you won't.'

'Who's going to stop me?'

'I am,' she cried, snatching a carving knife from the table and brandishing it. 'I'm serious, Jake. It's all over. I'll never go back to the old life.'

'Selina!' he said, spreading his arms. 'You'd never harm me, would you? I'm your husband. We belong together.'

'Keep back!' she ordered as he took a step towards her.

'What's come over you?'

'I finally found a way to escape that monster I was married to.'

'But I gave you everything.'

'It was always on your terms.'

'They can easily be arranged to suit your wishes.'

'You're a control freak. You only ever have what suits you.'

'I'll be a good husband to you, Selina. I promise.'

'Good husbands don't abuse their wives. They don't treat them like a prisoner. They don't go chasing after other women.' He was startled. 'I've known about them for ages, Jake. You're not the only one who can hire a private detective.'

'Those affairs were meaningless,' he said, flicking a dismissive hand. 'They don't affect what we have, Selina. I need you. I want you.' As he took another step forward, she jabbed his hand with the knife and drew blood. Jake was enraged. 'Right,' he yelled, lifting a kitchen chair up, 'let's play it your way, shall we? Come on. We can fight on equal terms now.'

'I'm calling the police,' she decided.

'No, you're not,' he said, using the chair to knock the telephone off the work surface and onto the floor. 'We don't want any interruptions. Now what are you going to do— come quietly or keep waving that knife at me?'

'I'm staying here.'

But there was a quaver in her voice. Selina's courage was being sapped. Though she'd rehearsed the scene many times, she now discovered her part had been over-written. Instead of being able to frighten him away, she was in serious danger. Her knife would not deter him. Only a gun would do that and the revolver was in the bedside drawer. Selina would never reach it in time. The shotgun was in the cupboard next door. Her one hope lay in getting to that and turning it on him. After thrusting the knife at him once more, she dashed through the door to the living room and slammed it behind her, rushing to the cupboard and flinging it open. Jake was after her at once. He came into the room with the chair held high, as if about to smash it down on her head. Then he saw the shotgun pointing at him. The sight made him step backwards involuntarily.

'I always keep it loaded,' she warned.

'You'd never shoot me, Selina, surely?'

'Put that chair down and get out.'

'What have I done to deserve this?' he asked, hurt and bewildered. 'Was I really such a monster?' His tone softened. 'Let me make it up to you, darling. You can have whatever you want whenever you want it. I'll swear to that. Listen,' he went on, lowering the chair, 'I'll build that tennis court you always talked about. I know how much you love the game. We'll have tennis parties. You can invite whoever you choose.'

'I simply want to be left alone,' she said, keeping the shotgun on him.

He shrugged. 'Very well—you win, Selina. I'll be off.'

Pretending to turn, he suddenly hurled the chair at her and knocked the gun from her hands. Selina let out a scream of horror. As she tried to pick up the weapon, he stabbed a foot down on it and cuffed her across the face, making her reel against the front door and bang her head on the hard timber. She was back in an all too familiar situation, cowering in terror and losing the urge to resist. Another blow rallied her. Gathering up her strength, she unlocked the front door and charged through it into the gloom beyond. Selina had no idea where she was going and no breath to call out for help. All she knew was Jake was after her, bent on revenge. Selina was alone and unarmed. She had no means of defence or of summoning aid. The panic button and the cell phone were back in the cottage.

Then she felt something lapping against her feet and

realised her situation was not as dire as she'd thought. The tide was coming in fast. She had a murder weapon, after all. Jake was no swimmer and the effort of chasing her was taking its toll on him. She could hear him grunting and wheezing. Though she was fast enough to outrun him, Selina slowed down to let him think he was gaining on her. They were splashing through water that was rising inexorably. Because she ran on the beach every day, she knew exactly where they were and she was aware of the treacherous undercurrents in the sea. Jake, on the other hand, was running blind, powered by the desire to catch, subdue and punish a wife who'd dared to desert him. Even when the water was up to his knees, he plodded on regardless.

Minutes later, putting in a final spurt, he got within yards of her. But it was too late. Selina dived forward into the incoming waves and began to swim expertly. All her husband could do was to stand waist-deep in the sea and wonder where she was going. Oblivious to danger and gasping with exhaustion, he went after her with murder in his heart. Selina, however, now had a watery accomplice. The tide had come in so quickly that her husband was trapped. Jake might overpower her but he could never withstand the might of the sea. As he plunged madly forward, the waves thickened, the foam spattered his face, the undertow strengthened and his legs turned to jelly. The next moment, he was swept off his feet and fighting for his life. A mouthful of salt water gagged him.

When Selina swam past him, he was floating helplessly out to sea.

The body was washed up a week later. Selina was feeding Rex in the garden of the Wyman mansion when contacted by the police. Informed of Jake's gruesome death, she expressed great surprise.

'Whatever was he doing in the sea?' she asked, innocently. 'My husband was such a poor swimmer.'

Daisy and the Desperado
Bill Cameron

"Hey, you still got your gun?"

For a second I thought Marcy was talking to someone else. But there was only one customer in the shop, a high school girl camped out at the table beside the fish tank, nursing an iced caramel latte and scribbling furiously in a notebook. Uncommon Cup Coffee House was so dead that overheated July afternoon I'd resorted to cleaning the pastry display—it was that or take a nap in it.

"Why? You thinking about robbing a liquor store?"

"That's a thought." Marcy sat on a stool behind the counter and stared out the front window, turbulence in her eyes.

It was a look I recognized.

"It's your Grandma Daisy, isn't it?"

Her silence was all the answer I needed. I sat back on my heels, the pastry case forgotten. Daisy Morgan was notorious among the cops of Portland's Southeast Precinct. Or legendary, depending on who you asked.

"You better tell me."

"Oh, Skin..." She let out a long, slow breath. "I think Old Long wants to kill her."

It wouldn't be the first time. Once or twice, I'd even considered it myself. Hell, my first encounter with Grandma Daisy was at gunpoint.

Not mine.

Hers.

It was during my patrol days, a typical call. Report of an attempted break-in, possible domestic disturbance. I assumed it was some ne'er-do-well showing up at his ex's house demanding whatever the hell these dirtbags think they're owed. The call came in just after midnight, the Drunking Hour, from a neighbor who didn't appreciate all the damn noise. Under the community policing model in force in those days, S.O.P. was de-escalate and defuse.

But this time it wasn't a girlfriend or wife—or raging ex— waiting for me when I pulled up. It was a fellow named George Long, and he was covered in multi-color, fluorescent paint spatter.

"Hey, man, you gonna arrest that woman?"

"What woman?"

He gestured wildly at the dark house next door—windows closed, shades drawn, porch light off. "The kook who shot me." At five paces, his beer breath measured at least point-one-five.

I looked him over. Fiftyish with thinning blond hair and a wispy neckbeard. His cargo pants were unzipped and his shirt was unbuttoned to his navel, revealing a tattooed unicorn on his chest. The rest of him was a Day-Glo rainbow. "With a paint gun?"

"Course with a paint gun! You think I done this to myself?"

In Portland's Hawthorne neighborhood in the mid-90s, there was no telling what a fellow might do to himself. "How about you start at the beginning?"

To his credit, he kept it short. "I was coming home from the Addition and when I walked past her house she ambushed me from her porch."

Sewickley's Addition was a bar a few blocks away on Hawthorne—I've busted up more brawls there than I can count. "Have you been drinking, Mr. Long?"

"You don't go to the Addition for the atmosphere, man. Doesn't mean she can just up and bust a cap in my ass."

"Shotgunned by Skittles is more like it." He actually chuckled at that. "Why don't you go inside and get cleaned up? I'll talk to your neighbor."

"Watch yourself. She's not called Crazy Daisy for nothing."

Crazy Daisy didn't want to open the door, even after I identified myself as a peace officer. When she finally did, the fact I was a cop didn't stop her from saying hello with the barrel of her paintball gun.

"Who said you could come up on my porch?" Her voice was a growl out of a cavern of shadows beyond a barred security gate. From somewhere inside, I could hear the burble of a television.

"Portland Police, ma'am. I need you to put the gun down so I can talk to you about your neighbor."

"Old Long?"

"Apparently, yes."

For a second, the barrel wavered, and I wondered if I was going to explain to my sergeant how I let a little old lady get the drop on me. But then the gun disappeared and she stuck her face between the bars of her security gate. After I dragged her name out of her, she said, "You gonna arrest that shit-bird?" Lights came on, one on the porch and another inside. She was of indeterminate age—fifty, seventy. I had no idea. Her hair was the color of old paper and her eyes were hard, but her round cheeks had the rosy glow of a character in a Christmas special. Standing behind her holding a bowl of popcorn was a little girl, maybe four or five.

"Did you shoot Mr. Long, ma'am?"

From the look on her face, maybe she thought it was a trick question. "I most certainly did. He bangs on the side of my house all night long."

"Why would he do that?"

"How the hell am I supposed to know? You're the detective."

Actually I wasn't. I had plans to be a detective—someday—but she didn't need a detective anyway. "Have you called us?"

"Why would I bother? All you numbnuts do is drive by shining your light so he knows to hide." The gun appeared for a second and I stepped back. "You're useless."

Through the security bars, I could see every surface was stacked with paperbacks. The little girl—Marcy, I would learn—followed my eyes and said, "Gramma Daisy reads *all* the books."

"Pretty late for you to be up, isn't it, sweetie?"

"We're watching *Little Mermaid*."

"Not that it's any of your damn business," her grandmother added.

I sighed and looked back at the street. George Long was long gone—either inside his own house or back to Sewickley's for more lubrication.

"Ma'am, if you promise to stop shooting people with that paint gun, I'll promise to do a better job of keeping an eye on things around here. Deal?"

"If you don't, Detective—"

"Officer."

"*Officer*—" She pointedly examined my name tag, never a good sign. "—Kadash, next time maybe I'll shoot *you*." With that, she slammed the door.

Not my most successful citizen encounter, but I'd escaped pigment-free. I drove away, relieved to put Daisy Morgan and George Long in my rearview mirror for good.

In my dreams.

"I'm not giving your Grandma Daisy a weapon. She can call the police like a normal person."

Marcy rolled her eyes. Like *that* was gonna happen. "You should talk to her at least."

"*I'm* not a cop anymore. I'm respectable now."

"Just talk to her, Skin."

I argued, but not only was Marcy my boss—she was the manager and I was a mere part-time barista—she was also damnably persistent. So after our shift, we strolled over to her grandmother's—far too short a walk from the shop if you asked me.

Daisy lived in a Depression-era shotgun house—three rooms in a line with a bathroom tacked onto the back during a mid-60s remodel. Apparently she had an outhouse before that. The house was set forward on a raised, narrow lot, with a shallow bank in front planted with strawberries. In back, a well-kept garden filled the yard all the way back to the overgrown alley. Wisteria grew over the narrow porch.

Next door, George Long's house was a study in contrasts. It was a largish Old Portland bungalow, the kind of place that even in its rundown state would be snapped up for a ridiculous sum the very day he could be bothered to put it on the market. The paint was ten years past its sell-by date, the front porch sagged, and the foundation along the driveway which separated the two houses was cracked—where it wasn't hidden by stacks of old tires, broken crates, and scrap metal.

"Curb appeal was never his thing, was it?"

Marcy's tight lips answered that question.

Daisy met us at the front door. Unarmed, thank God. "You a detective yet?"

"Not so much." I'd been retired from the police bureau almost five years. "How you been, Daisy?"

She waved dismissively. "I got the cancer and they chopped out half my guts. I told the doctor if it came down to me pooping into a bag he might as well let me die on the table, because if I woke up like that I'd have his balls for Christmas ornaments."

"I don't see you dragging a colostomy bag, so—"

Marcy smacked me on the back of the head and pushed me into the front room. The walls were still floor-to-ceiling paperbacks, but otherwise the place was tidy. I sat in a wing chair that was older—but in better shape—than I was. Marcy plopped down on the lumpy couch across from me.

"No bag, no, but I can't eat peppers anymore." Before I could protest, Daisy handed me a jelly jar filled to the brim with a viscous purple fluid. Wine—allegedly—homemade from Welch's concentrate. She'd had been selling it over her back fence for years. Ten bucks if you brought your own bottle, twelve if you took one of hers.

"Marcy says you have a little problem."

"She tells it better."

I let my eyes stray to Marcy. She shrugged, as if dragging me over here just to spin a tale she could have shared back the shop was her plan all along.

I sighed. "Spill it."

"I stopped by on my way work today. Grandma Daisy was

making a pie, and asked me to pick some rhubarb. I knew something was off when I saw the raccoon in the yard in broad daylight."

I sipped from my jar. The wine was thick as syrup and packed all the punch of rubbing alcohol. "Did you scream and run away?"

Marcy didn't bother to roll her eyes. She's more badass than ten of me. "I chased him off with a rake, and then, under a rhubarb leaf I found..." Her eyes strayed to her grandmother, "...it."

"It."

"A foot."

"What do you mean, a foot?"

"A human foot." She swallowed. "The raccoon was eating it."

"Did I need to know that?" But I was actually relieved. Before I was a barista, I worked homicide. When it came right down to it, I was more at ease with a dismembered foot than a giant rat with thumbs.

"So what do you want from me? To run interference with the cops?" They should have called the police immediately, but I'd known Daisy too long.

They exchanged a look.

"Where's the foot now?"

Daisy *tsk-tsk*ed dismissively. "I wanted to chuck it right back where it came from, but she wouldn't let me."

A memory tickled at the base of my neck. "Where it came from."

"Yeah, right through Old Long's front window."

"You're telling me it's George's foot—his *actual* foot?" I closed my eyes for a second and imagined myself somewhere else—say, on a rocket being launched into the sun.

"It gets worse, Skin."

I down my wine and hold out my jar for more. "Tell me."

"There was a note. He said he we've gotta hand over Grandma Daisy's pot, or else."

* * *

Over the years, I would cross paths with Grandma Daisy and George Long many times. Usually, it was more of the same. A neighbor would call about some ruckus and I'd arrive to find her accusing him of banging on her house, or throwing crap in her yard, or stealing her returnables right the hell off her enclosed back porch. His defense, offered with a grin, was always the same.

"She's a kook, man."

And he was a drunk who, near as I could tell, had no visible means of support. But there was also no visible evidence he was doing any of the things she claimed—aside from the stray bowling shoe which, in this neighborhood, was one of the least weird items which might mysteriously turn up in your yard. I never found any other trash or debris. The enclosed porch showed no signs of forced entry. Part of me was willing to believe he banged on her house—a kind of middle-aged souse's version of Ding Dong Ditch—but no one ever caught him in the act. When I suggested Daisy install security cameras, she scoffed.

"What am I, made of money?"

During the years before she grew up to be my manager at Uncommon Cup, Marcy visited often. Once, when her grandmother went to the back room to answer the phone, I asked her if she ever heard the banging. Her answer was an icy stare, and the solemn declaration, "Grandma Daisy isn't a cop. She doesn't have to lie."

Ouch.

The closest to a legitimate call was the time Long was doing a little archery, his target tacked to the cedar fence which separated the two yards. One of his shots went high and the arrow lodged in a birdhouse in Daisy's yard. Fortunately no one was home.

Except for Daisy, of course. She was screaming bloody murder when I pulled up. "He's damn lucky he didn't hit one of my fledges!"

The arrow sticking out the birdhouse was a rare piece of hard evidence.

Even so, Long insisted it was an accident. "I was just practicing. A man has a right to defend himself."

"You expecting the Battle of Agincourt to break out around here, George?"

I gave him a choice: hand over his bow or answer charges of unlawful discharge of a dangerous weapon within city limits. He tried to argue, so I quoted the relevant statute in detail until he threw up his hands in surrender.

But as he made his way back into his house, he emitted a braying laugh. "Joke's on you. That's not even my good bow."

The door slammed before I could formulate an appropriate retort.

Most of my visits were little more than counseling sessions. I tried to get the neighborhood mediator involved, but Daisy would only talk to me, and Long insisted there was no problem. She was just a kook.

It was a stalemate, until the spring of 2003. I was a detective by then, and had worked my way from property to person crimes. I'd been out of a patrol car long enough my memories of Grandma Daisy and George Long had faded to the stuff of half-forgotten nightmare. Then I got a call-out to the scene of a shooting in southeast Portland. Hawthorne neighborhood, a few blocks from Sewickley's Addition.

Sure enough, Crazy Daisy had tried to plug her shit-bird neighbor.

I insisted on seeing the weed before the foot. It was a matter of priorities. I needed to know what we were dealing with.

The house sat on a cinderblock foundation which had been insulated as part of the addition in the 1960s. More recently, Daisy had excavated a ten-by-ten pit under the trapdoor hatch deep enough for me to stand upright when I climbed down from the kitchen. She'd lined the excavation with landscaping blocks and sealed them with a skin of concrete, leaving a hole in the center to serve as a drain. Grow lights hung from the floor joists overhead, and a hose ran under the house from the backyard tap. Sacks of potting soil, empty pots, and fertilizer were heaped on the dirt floor of the crawlspace around the grow pit, home to a dozen squat specimens of *cannabis indica.*

"Daisy, are you out of your flippin' mind?"

"You try living on Social Security. Lord knows what I'll do if Oregon pulls a Colorado and they start stocking weed at the Plaid Pantry. Not that I'm copping to anything."

I climbed out of the pit and polished off my second jar of wine, then regretted it and asked Marcy to make me some coffee. "Strong." While she fussed with an ancient percolator, I followed Daisy into the backyard.

They'd covered the foot with a terracotta pot to protect it from the local wildlife. The skin was leathery and the exposed ankle bone looked like a knob of cracked ivory. I straightened up and peered over the fence at Long's house. "How is it he even *has* his foot?"

Daisy shrugged. "He wanted a keepsake. I guess he knew a guy who worked at the hospital."

"When did you talk to him? I thought he was your arch nemesis."

"You think Superman doesn't talk to Lex Luthor from time to time? We share a fence. He buys wine. Even taught me a few things about...gardening."

"That's true, Skin," Marcy said from the back steps, "Grandma's crops used to be no better than grass clippings."

"I'm not copping to anything."

I shook my head, wondering why I was even here. "So this friend somehow salvaged his amputated foot?"

"Who said they were friends?"

I didn't want to know why Long felt compelled to chuck his "keepsake" over their shared fence. Not eager to touch the offending appendage, I covered it back up with the terracotta pot. Back inside, Marcy offered me an iced coffee and a sheet of greasy bakers parchment. Someone—Long, I presumed—had scrawled on it with a black Sharpie.

I know wats growing in the crowlspace. Hand it over if you dont want any trubel.

"It was on the ground near the back door," Marcy said. "I assume it was wrapped around the foot, but the raccoon must have pulled it off."

The page was none the worse for wear.

"No instructions? Call a burner phone at midnight? Leave the weed under the Portlandia statue? Scratch your head and hop on one—?"

"Skin, you really ought to take this seriously."

The note—and the foot—struck me as more prank than threat. "I still don't know what you want me to do."

Daisy snorted. "You could drive by and shine your light."

Marcy put a soothing hand on her grandmother's forearm, then turned back to me. "A show of force might scare him off."

"So would the *police*, Marcy. Sheesh."

"They'll ask questions."

"I'm not copping to anything. I'm just saying you try living on Social Security."

I sighed. I'd heard her the first time.

I was between partners the night Daisy shot her neighbor, but three uniformed officers were on hand along with a pair of EMTs. George Long lay on an ambulance gurney, howling to the skies about his damn foot. Daisy sat on her porch swing with Marcy and one of the uniforms, content as Buddha.

Lights from the ambulance and two patrol cars bathed the chattering onlookers gathering in the street in front of the house—the usual crowd, faces I'd grown familiar with over the years, a few I'd even met. The Hawthorne neighborhood was home to an eclectic population, from soft-voiced earth mothers to larval hipsters and everything in between. I saw a fellow who might have been the leader of an outlaw biker gang, holding hands with a Vietnamese woman half his size. Kids poked their faces between the legs of their parents, or ran back and forth from yard to yard. Across the street, a cheerful couple named Diane and Janet sat in lawn chairs on their front lawn and raised beer bottles in salute when they saw me look their way.

Oh boy.

The first responder was a friend from my patrol days.

"What happened here, Jeff?"

"The old bat says someone was trying to pick her lock and she stuck her gun between the security bars. The desperado—her word, not mine—hollered loud enough to startle her, and the gun went off."

"Magically, no doubt."

Jeff gave me a wry smile and consulted his note pad. "The intruder fled, but she called 'useless as a chin dick 9-1-1' anyway—her words, not mine. First and last time, she insists. My guess is this guy—" He pointed over his shoulder at Long, "—jumped the fence, but got his foot caught between the pickets. He was hanging there when I pulled up."

I wondered when Daisy upgraded from paintball to lead.

"Where'd she hit him?"

"She didn't. Not exactly. There's a hole in his boot heel, but his injuries are all from getting tangled up in the fence. Compound fracture, lacerations, damaged pride, you name it."

I wasn't aware Long had any pride. "How many shots?"

"Just the one." Officer Jefferson held up a plastic evidence bag containing the offending weapon, a single-action .32 revolver. "She must've come to the door cocked."

I didn't bother to make the half-cocked joke. It was time to talk to Long. I forced myself over to the gurney and told him to put a sock in it. Give the man his due, he shut up.

"What were you doing up on Daisy's porch, George?"

"I was just—I wasn't doing anything wrong."

"We both know better than that."

He pooched out his lip. "I don't have to talk to you."

"Tell it to me, tell it to a judge. Your choice."

"Who says I was up on the porch anyway? Maybe it was someone else."

I sighed. "Daisy does?"

But Jeff cleared his throat. "She's actually not certain of that. Says she saw a figure, but never made out who it was."

"You found him tangled up in her fence though, right?"

"Yeah, but..."

"There's a *bullet hole* through his boot heel, right?"

Jeff had the same look of exasperation I no doubt wore

whenever I dealt with Daisy and Long. I put a hand on his shoulder.

"Okay, okay. Let's get this dingbat to the hospital, and I'll check for witnesses among these fine neighbors, see what I can sort out."

But none of the fine neighbors stuck around for question time. Janet and Diane took their lawn chairs inside, the children all vanished into their squirrel holes. The outlaw biker went one way and the Vietnamese lady another.

In the end, I managed to sort out very little. Daisy offered nothing more and Long insisted it was a misunderstanding. He was just trying to be neighborly. In what way, exactly, he never made clear. The DA managed a plea deal for criminal trespass—suspended sentence—and was damn grateful to get that much.

As for Daisy, we held her revolver for several weeks while the DA waffled. In the end, no charges were filed against her. A divot in the concrete of her porch suggested she'd fired before Long fled, and the DA was willing to concede Daisy reasonably believed she was defending her home against burglary. Still, the gun never made it out of evidence— conveniently lost in the kind of bureaucratic mix-up big city police departments excel at. Seemed to me the last thing Daisy Morgan needed was another opportunity to shoot at George Long.

Not that he was going to be hopping around her porch anymore. By rights he should have made a full recovery, but not George. He flaked out on his wound care, went septic, and ended up back in the hospital.

The gangrenous foot couldn't be saved.

"So, Skin, you gonna go get your gun now?"

It's been my experience if you have a gun you'll find a reason to use it, whether you need to or not. The last thing I wanted to do was throw water on a grease fire.

"Actually, I thought I would just go talk to George."

But when I knocked on Long's door—his doorbell was two loose wires held in place with chewing gum—there was no answer. I walked around the side and even stuck my nose into his backyard, but the house was buttoned up tight. The lone sign of a life was an air conditioner wheezing and dripping condensation from an upstairs window. Likely as not, Long was holding down a stool at Sewickley's, oblivious to the drama unfolding across his cracked driveway.

Back at Daisy's, I pulled out my phone. Marcy stopped me. "Just wait and see. You'll catch him in the act, I guarantee it."

"That's what I'm afraid of."

"Skin—"

"Fine, fine." I knew when I was licked. "But if things go sideways, I'm calling the cops. I'll try to keep the crawlspace out of it, but I'm not taking any chances with your grandmother's safety. Or yours, for that matter."

For a second I thought she'd argue with me, but instead she let out a long breath and nodded. "It's settled then."

The heat held on into evening. Back in my cop days, July and August were when I got most of my calls to that side street off Hawthorne, the Daisy Days of Summer. Most of the year, the little shotgun house was front room/bedroom/eat-in kitchen. Come the Daisy Days, it was sauna/sweat lodge/smokehouse, and where-the-hell's-the-damn-door.

"Daisy, you ever consider opening a window once in a while?"

"I could do that, sure. Or maybe I could just put out a neon sign. Desperadoes Welcome."

"Grandma," Marcy said, "how about I turn the fan on and open the front door?"

"Just make sure those burglar bars are locked." With that Daisy trundled off to the back of the house with the speed of a mouse escaping a house cat. It struck me she might be afraid. I'd always seen her as irascible, short with fools, and fiercely independent—a woman going her own way. But now I wasn't sure that was the whole story.

Marcy misinterpreted my look. "She's been here a long time. Raised my dad and my aunt in this house." She looked around the cramped room at the lumpy sofa, the two wing chairs, piles and piles of books. "This was the kid's bedroom. Grandma Daisy and Grandpa Moon—when he was around—

29

slept in the next room. Dad said they actually used a chamber pot if they had to go to the bathroom in the middle the night. In the morning they'd have to haul it to the outhouse. When Moon died, Grandma bought a bargain cremation and used the rest of the life insurance to add on the bathroom and back porch."

"She and your grandpa didn't get along, I take it."

"By comparison, George Long is her soul mate." She dropped back into one of the chairs. "Skin, I know what we're *supposed* to do. It's just..."

"The cops wouldn't do anything, not to a woman her age. At worst, they'd pretend she thought she was growing house plants and seize the stash, then have a good laugh once she was out of earshot."

"She's not kidding when she talks about how hard it is to get by on Social Security. The wine and the weed are all that keeps her from losing this place." Marcy pondered her hands for a long moment. "She won't take money from me."

I didn't know what to say. After a while, Marcy went to check on her grandmother and I settled in for what I hoped would be an uneventful night.

Yeah. Sure.

As in the old days, Daisy slept in the middle room. Marcy set up a cot beside her. Before bedding down, she offered me a headlamp with a red light setting. "For surveillance, or whatever. Save your night vision." Then she pressed the key to the burglar bars into my hand, patted the top of my head like I was a good dog, and left me with the front room to myself.

I kept the door open—burglar bars locked—and listened for lurking ne'er-do-wells. All I heard was the distant chatter of an outdoor party. The night air in the close little room was still and stifling. Every so often I'd doze, but the couch was lumpy and some noise—a dog barking or a car passing— would startle me awake. As evening melted into night, my nerves stretched wire-snap tight. I flipped on the headlamp and grabbed a book at random, anything to distract myself.

The cover featured a shirtless man with intimidating abs wielding a hockey stick. Turned out he wasn't beating people to death with it, but playing actual hockey—when he wasn't romancing an up-and-coming fashion designer. I was a dozen chapters in when a sound from the front porch jerked me back to reality.

In the red glow of the headlamp, the room—with its ceiling-high stacks of books—looked like a scene out of a Poe tale. The scrape of a shoe on concrete squirreled through the burglar bars. Hardly breathing, I set the book on the floor and sidled up to the door. Outside, I could hear a heavy breath.

Just as I turned the key in the lock on the security gate, Daisy howled from the next room. "Loooong!" There was a crash—Marcy falling off her cot from the sound of it. An instant later, she materialized at my side.

"Get him!"

I gestured for her to pipe down. Whatever was on the front porch—George Long, rabid raccoon—suddenly went quiet. Through the burglar bars, I had a better view of the street than the porch itself, which helped me not one iota. Another scrape sounded right outside the door.

Marcy put a hand on my back and gave me shove. There was nothing for it but to confront the intruder, footless drunk or rabid bandit beast. I threw open the gate and leaped out onto the porch.

"Ah-hah!"

A man roughly the height and girth of a mature Sitka spruce confronted me. I raised my head, but all I could make out in the headlamp's rufous glow was a bushy beard and all but visible halitosis.

"Wait. You're not Long."

Not-Long responded with a roar. He lunged, and his barrel belly struck me chest-high with the force of a falling boulder. I stumbled backward as he raised arms like gnarled tree branches. *Just fall down*, I thought stupidly. But before either one of us could make another move a *thwock* split the sultry night.

For a second, nothing happened. Then, the giant yowled

and started hopping on one foot. As he pawed fecklessly at his rear end, he lurched side to side. For a second I thought he would fall on me, so I gave him a hard shove. Eyes bulging, he struck the porch rail and tumbled ass over kettle into Daisy's strawberries.

The porch light came on. The sudden glare fell on the shaft of an arrow protruding from the giant's ass. When he tried to get up, I stepped off the porch and onto his back. "Stay down."

"Who is it, Skin?"

Daisy joined Marcy at the door. "I know who it is."

I studied him with increasing irritation as he wriggled under foot. Then it hit me. He was one of many neighborhood witnesses to the George and Daisy show over the years, the biker dude.

"I don't remember his name." If I ever knew it. It had been a long time since I tried to question the neighbors. "I'm guessing he heard what your grandma was up to—"

"I'm not copping to anything!"

"—and came sniffing for what he thought was easy pickings." He continued to squirm, so I pressed some weight onto him. "You're gonna have to call the cops, I'm afraid."

"I already did."

Daisy's tone was resigned. My face must have registered my surprise.

"She was worried you might get hurt," Marcy said.

Out on the street, the usual cadre of gawkers had started to gather. "Howdy, Officer," Diane, or maybe Janet, from across the street called. I waved, didn't bother to correct her. The Vietnamese woman came to stare at the thrashing giant. "I told you not to mess with these people. Buy a lottery ticket next time. The odds are better!" He only groaned as she stormed off.

"Go on inside," I said to Marcy and Daisy. "I'll stay here till the cavalry arrives."

"They'll just shine a light and drive past."

The burglar bars closed with a clang. I chuckled, then movement caught my eye from across the cracked driveway. Next door, George Long stood on his front porch, compound bow in his hand. His good bow, no doubt. Down at my feet, the writhing giant wreaked havoc on Daisy's strawberries. "Settle down," I said, "unless you want one in your other cheek."

I turned my gaze back to George, who raised the bow in a kind of salute. I nodded in acknowledgment, and he turned and hobbled back into his house just ahead of the patrol unit which screeched to a stop in front of Daisy's shotgun house.

The next morning, Long chose not to pretend he wasn't home when I banged on his front door. He yelled for me to come in, and I made my way through a short foyer hallway to a living room last seen by outsiders during a *Hoarders* marathon.

"Officer!" he greeted me from a swollen, puke-colored recliner.

"I'm retired, Mr. Long."

"Mister, then. Uh...what the hell's your name anyway?"

Already, I could feel the headache developing behind my left eye.

"So, Crazy Daisy gonna give me my foot back?"

"The one *you* threw into her yard?" I noted with mild surprise he was wearing a prosthetic. I half-expected a peg leg.

"I was aiming for the giant."

I scanned the room. Like Daisy, he had his share of books, but mixed in with the reading material was an eclectic collection of detritus. Empty wine bottles, Daisy's Sharpie scrawl in place of labels. A silver Elvis letter opener sticking out of a wig form. A suit of armor hung with scarves and bandanas. Less surprising were the dozens of mismatched bowling shoes in various states of wear, left to gather dust in the intervening years since his foot came off.

"You couldn't throw a shoe instead?"

"I'd tried that the last time I saw him poking around her back door."

"I know."

"The foot was a calculated escalation." He reached out with a hand which might have been once attached to a Nazgûl and picked up the compound bow from beside his chair. "I didn't wanna go all Henry the Fifth on him unless I absolutely had to."

"You wrote the note, too, didn't you?"

"It's not like that guy can write."

"But can he spell?"

Long stared at me. "Huh?"

"Never mind." I wondered why he didn't just tell Daisy what was going on, but just as quickly recognized the folly of that notion. Daisy would never believe him, but the note was a different matter. "You knew she would call me."

"Or her granddaughter would."

"And you could have retrieved the foot when you left the note, but—"

"Emphasis."

As I stood there chuckling, an object on the mantle amidst a collection of bowling trophies an item caught my eye. I studied it for a long moment.

"George, how long as this been going on?"

"What do you mean?"

"You, Daisy...all the acting up?"

"I don't know what you mean."

"I think you do."

He was quiet. Somewhere under the collected debris, a radio offered the weather report. Portland's usual forecast, more of the same until suddenly it wasn't.

"I appreciate that you've been looking out for her. But you can't keep acting like lovesick grade schooler pulling some girl's hair to get attention. It's creepy."

"It's not like that," he grumbled. But there was no conviction in his protest.

"So you say." My eyes remained on the mantle where, in the place of honor, stood a cowboy boot mounted on a polished wooden stand. The bullet hole was plainly visible in the heel. "Next time, George, call the police when you see someone lurking around her house."

"I'd rather throw shoes."

I remembered Daisy telling me he'd taught her about gardening. "If you've got your own grow operation to worry about, pick up a burner phone to make the call."

"I can't begin to imagine what you mean."

"Not copping to anything?" He stared me down. I got to my feet and headed for the door. "Gotta supplement the Social Security somehow, I guess."

Not much more than a year later, Marcy found Daisy lying on the couch in the center room of her little shotgun house, thumb tucked into a racy paperback on her chest. Half a glass of homemade wine on the bedside table, the television tuned to Cinemax. She'd passed away in her sleep.

At the wake, George Long rolled in on a cherry red scooter and pulled to a stop in front of the open casket. For a moment, I watched the old desperado, his gaze remote and fathomless, then joined him.

"That's a nice ride, George. Must've set you back a few bucks."

"Medicare paid for it," he snapped. "Not that it's any of your business."

"You're right. It's not."

"What do you want, copper?"

"Just wondering how you're doing is all. It's been a while."

I thought he was going to tell me "Not long enough." Or hit the throttle and torch his way out of there. Instead he let out a long, heavy sigh and leaned back in his chair. I saw he was clutching the cowboy boot against his chest.

"I dunno." He reached down with his free hand as if to scratch his missing foot. "I guess I figured she'd outlive us all."

Life's a Beach
Judith Cutler

Two senior employees—head of Information Technology and head of Human Resources—in a relationship: that's rarely good news for any organisation. But since it's usually the head of HR that casts an imprimatur on such goings on, it was hard for anyone to veto my romance with Taylor, head of Human Resources. In fact, once Taylor set her mind on anything, it was as hard for anyone to change Taylor's course as it was to turn a great ship. Not that she looked like a container vessel: she was once described, as she took pleasure in telling me, as a pocket Venus. I suspect, however, she preferred her last CEO's description of her—an Exocet missile.

In any case, Taylor solved the problem of us being in a mere relationship. Whisked away to Mauritius for our first extended romantic and alcohol-fuelled tryst, I found myself taking part in a beach wedding. Ours. Total heaven. Neither of us had any family to offend by such a spontaneous and private ceremony. I'd lost both my parents while I was still at university; Taylor simply never mentioned hers. Or any other family, for that matter. It was as if she'd emerged, fully formed with feet in Jimmy Choo heels, from a prestigious office block.

If I hadn't expected to be married, even less did I expect to be given my redundancy papers, personally signed by my new wife, when we came back to England. The very day we returned, actually. I was inclined to be upset and resentful. She pointed out that life was like that in business: hadn't one famous football manager once sold her husband to another club? Hardly appeased, I told her the timing was odd to say the least. Astonished at my stupidity, she assured me it made absolute sense. My redundancy package, when it had been fully negotiated, would mean that if we both sold our apartments we would be able to buy the house of our dreams.

I didn't argue about selling my bachelor pad. It was roomy enough for one, with nice views over Kingston on Thames, but I had an intractable neighbour who insisted on letting a stray cat into the lobby but never deemed it necessary to deal with what the cat left behind. Fur-balls. And worse.

I never understood how Taylor could even dream of abandoning her London apartment. It was big enough to absorb me and my possessions without blinking; it had views over Lord's Cricket Ground. Perfection. But Taylor decreed we must sell it. Someone desperate to watch some vital test matches had made an offer to any potential seller in the block so outrageous she told me sentiment simply could not get in the way. In any case, who had time to sit and watch anything?

Not Taylor, that was for sure. She was too busy overseeing the other redundancy deals. It was my job to locate the dream home—her dream, it soon transpired, rather than mine, which was less grandiose than hers. I favoured an environmentally-built new home, and used my spare time touring round commutable areas hunting for one: I found a perfect example in Kent, built deep into a hillside with the windows and solar panels angled to get the best of the sun. She didn't like the idea of my having to mow the grass on the roof and rejected out of hand the notion of buying some sheep to do the job. Next on my wish list was an understated Georgian rectory near Tunbridge, though its price tag was the opposite of understated, as she scathingly pointed out. We needed an investment property, she said: if it needed some TLC, I'd be at hand to do minor jobs or be a site manager for any major ones. I was wasting time: we'd lose our buyer if we weren't careful.

At last I did what I should have done in the first place. To save time and energy, I took to my computer and merely printed off details of likely properties for her cursory inspection. They were rejected out of hand: too far from London, too close to London, too old, too modern.

The cricket season began. I watched the games from her

balcony; her potential buyer waxed furious.

When rain stopped play, it was back to the computer. And I found a place I fell in love with. Knottsall House. A Regency gentleman's country residence. It was too far from London and too expensive, as I explained to Taylor when she picked up the torn pieces of printout from my waste bin.

'No problem,' she declared. 'I've accepted a redundancy package for myself.'

That was news to me, but probably shouldn't have been.

'We sell this place. Add in your redundancy pay-off and the money your studio flat realised. The vendors will drop the asking price by—what, twenty percent?—for cash.' She dared me to argue.

Perhaps I breathed the words *upkeep* and *maintenance.*

'I've already lined up months of freelance work at twelve hundred pounds a day, double that for weekends.' She ticked off the house's attractions on her fingers. 'Tennis court? Good. Swimming pool—too small, but we can enlarge it. Parking? We'll need a bigger garage.'

'We'll never get planning permission.'

'Not for anything above ground, okay, so we go underground. Croquet lawn. A lake. Check if it needs dredging, will you? Yes, it all looks good. What's this about contemporary furniture? Oh, I thought they meant modern, not made at the same time as the house was built. We'll buy as much as we can from the vendor. We can pick up the rest at auction.'

For *we* read *you,* of course.

It was possible to view auction lots on line, but I wanted to become properly acquainted with items I proposed to spend the rest of my life with. North Yorkshire: there I found a portrait of a horse that was good enough to be a Stubbs which would look lovely in the hall. Devon: in the unpromising surroundings of what was normally an indoor stock market there was a collection of early editions ideal for the library—Jane Austen, the Brontes, Scott and George Eliot (I know she was too late for the house but *Middlemarch* is set at the time of the 1832 Reform Act and just qualified). For the kitchen came gleaming copper pans and moulds from a village hall near Harlech. An early Worcester dinner service to display—not use!—in the dining room came from Birmingham. And in Cirencester I found a sampler I put hurriedly back on the table—someone had carefully embroidered the legend, *Marry in haste; repent at leisure.*

Not that I was repenting at anything. Finding time to teach IT at a local school—volunteers with my background were, after all, like hen's teeth—I developed a pleasant enough routine. On days when I wasn't at auctions I would stroll into the local town, and buy supplies from local traders. Moatham was undistinguished in appearance, but I liked its people, from the ex-serviceman Big Issue seller for whom I always bought a corned beef sandwich in exchange for the next episode of his life story, to the tradesmen I consulted about work I needed to do on the house or employed for more serious renovations. I enjoyed working in Knottsall House's grounds (no mere garden for us) and kept the now huge pool and unused tennis court pristine. I was fitter than I'd ever been.

As for Taylor, I hardly saw enough of her to discover if she was still happy. I knew from our joint bank account that she was making eye-watering amounts by descending on big organisations and telling them how many hundred employees they should shed. I doubt if any of their settlements were generous. At first, at her suggestion, as it happens, we banned phones from the meals we managed to share—I was becoming an expert on high energy, low calorie meals so she could work fourteen hours, take no exercise and still look like Victoria Beckham. Later, however, there came texts she had to deal with, calls she had to take, and tweets she needed to giggle over.

By now her work as corporate executioner was taking her further afield; she roamed the multinationals, making them leaner and fitter. Work fled from the UK and Western Europe. Ted, the Big Issue seller, got a job with accommodation attached—in other words a prison sentence—and was replaced by Karl, an unattractive Polish specimen whose saving grace was his love for a mangy dog. He thanked me for forking out for vet's bills by simply walking away from his pitch: I never knew what happened to him.

Occasionally I was invited to tag along with Taylor to some jolly or other, either in the city or even abroad, a corporate husband with all the corporate wives. The amount of flesh they displayed seemed to be in direct proportion to their husbands' income. Thank goodness men could withdraw into the carapace of a DJ or a tux. It was surely only their wives' eyes who appraised the jacket to see if it was the latest style. No, champagne and jet lag were not for me.

But our life together was still excellent. For one thing we never had enough time to quarrel. Furthermore, it was as if the itinerant nature of her life made the marriage bed more special. So I could tell myself that though my career path was far from the one I'd envisaged, it was one of contentment and fulfilment. If I was becoming, in my own quiet way, the lord of the manor, I wouldn't argue. Church fete? Hold it on our lower lawn. Fundraising drinks and nibbles? Use our terrace or if it's wet the grand entrance hall. Model yacht club? Feel free to use our lake.

I lived, however, with two fears. The first was the economic bubble would bring along a Russian oligarch so eager to add to his property portfolio that he made Taylor an offer she wouldn't hesitate unilaterally to accept; the other— the flip-side of the coin—was her work would dry up, and we would be forced to sell. In the event, it looked as if neither would be realised: Taylor decided we should have a baby.

Georgiana, named, poor child, after that unhappy Duchess of Devonshire, was the joy of my life. Unfortunately Taylor and I were unable to agree on how Georgiana should be pronounced: *Georgi- a-na* or *George-ayna*. It was hardly worth arguing about: to me she was always Georgie, although Taylor stigmatised the name as passé middle-class nineteen-fifties. I never could be bothered to Google it to see if she was right. I had to share Georgie with a nanny—a succession of nannies as it happened, changed according to whichever theory of raising toddlers was propounded by the magazine Taylor happened to be reading at the time. The baby became a little girl: she held my heart in her grubby little hand. I knew from the way she ran to me with each new discovery, from the pain of a gravel-rashed knee to the wonder of a May-fly, that she worshipped me in return. If Georgie'd been as studiously polite to me as she was to Taylor it would have broken my heart, but Taylor seemed to think that was how children should treat their mothers. She also thought the best way to treat Georgie was to send the little mite to school. Not the local primary school. Away to school. Aged six. Her main motivation appeared to be the cuteness of the little uniforms with the curly-brimmed straw hats.

To say I objected is a masterpiece of understatement. I argued. I explained. I raged. I pleaded. And I gave up on the marriage.

Taylor sensed something was wrong, but probably couldn't understand what it was. She knew the major changes she'd told me to make to the house weren't being done; they wouldn't be, because every day I could, I headed off into the next county to spend time with Georgie. Incensed by my apparent inefficiency, she started to leave me the sort of lists she'd left the cleaning lady, who'd left because she could stand them no more. I suspect Taylor never realised she'd gone, because I simply did her work to fill the emptiness of my days. I pocketed the inadequate pay, too.

The latest Big Issue seller was a pretty girl, Mina, who said she liked egg mayo sandwiches but really loved smoked salmon with cream cheese. One day, tucking into a Fair Trade chocolate bar I'd brought as her dessert, she observed she'd make more money back home. It seemed that she was highly qualified—she was a nurse who'd lost her job when the local hospital trust was merged with another to meet efficiency targets which might or might not have been set by Taylor. I asked why she stayed—I'd even have helped with the air fare home myself. But Romania wasn't her target: her boyfriend, a tennis coach, who'd been working in South Africa, was now in America. I worried about her safety: what if Georgie was ever in the same awful situation? Something must be done. If she couldn't go home, home must come to her, one way or another.

I'd had time to clear out and refurbish—heavens, the place now met the highest environmental criteria—what had once been a stable block. Taylor's briefly evinced desire to ride had come to nothing, so I was reasonably sure Mina would live there undetected. All those unused rooms in the house, and she lived in a stable! She was probably warmer where she was, but my conscience was still wrung. But she insisted she was fine, even though she refused to give up her Big Issue pitch and set off before eight each day.

I also made time to refresh my IT skills: a return to the job market was becoming more of a necessity each day. I needed to be able to prove to a family court that not only was I a fit person to have custody of Georgie, I was able to provide for her, too. I improved so much I was able to sort out a glitch in some software Taylor was using which had defeated the IT section of her current employer. I should have felt guilty, I suppose: while I was repairing it I couldn't resist having a look at some of her files. What I found made interesting but unsurprising reading. In addition to the money she regularly put into our joint account she put an even greater sum into an account of which I knew nothing. It would have been the work of moments to syphon off an insignificant but regular amount into a new account for myself, but I resisted. It was Georgie I wanted, not money. Georgie and the house. Not just any house. The house I'd put my heart and soul into.

On rare days between jobs Taylor would walk round the grounds with me. I was terrified she might detect some sign of Mina, despite our agreement that each day before she left for her pitch the rooms she occupied must be forensically clean. Mina obviously wanted even less than I did an explosion from a wife who might consider herself betrayed. Not that I'd ever touch Mina: I felt she was a grown-up version of Georgie, to be cared for and cherished.

One bright, warm morning was so lovely I wondered why I'd ever toiled in an office, when working in the grounds was so rewarding, I accompanied Taylor on a swift tour.

She nodded: yes, they could have stepped from the pages of a heritage magazine!

In the middle of the largest lawn, she stopped dead,

pointed at the lake, which for safety's sake I'd fenced off the moment Georgie started walking, and declared, 'We should have a party. A big one. With a theme. A beach party.'

'We haven't got a beach,' I objected foolishly.

I had to admit she had more vision and imagination than I did. 'That bank over there, where the geese kept coming ashore last winter,' she said pointing.

Marvelling that she'd even noticed such a detail, I nodded. 'They didn't do the grass there much good, did they?'

'So we get rid of the grass.' For *we* read *you*, of course. 'Dig it out to a really good depth—a couple of metres. More. We need a beach at least thirty metres wide, five or six deep. A little platform for a life guard here. Some beach huts over there. A volleyball net there. The sand will have to be top quality, of course.'

'What about the displaced soil? Any plans for that?' I asked, desperately keeping irony out of my voice.

'What about making an island in the middle of the lake? Maybe the damned birds would nest on that instead. And now Georgie can swim, tear up that hideous fence—it'll make a good bonfire and we can have fireworks at the end of the party.'

It didn't take me very long to master the controls of the digger we hired, at least as far as the excavating was concerned. I was less pleased with the island I'd been told to create, but when it was turfed over and a few maturing trees planted, it would look good enough at dusk. It was the work of moments to work out how many cubic metres of sand I'd need, to achieve a nicely sloping beach, but Taylor came and peered over my shoulder: 'Double that,' she said.

'Not if you want a slope—a nice gradient into the water. The amount you suggest would practically make a sheer drop—a sand dune at least,' I conceded, trying to laugh her out of her folly, but only reinforcing her intransigence. 'It'd be far too steep for beach cricket or volleyball. Now, what about a few canoes?'

We worked out the guest list together, nominally at least, since I'd lost touch with many of my old friends and she had plenty of contacts she needed to cultivate. Then there were decisions to be made about food.

'I'd be happy to run the barbecue myself,' I said mildly.

'If you want the best you hire the best,' she said.

We compared quotes from three catering firms and agreed on her choice. I also booked a couple of marquees, in case it dared to rain.

Then I turned my attention to new beach. For some reason the contractor simply dumped a mountain of sand some twenty metres from the edge of the lake. Fortunately I could hire a dumper truck before Taylor came back from her latest trip—the Channel Islands, I think—and I was more than half way through the mound when she came down to inspect my handiwork.

'You've not distributed it very evenly,' she observed, as I trundled up with the latest load. 'You should have raked it over more often.'

'I think I'll need the JCB to do that,' I said, hoping to play with a familiar machine rather than continue my wrestling match with the controls of a decidedly contrary one. She'd been right, of course: the beach was no more than an intermittent series of humps.

'For goodness' sake, you've got a rake, haven't you?'

I parked the dumper truck and jumped down on to the beach, looking up at her irate features. 'It's hard work,' I said, doing my best. At last, having made very little impression, I started to scramble out. I might have been trying to ascend a down escalator. With each step I took, I slipped nearer the lake. A last a crabwise approach worked, and I hauled myself back up, ending in a gasping heap beside the dumper truck.

'I'd forgotten what a wimp you are,' Taylor informed me. She looked at her watch. 'I've got an hour or so before the taxi to the airport is due. You tip and I'll rake.'

'You don't want to hurt your back, Taylor; it's not just dragging the sand around, it's getting safely up and down.'

'Just get on that damned truck and do it.'

'I've got a full load. At least let me empty most of it first. It always goes with such a rush.'

'What part of *do it* don't you understand?' she demanded icily, leaping down on to the most recently dumped pile of sand and disappearing, of course, from sight.

Very well, I'd tip and she'd rake. Pulling the tip lever gently, I hoped to release a steady, gentle stream. Instead, I released a cascade. I did my best to halt it. The hopper hovered in mid-air. But there was still enough momentum in the remaining sand for tonnes of it to pour remorselessly down.

Bracing myself for the sort of scathing criticism I realised Taylor enjoyed delivering, I slid nervously down from the seat and peered over the lip of the beach. 'I'm sorry—the lever's not very easy to control. Why don't you do the next load and I'll do my best with the rake?'

There was no reply. No doubt she was speechless with anger. Or perhaps—there were dents in the soft dry sand that were the nearest you could get to footprints—she had stomped off in anger, and gone to do her packing. Like a guilty schoolboy I tipped three or four more loads. Better make it five or six. If I could have found the rake, I'd have had another go at smoothing it out myself.

I checked my watch: she should have calmed down by now. Tail between my legs, I trudged back to the house, calling my apologies the moment I'd pulled off my wellies by the back door.

Silence. I really had offended her, hadn't I?

I made some coffee and took it up to her bedroom. It had become hers when Georgie had had a terrible attack of croup and needed night-time caring. Naturally I'd moved to the bedroom next to hers, so Taylor could sleep in peace. Her case—the largest she could wangle on board as cabin luggage—and her computer bag stood neatly beside the door. Her travel outfit lay on the bed. Of Taylor and her sandy jeans there was no sign.

With cold horror I knew where she was. And I also knew that no amount of frantic digging would move those tonnes of sand which would have crushed or suffocated her.

Which would do Georgie more harm, knowing her father had killed her mother—however accidentally—and might serve time in jail for manslaughter, or believing her mother had simply not returned from a business trip?

No contest. But first I needed Mina, not to confess to, heavens, no. Just for a little chat, which took place over not her everyday egg mayo but over her real favourite, smoked salmon on wholemeal. Had her boyfriend found another job?

She nodded, a little cream cheese on her lip. 'It gets worse. He's been head hunted for a club in Ecuador. Sometimes I think I shall never see him again.'

'I think I may be able to fix it. In fact, I know I can. Pack up and come back to the stables in about an hour. No fuss. Just knock off early. Okay? All you have to do is trust me.'

It didn't take very long to make a few changes on Taylor's computer. Firstly, I rebooked her ticket: she no longer wanted a return to Monaco, but chose a single to Ecuador, a country with which of course the UK had no extradition treaty. Then I gave her reason to go to Quito: once I'd accessed her secret account (it held a great deal more than I'd expected) it was easy enough to move funds to a company there from a couple of the blue chip companies for which she'd worked. In view of her savings, perhaps escape had been on her agenda anyway, if not to South America. As for her passport, if Mina pulled back her pretty hair into a tight and forbidding knot and looked angry, she was a dead ringer for Taylor. From her purse I extracted the bank card operating the secret account. Oh, she was so careless with her passwords—how often had I warned her?

I intercepted Mina before she could return to the stable and explained.

'You mean I can draw money using this card?' she squeaked. 'As much as I want?'

'As much as you feel you ought,' I said. 'You'll need an apartment, a car—don't stint yourself. The only condition is you must promise me that within a year you will change your name. You must never try to leave Ecuador in your own name or using this passport—come on, Mina, there are enough drugs criminals over there to sort out your ID. You—and this woman—have to disappear.'

* * *

As the deserted husband, I had two choices: to continue with the party, putting on a brave face, or to call it off. By the time the JCB had flattened the beach down to a compact smooth surface, with Taylor some four metres beneath it— though I couldn't be entirely sure how far or under which mound she lay—I did what she'd have done in similar circumstances. First I reinstated the fence. Next I confirmed all the arrangements and the show went on, with the caveat that I thought the contractors had messed up their beach-laying and it was unsafe to venture on to the sand. I might not have liked Taylor very much but I drew the line at dancing on her grave.

The future? I'm not sure yet. Naturally I shall report to the police that Taylor's gone missing and will show them her accounts, as amended by me, of course. With the stout fence still in situ, I can't imagine there'll ever be any danger of Taylor making an unwelcome reappearance. Should there ever be any sign of a landslip, however, it's just possible that when I hear Mina has left Ecuador for good, I might just take Georgie there for a long holiday. And we might come back to a new home. With completely different identities, of course.

Rounder Jon
Eldon Hughes

"Rounder Jon never escaped the Meska Té."

I'd muttered it the first time. I'd been listening to these three slick-suited strangers at the end of the bar, egging on the locals. They'd wandered in an hour earlier and made a run at me. I'd shrugged like I didn't know what they were talking about and moved off down the bar. I was hoping they were just fishing. Maybe they'd get bored and go try somewhere else. Plenty of other bars on the beach, right?

No such luck. They settled in and started buying drinks for the regulars, trying to drum up stories about the old tide runner. They were looking for gossip, trying to dig up a lead. Now, I'm all for good conversation. A spirited discussion sells more booze. But the less they heard what they wanted, the pushier they got. They'd already stomped right past rude and on into boring. This time I announced it for the whole bar to hear.

"Rounder Jon never escaped the Meska Té."

"What was that?" The youngest and loudest turned to face me, trying to assault me with the question. "What would you know about marsh crawlers...grandpa?" He sneered at me, actually sneered, like we were all in some late night B-movie.

I shrugged. "I know they don't like being called marsh crawlers. I know the story's nothing but a legend. The Jonny Man never escaped from the Meska Té. I know," I said, "because I was there." I announced that last line to the room, too.

The place got so quiet you could hear the smoke haze drifting in the air. I turned my attention to wiping a small puddle of spilled beer off the bar, working the rag in slow circles across the deep red grain of the old wood.

It didn't take long. The three of them rearranged themselves along the bar, coming to rest in front of me. I looked up and everyone else went back to their own conversations.

The older gent with the antique slick-backed hairpiece was in the center now; the man in charge. He rested himself on a stool and glanced, left to right, at his companions. Then his gaze came back to settle against mine. I heard a quiet thud and the subtle ring of soft metal as a coin was pinned between the wood and his well-manicured fingers.

I knew that sound. I'd heard it a few times before. Very few people these days have ever seen a gold coin outside the souvenir ads in a magazine. A man drops one in front of you, he's not fishing. He's hunting.

"Another round for the three of us, friend. One for yourself, if you've a mind," he said. "You can keep the change, if your story's good enough."

His voice was so smooth, his manner dripping with class. But even homicidal maniacs can look classy until the knife comes out. I sighed, a deep breath that left me hollow even as a lead weight formed in the pit of my stomach.

There was the tiniest glint of a cold humor in his eyes as the old man eased his hand away. I made a casual pass with the rag and the gold piece disappeared into my apron pocket. My arm hadn't hesitated, but I was pretty sure he'd caught the single eye blink.

It'd been a half dozen years since the Jonny Man had stumbled ashore with a strong box half full of raw gold ore. Said he'd gotten it from some mine in Mexico. Anybody else would have raced to a safe deposit box, or sold it. Not Jon. He'd found some guy to melt it all down and turn it into gold coins. One side had a tiny island, with an even tinier palm tree silhouetted against a full moon. The other featured a giant, slanted "J" with a pirate flag flying from the top of the letter. It was Jon all over, pure braggadocio—bold, foolhardy, romantic. He used them as calling cards for serious clients. If the old man had one of Jon's coins, then he was unfinished business. The weight in my stomach grew a twin.

"That drink?" the jittery boy with the sneer said.

"And the story, of course," the old man followed.

I nodded and set us all up with a round before leaning against the back bar.

I stopped with the glass not quite to my lips. Business was business. But a good drink...

In my book, the air of a good whiskey is the best part. It's a promise of what's to come, carried on the aromas of the past. This wasn't some corporate, manufactured liquor, batched together in clean rooms by some sterile computer and then focus-grouped out of any character it had ever had. This was the real thing. Single malt, made by hand, by people who had seen grandchildren grow up since then, or died trying. Drop for drop it was worth a hundred times what it cost to bring it to my glass. But price doesn't determine value. Memories do.

I let the aroma take me back to peat and rich dark earth; to salt carried on the wind of a distant sea. I felt the rhythm of the blood in my veins as it slowed to match the dull low thumps of the ocean breakers outside and waited for it all to sync up, beat for beat, tide for tide, remembering when.

The smallest sip and the world sped up again.

A mirror ran the length of the bar behind my head. I turned to face it, looking around over their heads, taking the time to see what the three hard cases behind me could see in the reflection. Lots of real wood, not that fabricated crap. There was just enough light to keep the shadows alive. Crowded, but not too crowded. No one appeared to be listening, but I knew half the house was hanging on every word.

Discretion. Nice. I admire both the deed and sound of the word. Be a good name for this place.

"Come on, old man. We don't have all night," the young one said.

I looked at my new drinking companions, then at my watch. "It's not quite night yet, lad," I assured him. "And this won't take all of it. But, a true tale does require a bit of telling."

I gestured to the empty bar stool in front of him, and looked to include the other man among them. He was still standing, his gaze keeping a steady bounce between the crowd and the door.

"Relax, gentlemen. Take a load off."

"We don't have time for—" the boy started. I'd decided to call him Ferret. He looked like a ferret; jumpy, eager, head yanking around trying to find something to pounce on. He might have finished the sentence, but the elder statesman laid a hand on his arm.

"Come on, Mister C, this old guy don't know nothin'."

A bony hand squeezed the arm once. Ferret shut up and sat down. Not that he stopped moving. There was something weird going on right beneath his skin, like he couldn't keep his bones from vibrating. Maybe it was just imagination, but I thought I could feel him, humming down the stool and across the old plank floor, a soft staccato rumble reaching underneath the bar to where I was standing.

Mr. C said, "Please, tell us more about Rounder Jon, and what you think you saw."

I took another sip and started in.

"There are a thousand tales about Rounder Jon floating all over the Back Bay. Folks'll say Rounder Jon once made the run to Cuba and back in a single night, all by the dark of the moon. Or that he escaped from the palace in the old capital with a box of cigars off the desk of old Castro himself. Heck, most of the tales are probably true. But he never escaped from the Meska Té. No one does. That's not to say he didn't have dealings with them."

Ferret said, "Well, I heard he got involved with some strangers from up north, got scared and ran off with the wrong man's money."

"First off, son, best to remember you're the stranger here. And hearing things is a sign of mental illness. You might want to have that looked at."

I thought Ferret was going to come across the bar, but the old man had a hand back on his arm and some stern words in his ear.

He sat back down and Mr. C nodded at me. "And what do you know of these marsh crawlers?" He raised a hand. "The Meska Té. Please. Tell us."

"The Meska Té are an old race. Not old like we think of it—founding fathers, moon landings and such, but old like before Columbus got his first boat."

"You mean Indians, First Nations."

"I don't know," I said. "They might be even older. They're ancient. Like they were around to give the world a push, start it turning the first time.

"Some say they might have been nomads, once. Centuries ago, before anybody else floated in from the sea, the Meska Té were already settled along the Back Bay. I've heard some folks say there aren't many left. Others will swear there are thousands of them out there, living in secret up and down the coast, hiding in the marsh grass that runs between the beach and the swamps. I don't know what anybody knows for sure. If some government official ever tried to make a count I'd bet it was never recorded anywhere. That is, if they got back out to tell anybody."

"What's that supposed to mean?" Ferret asked.

"The marshlands can be deceptive. Some places you walk off into the high grass and think you've stepped into another world. Might be, you have. You can wander for the rest of your life and never find your way out again, unless you're one of the Meska. That's kinda how they want it. See, the Meska Té consider themselves to be a part of the Back Bay. They are its protectors, in particular, the areas where the tall grass meets the sea.

"That made things difficult for the Jonny Man. Rounder Jon's chosen occupation had him running boats in and out of the marsh lands and glades. High powered boats have never been too kind or considerate of the natural way of things. Put him in a hard place with the Meska. After all, the marshlands are more than just their home. They are their food source, their temples."

"Their temples?" Mr. C asked.

"Sure, every culture revolves around food and survival. That which nurtures and protects us becomes sacred."

"Pretty deep thoughts for a bartender." It was the third guy. The one with a voice that sounded like it came from the deep end of a mine. He talked softer and slower than either of the other two, but the voice was solid. Like something you'd build a house on, or a prison.

I shrugged. "I used to read a lot. Anyway, the Meska Té aren't much different from you and me, once you get past what they look like."

"I heard they run around on all fours," Ferret said.

"Sometimes they do." I nodded. "When they are taking down prey, for example. They are faster on four limbs than anything that runs on just two."

"That's weird." There he was, sneering again. "Standing like a man, but crawling around like a crab. How fast could they be?"

"Crabs have eight legs, son," I said. "Panthers have four, though. How far you think you'd get in a foot race with a panther?"

The elder statesman cut us off before I could talk Ferret into making the bet.

"Tell me more of what they look like. Describe them for me," he pushed.

"Mostly they're shorter than the average man. Kinda like we used to be, two centuries ago. They can be paler, or darker, sometimes both. Their skin tends to change, patterns and shades that blend with the colors of the beach in the moonlight. And they only have four fingers...well three fingers and a thumb, when they're adults."

"Adults?" the old man asked.

"It's a rite of passage," I nodded. "The pinkies get sacrificed to prove their faith and commitment to the family."

I held my right hand up, open, in front of me. "Their hands are long and thin, much thinner from front to back than yours and mine are. And there is a flap of skin that webs the gaps between each digit."

Ferret snorted. "Yeah, right."

"Hey, friend. You asked, I'm telling. You don't want to hear? Your fingers fit the door handle just fine."

"I knew a guy had webbed fingers once." It was Gravel Voice again. He looked at Mr. C and nodded. "His father and mother were cousins or something."

"Anyway," I said. "There must have been a hundred of

54

them waiting for us that night when they dragged us off the beach, who knows how many hiding out in the shadows."

I gestured with my glass, asking them if they were ready for a refill. Mr. C shook his head.

The other two pushed their empties toward me. I poured while I continued.

"Everywhere I looked I saw these big, round eyes shining back at us. You ever catch an animal in the glare of a flashlight in the middle of the night? Even when they're in the shadows, the Meska Té's eyes glow, like they're mirroring back light you can't even see.

"And strong? Let me tell you. I'd bet not one of those guys topped out at a hundred pounds. But two of them had hold of Rounder Jon and had him stuck solid. That's saying something. You know how big the Jonny Man is."

"I don't," Gravel Voice said. "Never had the pleasure of dealing with him, at least not face to face."

"No? Huh. Well he's half again bigger than me, and a lot stronger. I'm just an old guy; but even when I was at my best I wasn't as strong as Rounder Jon." I slid their glasses over and plugged the bottle.

"One time we were out in a cigarette boat, forty plus feet long. Man that thing could move. Twin inboard turbos and extra-long range fuel tanks, all of them near to full. We ran up hard on a sandbar. We were going way too fast, trying to get shut of some unfortunate business associates. You understand." I looked at Mr. C, but he didn't even blink.

"He climbed out of the boat and stood there, waist deep in saltwater and sand. He reached down and lifted the nose of that big ass boat clear out of the water. Dropped it down free of the sandbar, jumped up behind the wheel and off we went. Got away clean as a baby's dream."

"Is that what you were up to the night they grabbed you?" Gravel Voice asked. "Did they interrupt you...doing business?"

I shook my head. "No, we were settling a social matter. I was there to be a witness."

"A witness," Mr. C repeated.

The bells over the front door made an old fashioned jingle,

just before the door opened. The sound of the ocean surf got suddenly louder, and an orange red glow from the sunset bathed the front of the bar, making the scuffed wood floor look like smoldering coals. A tall, thin shadow walked toward us. The shadow and the glow slid sideways out of sight as the door closed behind him, revealing a craggy, friendly face.

"Hey, Joe," I called. "Sound system's warmed up, ready for you to plug in."

"Cool." He was carrying a battered guitar case. "Franky Fingers and Willie ought to be around in a bit." A round of applause went up from the house.

"You want one to get you started?"

He shrugged. "Wouldn't hurt my feelings any."

I looked at Mr. C. "Gimme a sec."

I grabbed a mug and pulled the tap, then met Joe at the end of the bar. He took it and drained it in one long drink.

"Cools the blood, warms the soul." He sighed and handed back the empty mug. "Anything I can do for you before I set up?" he asked.

"Call the boys and tell them to shake a leg. The natives are getting restless."

"Sure thing." He popped his guitar case open and I went back to the gents down the bar.

"You're in luck," I said. "Franky Fingers, Willie and Stringfellow Joe. The place is gonna swing tonight."

"What did you mean about being a witness?" There was that deep, gravelly voice again, cutting right across any thoughts of the night's profits. "Are you saying you gave Rounder Jon up to the police?"

I looked at him, then at them. I smiled and shook my head. "Getting caught by the cops might have been a blessing. Rounder Jon got caught by an angry father."

"A father?" Mr. C asked.

"Tenecate, ruler of the Meska Té. And, the father of a certain grassland princess, Neeshawah."

"He did her, didn't he?" Ferret said. He was so excited he reached across and grabbed my arm. There was this slimy wet smile on his narrow face. I looked away. I didn't want to follow where the gleeful look in his eyes would take me.

I shook him off. "No. If he had, they would have staked his body head down on the beach, sliced him up and left him alive so he could watch the tide roll over him."

"That's pretty dramatic," gravel voice said.

"Remember the finger thing? They're big on dramatic. Probably why they put up with Jon." My grin was small, and didn't last long. "The Meska would see it as a sacrifice, an offering. Give him one last chance to make amends. He could make his peace, feed the crabs and, through them, the marshlands."

I refilled Ferret's glass and set it back down in front of him, just to show I'd taken no offense at the contact. "No, what the Jonny Man did was much worse. He fell in love with Neeshawah, and her with him."

"This Tenecate wasn't too fond of the idea," Mr. C said.

"I should say not." I refilled Gravel Voice's glass without asking.

"He'd been caught more than once on their land, and been told in no uncertain terms to stay out. But Jon? Well, he always said the safest place to hide was where folks were afraid to look. So, whenever he was pursued, especially by the law, he'd lay up in a cove, cover the boat over in high grass. The damage his boats did to the wildlife and the way he defied Tenecate would have been enough for them to feed him to the sea.

"But somewhere, during one of those times, he met Neeshawah. After that, there was no keeping him away. Couldn't get her out of his head."

Ferret started giggling. It was a creepy sound. It got louder, and faster. Then he snorted.

"Come on!" he said. "A head for some head? This Rounder guy wanted some head, so the old guy took his. That's funny!"

"Tenecate didn't take Rounder Jon's head," I said. "I bet he thought about it a few times, though. Just shows you have no kids of your own."

"What's that supposed to mean?" he asked.

Huh, maybe he does. Now, that's a disturbing thought.

At least he'd stopped the weird giggling noise.

"Tenecate could have taken Jon's head, but what about Neeshawah? She loved Rounder Jon. No father would cause his only daughter that much pain. So, he made Jon give his hand instead."

"Marriage," Gravel Voice said. "Tenecate made Rounder Jon marry Neeshawah. That's what you were there to witness, a wedding."

I nodded. "A hand fasting but, yeah. Jonny married Neeshawah. He swore to stay by her side for the rest of their lives." I tipped my drink back and swallowed the last of it. Then I pointed at them with the empty glass. "The result is the same. Like I said, Rounder Jon never escaped from the Meska Té, and he never will."

"Guess we'll just have to go find him, then, and take what he owes us," Ferret said.

"You gotta do what you gotta do." I shrugged.

"Oh, I don't know that we need go to all that trouble," Mr. C said. He leaned back on the stool and looked at me. "I believe we can accomplish our goals right here."

"How so?" I asked.

"I notice the little finger is missing from your left hand," he said. "Something tells me it wasn't an accident. So, what did you get for delivering Rounder Jon to the Meska Té?"

I was gonna protest, but hey, the truth is the truth.

"This place," I said, motioning around me.

"Not entirely accurate, I suspect," he said. "I think you got money. I think you purchased this establishment with the money from Rounder Jon's boat, money that he was to have...invested for me."

Like I said, truth is truth.

Ferret jumped off his stool. "So maybe what I do is come around the bar and start taking the money out of your ass?"

Mr. C raised his hand again. "Be still! Look around you. Try to think instead of speak."

More people had been arriving while we talked. The word was already out about the night's music. Folks were still leaving us alone, giving us an ever smaller bubble of space. I was going to have to get back to work pretty quick.

Mr. C's hand returned to the bar. "My nephew is slow to

learn the value of patience. I, however, was not. This would appear to be a very useful establishment to own a piece of," Mr. C said. "Or all of."

"Now, wait a minute..." I started to object, but he stood up next to Ferret.

"The money was mine. So, this bar is rightfully mine. However, for now let's consider ourselves partners, eh?" That cold humor was back in his eyes. "Take the night to get used to the idea," he said. "Mull the alternatives. You won't like them. We'll come back tomorrow and work out the details."

Ferret said, "Maybe one of us should stay here and keep an eye on him tonight?"

"Oh, I don't think that is necessary." But then he paused. "On the other hand, it would be worthwhile to have a firsthand account of the night's business." He turned to Gravel Voice. "Would you mind staying behind?"

"Shouldn't I stay close to you. I mean, just in case."

"Hey, stick around," I told Gravel Voice. "The music's gonna be good, and you'll have more fun here. Uh, no offense," I said to the other two.

"None taken," Mr. C said, with a thin smile. He looked at Ferret. "Let's go."

I stood there behind the bar, making a fist around the rag in my hand. As they left, Franky Fingers and Willie came in.

Time to get this party started.

I turned my attention to the people lining up at the bar. It was awhile before I found myself back in front of Gravel Voice.

"Why'd you want me to stay?" he asked.

"Figured you'd be more fun than the other guy."

"Maybe." He nodded. "Then again, maybe not."

"Consider it a favor, then. Where they're going is no place for a cop."

I had to hand it to him. He didn't even try to deny it. We didn't have to go through all of the "What gave me away?" or the "Where have we seen each other before?" crap.

"Besides, I have a confession to make," I said. I motioned toward a new group gathering at the end of the bar. "Just give me a couple minutes."

I poured him a fresh one and went down the bar to fill some drink orders. Up on stage Stringfellow Joe and the guys started in on some vintage Django Reinhardt riffs. Joe's fingers danced up and down the neck of his guitar. I could feel the crowd getting into it.

It's gonna be a good night. I glanced at the door. Better for some than others, of course.

I went back to Gravel Voice and pointed at his glass.

He shook his head and said, "You were gonna confess something."

"Forgive me, Father," I began, and he gave me a tight smile. "It's like this. The Meska Té weren't gonna just let me go after the hand fasting. It wasn't some 'Hey, thanks for coming. Be sure and take a piece of cake.' affair. I had to make them a promise, and I had to swear I'd live up to it."

I raised my left hand. The skin was still pink and healing. It was going to be an ugly scar. "Even that cost me my pinkie."

"What was the promise?"

"You ever heard of a bride price?"

He shook his head.

"You know what a dowry is, right?"

He nodded.

"Bride price is like that, except it's paid by the groom, to the bride's family."

"Ahh." He nodded. "So, you didn't buy this place with the money after all."

I shook my head. "Sure I did. The Meska don't care about money. I doubt they even know what it is. They care about the land, and about family. The groom has to prove he's worthy of marrying the bride, prove he has the strength and position to protect her and support her at least as well as her father. Among the Meska, that's proven by sacrifice. The bride price is paid with a soul, a life. The body is returned to the land. The soul stays behind, a spirit bound to protecting the bride, and later, her own family."

"That's just..." he started, then trailed off.

"Yeah, like you or I don't have any weird relatives," I said. "The more valuable the bride, the bigger the price. Sometimes it's just the soul of an animal—livestock, say. Sometimes it's the life of a servant, or even a lesser family member. In rare cases, like with royalty, it requires two souls."

"Two souls? You mean two people?"

I nodded. "It's worse if a guy has no holdings, no servants. Then he has to find two friends or family members who love him enough, and believe the marriage is important enough to the village or the family, to sacrifice themselves for it."

"Then shouldn't you be dead?" he asked.

"Believe me, I would be, and Jon would still be one short. But he and Tenecate made a deal. As part of marrying Neeshawah, Jon offered up an alternate sacrifice, one that would help put a stop to the illegal boats running in and out the marshlands."

"Just how was he supposed to do that?"

I looked away from him. "Well, that's where the confession comes in..."

He jumped up and started for the door.

"It's too late. The Meska Té were waiting outside. They're already gone. And you'll never find what's left of them by morning."

He stopped and turned to look at me. Then he came back and sat down.

"So. What happens next?"

I shrugged and poured him a drink. "The world turns. The tide rolls in."

Tsunami Surprise
Delaney Green

Why did it have to be an arm?

The other garbage that had washed up in the last fifteen months had been stuff Frank could tag for the tsunami debris team if it was big or leave for the cleanup volunteers who showed up every weekend to pick up the beach. They picked up shoes. Dolls. Plastic. Construction waste. Oceanographers said tsunami trash would be washing ashore in Washington State for a generation.

"Who was that?" Doris yelled from the lab.

"A kid found an arm under that dock on Ruby Beach."

Doris stepped into the doorway. "A Japanese arm?"

"I guess. He said it was chained to the dock."

"How come nobody saw an arm chained to a dock?"

"It was buried. The kid's dog dug it up."

When Japanese debris first started washing ashore, a few men in Forks had talked about scoring a free boat, but Frank only knew of one guy who'd actually scraped off the layers of marine slime and gooseneck barnacles from the little runabout he found. Nobody else wanted a boat that bad, including the original owners in Japan.

By the time that big dock from Misawa washed up in Newport, the novelty had worn off. Nobody wanted any part of any Japanese junk. The Newport dock was cut into pieces and hauled away, but the state park commission still hadn't awarded a contract to remove the dock in Frank's back yard.

And now a kid in Queets had found an arm under it. Frank hadn't even had his coffee yet.

He emptied yesterday's leftover joe into a mug. "I gotta drive down there."

Doris said, "Don't drink that. Stop at the coffee shop on

63

the way out of town."

Frank took a mouthful and spit it back in the mug. "Why does it turn to battery acid overnight?"

"It's day-old. I'll make fresh before you come back. Don't forget the bolt cutter."

"Right," Frank took it down from its peg by the door. "Did Wally come to fix the freezer yet?"

"No. He said he was sorry."

"Well, where am I supposed to put the arm when I bring it back?"

"Your house I guess."

"Mel told me no more evidence at our house."

"We got no choice."

"Why can't you put it in your freezer?"

"Frank, you know I just bought a quarter of a pig. Bring the arm here first so I can get the prints off it. Have you got your camera?"

Frank took the digital out of his desk drawer and dropped it into his pocket. "Yup."

Doris said, "I'll figure out who to contact in Japan. Take an ice chest along."

"What, mine?"

"I won't tell Melanie if you won't."

Frank parked the squad in the gravel lot next to Ruby Beach. He grabbed the bolt cutter and the ice chest and took the path that led to the water. The beach would be crawling with cleanup volunteers tomorrow and Saturday. Lucky the kid found the arm today.

He heard barking when he stepped to the sand. Sounded like a big dog. He squinted at the dock and saw a black lab galloping toward him. Heard a kid yell, "Stop, Joe! Friend." The dog paced, waiting for the boy to catch up. Frank heard the growling from fifteen feet away.

Frank waited for the boy. "Hi. I'm Tommy Jeever. This is Joe." Joe growled. "Friend, Joe. Sit." Joe sat, but he had the same look on his face Doris wore all day every April 1st. Tommy panted. "It's a good thing you're here," Tommy said.

"Two guys down the beach had metal detectors, but Joe scared 'em off."

"So nobody knows about this yet?"

"Nope. Man, am I lucky school got out last week. Otherwise, those two guys mighta found it first."

"Lucky. Take the cutter, will you?" Frank handed it over. They started for the dock. Joe nosed between them.

"Wow, is this police equipment?"

"Sure. Special issue. So, what made you decide to dig under the dock?"

"Joe started digging. I let him go because Mom never lets him dig at home. Then I saw what he had. Then I called you." Tommy held up a track phone. "Check it, Chief. My very own phone. So far I got numbers in it for Forks police, Mom, Dad, my cousin, and the casino."

"Sweet. Can you hold the dog? I've got to take pictures." Frank got a long shot of the dock and a couple shots of the hole, then zoomed in for a close-up of the arm and the way it was attached to the dock. He shot a close-up of the plaque screwed to the dock. Then he put on gloves, cut the chain, and lifted the arm. Joe barked.

"Don't worry, Chief, I got him," Tommy said. Frank saw a black line on the skin. He brushed away the clinging sand. It was a tattoo. A bamboo leaf tattoo trailed from the severed elbow down the outside of the arm almost to the wrist. Frank shot a picture of the tat, too. He placed the arm in the ice chest.

"What happened to the rest of him?" Tommy asked.

"How old are you?"

"Ten-goin'-on eleven."

"Well, the rest of him could've stayed in Japan when the dock tore loose. Or he could've been eaten by a shark or something else. It's four thousand miles of ocean between here and Japan. Lotta hungry animals in that much water."

"Gross." The dog pawed the ice chest. "Leave it, Joe," Tommy said. "Sit."

"Well, Tommy, I've got to get this back to Forks so my deputy can lift some prints. Can I ask you not to talk about this just yet? Ongoing investigation."

"Can I tell Robbie I found an arm?"

"Robbie a friend?" Tommy nodded. Frank said, "I wish you wouldn't. Give me a week to get hold of the Japanese authorities and find out what they want to do, and then you can tell."

"How about my mom?"

"Would she let you keep coming down to the beach if she knew?"

"I won't tell anybody."

Back in the parking lot, Frank put the ice chest in the trunk. Joe growled. Tommy said, "He thinks you're taking his toy."

"Sorry, Joe," Frank said. Tommy handed over the bolt cutter. Frank said, "You did good. Someday you could be a cop."

"Thanks, but I'm gonna play basketball for the Blazers."

"I'll come watch you play." Tommy waved and Joe glared until Frank turned left out of the lot to drive back to Forks.

At the station, Frank hauled the ice chest into the lab. Doris put on a mask and gloves before lifting the arm to the stainless steel table. "Pretty beat up," she said. "I hope I can get prints. Ooh, check the tat. What is that, bamboo?" She flipped down her magnifier. "This is really fine work, Frank. This isn't your everyday tat."

"Let's take a couple more pictures and get prints off the hand. Wouldn't hurt to dust the rest of the arm just in case." Frank zoomed his camera in on the tattoo.

Doris said, "I contacted the National Police Agency in Tokyo. They sent the address for the cops in Misawa, since that's where the dock came from. All the prefectures handle their own cases. Prefecture's like a state."

"Doris, I am not keeping this thing until somebody gets around to calling us. Their whole city was wrecked. They may never call. Let's mail the arm and let 'em keep it in their freezer."

"Human remains. It'll have to go from Seattle to Hawaii and on to Tokyo. It'll cost us a grand, and we'll have to get a ton of documents."

"You looked it up already."

"Sure."

"Dammit. I should've let the kid's dog have it."

"Frank McCormick, you don't mean that." He looked at her. "Okay, maybe you do. Let's just get the prints, send 'em to Misawa with the pictures, and see what they say. They might be too busy to deal and just ask us to handle it."

An hour later, Frank had uploaded the pictures and was filling out a report. Doris came in and thumped the ice chest next to Frank's desk. "Done. Got prints off the hand. No prints on the arm. Everything's pretty waterlogged. Got some marine crawlies wedged in there, too."

"And now they're in my ice chest."

"Clean it with bleach. How do you suppose a guy got cuffed to a dock?"

"Not my problem. My problem is hiding that thing from Melanie."

"I'll send the email and pictures to Misawa if you want."

"Forward the email to Tokyo, too."

Back home, Frank wrapped the arm in butcher paper and labeled it "Tripe," which he was pretty sure was cow stomach. He put it in his big freezer under packages of salmon and beef. Melanie wouldn't take it out. She never cooked tripe. Nobody he knew cooked tripe.

On Monday, Doris met Frank at the door of the station first thing in the morning. "Frank, guess what?"

"You made me coffee. God bless you."

She handed her cup to him. "No—yes, here, take mine—about that arm. Misawa City is sending a guy here to pick it up."

"You're kidding me." Frank preferred Doris's coffee to his own and sucked down a heart-jolting swallow. "Oh, that's good, Dorrie."

"You're welcome. The guy is an agent. He'll be here on

Wednesday, the email said."

"Wow, what's the hurry? Must be a big case."

"They said it was something they'd been working on before the tsunami. They had a guy that disappeared, a businessman, rich guy. He was supposed to come in for questioning, but the tsunami hit and nobody's seen him since. The police thought this guy was mixed up with the Yakuza. Anyway, they want the arm."

On Wednesday, a rental car pulled up outside the jail. Frank watched a small, neat man in an expensive suit get out. Frank said to Doris, "Looks like Misawa cops get paid a lot more than we do."

"Figures," Doris said.

The Japanese agent walked in showing his ID. "You must be Chief McCormick," he said, sticking out his hand. He had an accent, but not so thick Frank couldn't understand him. "I'm Special Agent Matsushita."

Frank shook his hand, gestured to Doris. "How are you? This is Doris Glick, my deputy."

"Nice to meet you," Doris said.

"Where is the evidence?" Matsushita said.

"Our freezer here is out, so I've got it at my house," Frank said.

Matsushita's eyebrows met. "I see."

"Don't worry," Doris said. "Frank's freezer is brand new."

"I am certain Chief McCormick's freezer is adequate," Matsushita said. "But I am expected back on Friday, and I have a long drive back to Seattle. My superior wants to close this case, and we think the arm will help us to do that. Also, we are still cleaning up from the quake and the tsunami. You understand. I am needed at home."

"That terrible tsunami," Doris said. "And all those people washed out to sea. And that nuclear plant. I can't even imagine it. My sympathies to you and your country."

"Thank you, Miss Glick."

"It's 'Mrs.'"

"My apologies, Mrs. Glick."

Doris flapped her hand. "I'm a widow."

"I am very sorry for your loss." Matsushita bowed, then turned to Frank. "If I may ask, where was the arm found?"

"Chained to the front of the dock that washed up on Ruby Beach. Didn't your supervisor tell you?"

"Of course. But we like to hear firsthand accounts from witnesses."

"Me, too," Frank said.

"Did you find the arm?"

"No. A kid found it. Well, his dog did."

Matsushita took out a little notebook and jotted something in it. "And the boy lives here in Forks?"

"He lives on the rez. The Quinault Indian Reservation. On the coast. Junior high kid."

"Did he or the dog touch the arm?"

"No. He called it in right away."

"Good. Did you lift any prints?"

"Not from the arm," Doris said. "I just got the prints we sent to you."

"Your captain said it was a businessman," Frank said.

Matsushita nodded. "Very unfortunate. We believe he had joined forces with the *ninkyō dantai*—I think you Americans call it Yakuza."

"Organized crime," Frank said.

Matsushita nodded. "We had invited him to come in voluntarily to answer some questions. We planned a meeting for March 15. But, as you know, the tsunami struck March 11."

"How are you all doing over there?" Frank said.

"It is hard work, Chief McCormick. So many thousands of people still have no homes. Schools are disrupted. Businesses are destroyed. We Japanese are a tenacious people, but we are weary. Every time we finish one task, two more take its place."

"I know how that is."

"You conduct investigations, Chief McCormick?"

"Small potatoes compared to you. Stolen boats. School mascots dragged into the woods. Tourists re-enacting scenes from *Twilight*. That kind of thing."

"Of course. Not to cause difficulties, but if it is convenient, could we go to your house now? I have a plane to catch in Seattle."

"It's no trouble at all."

"Nice to meet you," Doris called as they walked out.

"And you, Miss—Mrs. Glick," Matsushita said. He bowed again.

In Frank's basement, Frank and Matsushita piled packages of meat into a laundry basket. Frank said, "I buried the arm under this stuff so my wife wouldn't find it. She doesn't like evidence mixed in with her groceries."

Frank passed a package labeled "salmon" to Matsushita. When Frank got to the bottom of the freezer, he said, "Agent Matsushita, we have a problem. It's not here."

"I do not understand. How can an arm walk away?"

"You're funny," Frank said. Matsushita blinked. "Never mind." Frank looked at all the packages again. "What the hell?" he grumbled. He punched up Melanie's cell. "Hey, baby. Where's the package of tripe we had in the freezer?"

"I brought it to the church for the Wildwood Banquet Saturday night."

"Why'd you do that? That tripe was evidence. I got a guy all the way from Japan here to pick it up."

"You did not put evidence in my freezer again."

"Mel, I'm sorry. The freezer at the office was out."

"I thought 'tripe' was some weird bird Cy Berg shot and gave to you. Serves you right if they cooked it up already, Frank McCormick."

"They wouldn't cook it once they unwrapped it."

"Why, what was it?"

"Tell you later." He tucked his phone in his pocket. Matsushita's face was like the clay warriors in those Chinese tombs. Waiting. Frank bared his teeth. He said, "This is awkward, Agent Matsushita. My wife thought the package was meat. She gave it to people preparing a big dinner for the town Saturday night. Fundraiser."

"It would be wise to retrieve the arm before any of the

cooks open the package."

Frank's cell buzzed. Doris said, "Frank, Tammy Munson called from the church. They unwrapped a package of meat somebody donated—I guess it was Mel—and found the arm inside. Tammy's pretty shook up. I told her to put it back in the freezer and that you'd come and get it."

"On my way." Frank told Matsushita, "Too late: they opened it. Can you help me get this stuff back in the freezer?" Matsushita handed packages to Frank, who stacked and piled and wedged until Melanie's groceries were jammed back in the freezer, probably not the way Mel wanted it done, but Frank was able to close and latch the lid. "Close enough for rock and roll," Frank muttered. "Let's go."

Tammy Munson was white-faced when Frank and Matsushita met her in the church kitchen. "I guess you thought this would be funny, Frank McCormick, but it is NOT."

"Tammy, I'm sorry. It was a mix-up with Melanie. The tripe is evidence."

"'Tripe?' Are you kidding me? Just where did you find an arm, Frank McCormick? You don't think people want to know when the police chief finds an arm in town?"

"I didn't find it in town—"

"And on top of that, I know for a fact that Melanie asked you not to bring evidence home any more. Poor Mrs. Armitage saw 'tripe' on the package and volunteered to cook it. Said she had a recipe from her Grandfather Beaumont in Lyon. She opened it up and fainted right there on the hard floor. Somebody had to take her home."

"I'll go by her house later. Where is the tripe now? Special Agent Matsushita has a plane to catch."

Matsushita dipped his head at Mrs. Munson. "My apologies, Miss. It is my fault. Chief McCormick saved the evidence at our request."

Tammy blinked at the stranger. She said, "It's not your fault. It's the chief's fault for taking the arm to his house in the first place. Frank, I don't understand why you don't just buy a freezer for the station."

"Tammy? The package?"

"Over in the walk-in. Just get it out of here. I've got to put my raccoon in the pressure cooker."

The other ladies prepping food for the Wildwood Banquet peeked up at Frank and Matsushita over their carving knives. The susurrus of their whispers was like sandpaper on a dry hull. Frank would be the butt of jokes for months after this: "Hey, Chief, how 'bout a little arm and eggs? My treat." and "McCormick, I hear they got shoulder roast on sale at Thriftway." Frank sighed.

Agent Matsushita peeked under the butcher paper. "Yes, this is it," he said. He zipped the arm inside a heavy-duty rubber sleeve and then placed the sleeve inside his shoulder bag.

"Can you travel like that? Doris said you need permits."

"Of course." Matsushita patted his breast pocket. "Permits. And now, if you would drive me back to your station, I can return to Seattle and catch my flight." Matsushita found Tammy and said, "Again, my sincere apologies for the trouble. And my thanks for your help." He bowed.

"You're welcome," Tammy said. Frank thought he might try bowing next time Tammy tried to chew him out a new one.

Back at the station, Matsushita placed his bag in the trunk of his rental.

"Stay for dinner?" Doris said.

"Thank you. No." He shook their hands. "Thank you for your assistance. We can let you know how the case resolves."

"Appreciate it," Frank said.

"Come back and visit sometime," Doris said.

"Thank you. Sayonara." He bowed. They watched his rental head south on Highway 101.

Doris said, "That was quick. Don't waste any time, do they."

"They sure don't."

"I'm outa here, Frank. See you tomorrow." Doris got into her Acura and spit gravel as she left the lot. Frank had asked her a hundred times not to do that. Matsushita hadn't done that. He'd been careful. Frank frowned. He went inside and sat at his desk. He clicked up something on his computer.

Then he picked up the phone.

On Saturday, Frank helped Wally move the new freezer in and the old freezer out. Doris manned the front desk. Frank and Wally had just got the old freezer heaved up to the back of Wally's truck when Doris called, "Frank, get in here. You better take a look at this."

"You good, Wally?" Wally nodded and shut the tailgate. Frank legged it to his desk. Doris fizzled and snapped and popped like she had a short. Frank said, "What's wrong with you?"

"Email from Japan. Read it."

Frank read: "Thank you for your telephone call. Your assistance in the matter of the arm allowed us to apprehend the suspect when he landed in Tokyo."

"What's all that?" Doris asked.

"Matsushita wasn't a cop. He was Yakuza."

Doris's jaw dropped. Frank hardly ever surprised her. It felt good.

She said, "He was a criminal? How the Sam Hill did you know that?"

"He had a tattoo. I saw the tip of it when we were pawing through my freezer. At first I figured Matsushita must be pretty high up to keep his job and a tattoo both, since the Japanese don't approve of tattoos. But then I figured that a country dealing with thousands of dead and missing and homeless and trillions of dollars of damage and a nuclear meltdown and all the other crap they're dealing with would never fly a guy halfway across the ocean to pick up an arm that took a year to get here."

"When did you figure this out?"

"I started to wonder when I saw that suit. When he held up his badge, I saw his left pinky was half sawed off. Yakuza does that if a guy gets in trouble with his boss or owes somebody money. Plus he called Yakuza '*ninkyō dantai*,' which is what Yakuza calls itself. The cops call Yakuza"— Frank glanced at his hand— "*bōryokudan.*"

"Let me see your hand, Frank McCormick. Cheater. Where'd you learn that?"

"Google."

She gave his hand back. "Why didn't you say anything to me? Why didn't you arrest him?"

"And put him where? In our jail? Deal with extradition? No way. So I called the cops in Tokyo and they called the cops in Misawa. It turns out the chief in Misawa never heard of Matsushita. In fact, he planned to ignore our email until he had time to deal with it. Besides, he had nobody to send and no money to send him with. But he knew somebody in his office was slipping intel to Yakuza because whenever they thought they had a charge that would stick, Yakuza always wiggled out of it."

"You don't speak Japanese. How'd you find all this out?"

"You know that high school Japanese teacher? The one whose salary we all chipped in to pay until her papers cleared the State department? Hiroko? I got her in here to interpret."

"Where was I?"

"Wednesday? You left at five o'clock like always. I called Sea-Tac after you left. Nobody named Matsushita was scheduled on any plane going west. He could have gone anywhere. He could've been traveling under a different name. So I got hold of Hiroko and we called Tokyo. They're sixteen hours ahead of us but it only takes twelve hours to fly there. I didn't want to risk their missing him."

"So they arrested Matsushita?"

"Yup, and they're tracing where our email pinged on its way to them."

"Whose arm was it?"

"Matsushita told the truth about that. It was a guy who was giving fifty percent of his real estate profits to Yakuza."

"So why'd they kill him?"

"He wanted to change their take to ten percent."

"Why did Yakuza want the arm back?"

"The same tattoo artist does all the Yakuza tattoos for the Yamaguchi-gumi syndicate big dogs. It's a special kind of tattooing. They do it the old way by hand using a metal needle attached to a wooden handle."

"I knew that was a special tat. I looked it up. It's called *irezumi*. It's a dying art."

Frank said, "Yakuza guys get body tats that cover their arms, back, legs and chest. Costs thousands of dollars and takes years to do."

"My little daisy was done in an hour, and I thought that hurt pretty bad. I can't imagine tattooing on a little jacket."

"Doris, you got a tattoo? Where?"

She looked over her glasses at him. "Need to know basis, Frank."

He shrugged. "If Matsushita had peeled off his coat, we would've seen his tats. The chief in Misawa figures Yakuza was afraid the tattoo on the arm would lead the cops to the artist, and then he'd identify the senior members of the organization."

"But everybody knows who the Yakuza are. Their pictures are on the internet."

"Apparently not all of them."

Doris mused, "I thought Matsushita smelled too good to be a cop." Frank waited for the punchline. "He was wearing Eau D'Hadrien. It costs five hundred dollars an ounce."

Despite having worked with Doris for fifteen years, Frank was still surprised by all the trivia she had squirreled away. He said, "Okay, I'll bite: How the hell do you know that?"

"You think I go home after work and knit? I got a life, too, Frank McCormick."

"I never doubted it."

Doris lapped her cardigan over her chest. "Last time I went to Seattle, I stopped at Nordstrom's for the beauty trend show. I got a smell of Eau D'Hadrien. Right out of the bottle, it smells like you're standing under a lemon tree in the sun drinking orange juice. It wasn't that good on Matsushita, but it wasn't bad."

"You smelled him."

"He was polite and elegant," Doris said, "and that bowing

thing he did? Tammy Munson noticed it too. It's refreshing. Respectful. People in Japan have a love-hate thing going with their criminals. Did you know there are six fan magazines over there dedicated to the Yakuza?"

"I did not know that," Frank said. "But did you know that my great-granddad in Wisconsin met Al Capone? Capone had a hideout in the Northwoods by that big lake—Superior. Granddad told me his father and all the neighbors played dumb any time the feds came looking for Capone."

"Why?"

"Capone was funny. A big spender. If you took care of him, he took care of you. Besides, it was Prohibition, and the only people who liked cops were Sunday School teachers. I guess people still love criminals more than they love cops," Frank said.

"Not once they get to know us," Doris said.

Frank pulled on his jacket. "Well, you got your new freezer, Dorrie, and Mel's talking to me again, and Tammy Munson called to say Mrs. Armitage got to thinking about her granddad's tripe and decided to make it anyway. I might try a little. I might even try a bite of Tammy Munson's raccoon. You up for a walk on the wild side?"

"As long as nobody makes me try tsunami surprise."

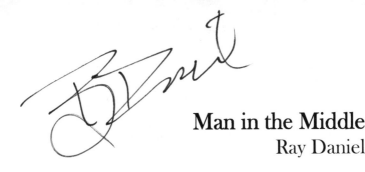

Man in the Middle
Ray Daniel

Fishing with Wi-Fi is a lot like regular fishing. You sit on the beach, put out the bait (in this case a hotspot called FREEWIFI) and wait. The fish come nibbling, drawn by the lure of free data access for their cell phones.

When a fish tries to log into Facebook through my hotspot, I present it with a fake login screen. The fish rolls its eyes and logs into Facebook, giving me its username and password. I store these and connect the fish to Facebook, letting it enjoy its free Wi-Fi. We hackers call this a Man in the Middle Attack, but I prefer to think of it as Fishing for Dopes.

One of the side benefits of my setup is that the kids today use an internet chat tool called texytext.com. The traffic is unencrypted, so I get to entertain myself by reading teenagers' texts. So much drama...

Ashley, stand up for the man.

The text came through as I was thinking of packing up from Revere Beach and heading home. The tide had been encroaching on the wet sand for the past hour and was threatening to flood my hotspot backpack. I would have ignored it if a girl in a white bikini hadn't stood at that moment and turned away from the ocean, shielding her eyes from the afternoon sun with her cell phone.

Okay. Now turn around and let him look at you.

The girl turned slowly, stopping so that whoever was up there could look at her butt, then continuing the turn until she faced the front again.

Stay there, this asshat wants to negotiate.

Negotiate? Who was this girl? I used Ashley's texytext handle, "ashgirl," and dove into my database of Facebook accounts. Sure enough I found out that ashgirl had also logged into Facebook, but there her account was an email address that started with the name ashley.greene.

Ashley sat back down on the wet sand, stared at the water, and chewed on a thumbnail. Angry sunburn blotches marred the pale skin of her back. Her shoulders were okay; apparently she had been applying sunscreen herself, or it had worn off somehow.

I glanced at the incoming tide, guessed that I still had a few minutes before salt water converted my hotspot to scrap. Opened my Facebook app and logged in as Ashley Greene.

Okay. Come on up.

The text had popped up as I scrolled through Ashley's Facebook feed. A couple of months ago her feed was all grumpy cat memes and complaints about her teachers. A few weeks ago it changed to a chorus of writings on her wall.

"Are you okay?" "Where are you?" "Please come back."

Ashley stood, brushed sand off her butt, turned, squared her shoulders and headed up the beach. A wave chased her and sloshed at my feet.

I searched for evidence of Mr. and Mrs. Greene. Found nothing. That was odd, but I had a theory.

Another wave hit me. I grabbed my backpack, lifted it above the water. It was time to go. I slung the backpack over my shoulder, followed Ashley's slow slog up the beach. The tablet vibrated in my hand. Another message.

Get your ass up here!

Somebody was impatient. Ashley increased her pace and so did I. I walked past her, reached the seawall first and sat. I needed to test my Facebook theory. I clicked through Ashley's privacy settings and found I was right. Ashley had blocked Donald Greene and Amy Greene. Since they were blocked, she couldn't see them and they couldn't see her. I unblocked them.

Heard a guy over my shoulder say, "Ashley, this is Stu."

Ashley said, "Hullo."

Stu said, "Jesus, you are a pretty little thing."

Ashley asked, "Where should we go?"

The guy making the introductions said, "The house. First

floor."

Stu's Red Sox T-Shirt spread across his gut, leaving a hairy little strip of flab resting over the spot where the T-shirt gave up and the bathing suit presumably began. I imagine Stu hadn't seen his own crotch in years. Ashley took Stu's hand, led him across Revere Beach Boulevard, looking more like his daughter than his whore.

Back on Facebook, Ashley's wall lit up with increasingly desperate pleas from the now unblocked Donald and Amy looking for their daughter. "We love you Ashley." "Come home Ashley." "If you know where we can find Ashley." "Go to findashley.info." The amber alerts, shared pleas for information, expressions of forgiveness all painted the same picture.

I typed, letting Ashley and Stu get some distance between us, then I closed the tablet, put it in the backpack, and slipped off the wall. A twenty-something guy wearing a backwards Bruin's cap caught my eye. I looked away, crossed Revere Beach Boulevard following Ashley and Stu. I could see them on the other side of the MBTA tracks, walking towards a triple decker.

I trotted after them, backpack on my shoulder. Lost them for a moment as I cleared the bridge over the tracks, but saw the door to a brown triple decker swinging shut. Ran towards it and slipped inside.

The triple decker's hallway smelled of cat piss and mold. I tried the door to the first floor apartment. As I had guessed, it was unlocked so that Bruin's-cap could have the only key. The door opened into a hallway. Doors opened off the hallway. One was closed. I threw it open, bashing it against the wall.

Ashley kneeled on mattress in front of Stu, her bikini top tossed to the side next to Stu's florescent orange bathing suit.

I said, "For Christ's sake, Stu, put that thing away. She's only sixteen."

Stu backed away, covering himself. "Who are you?"

"I'm the police, that's who." I'm not, of course, but Stu didn't know that.

"I never touched her!"

I said to Ashley. "Put on your top. We're going."

Ashley said, "But what about Mike?"

"I'll take care of Mike."

A voice behind me said, "You fucking will, huh?"

I turned. Bruins-cap stood right behind me holding an aluminum baseball bat. I backed away from him into the room.

Stu said to Mike, "Careful. He's a cop."

"He's no fucking cop," said Mike.

Ashley had retrieved her top and started to put it on.

"What are you doing?" Mike asked her. "You go blow that guy."

"She's just a kid, Mike," I said. "Her parents are looking for her."

"I've had enough of you," said Mike. He launched himself at me swinging the bat over his head. The bat arced up, glinting in the sunlight filtering through the dirty windows, came down right at my head. I turned, spinning away from the barrel to take the blow on my shoulder.

The bat smashed down onto my backpack, shattering the WIFI hotspot and laptop inside. Mike had lost his balance from the force of the swing and stepped forward. I whirled back towards him, planted the toe of my sneaker square between his legs. He grunted, stumbled onto his knees. I slipped the backpack from my shoulder swung it in my own arc, and finished destroying my laptop by mashing it into Mike's head. The ancient Dell with its massive battery did the rest of the work.

Ashley stood, bra in hand.

I said, "You put that on." Then to Stu, "You stay here."

Ashley did as she was told. I took her hand, dragged her out front.

She asked, "Where are we going?"

"We're getting you home."

"I can't go home," she said, "My parents hate me."

"No," I said, "they love you. Check your Facebook page."

A police car pulled up, no doubt a response to the Facebook message I had sent on Ashley's behalf to Donald and Amy naming the street where they'd find their daughter.

The cop asked me, "Is this Ashley Greene?"

I said, "Yeah."

"Who are you?"

"Just a guy who got stuck in the middle."

Nightshade
Tanis Mallow

For the past half hour, I'd studied Ivan Sadovsky through a thicket of privileged tourists. His huge head stood out as though he were another animal altogether, his face a slab of meat, fleshy, seared by too much time in the sun. The girl was late and his fingers, manicured but marred, knuckles knobby with scar tissue, tapped to the rising tempo of his rage.

She would pay for it later.

He narrowed his eyes at the bodyguard next to him as though the girl's tardiness was the man's fault. The bodyguard switched his considerable bulk back and forth, foot to foot, his obvious discomfort overriding any sense of menace he might have hoped to project.

Doing a much better job in the composure department, Rajani Dhar sat alone at a table near the door, hiding his deadly physique in a loud Tommy Bahama shirt, baggy plaid shorts and wire frame glasses despite the fact his eyesight was perfect. Props, all of it. He flashed a goofy grin at the hostess and engaged her in friendly banter, a thick Indian accent rolling across the room in an oral fog. More BS. He spoke with no accent and was neither goofy or friendly.

Why was he here? Part of Sadovsky's entourage? Doubtful. On the job? Likely. Here for me or someone else? A troubling question.

I slouched as far in my seat as my short sundress would allow, out of Dhar's line of sight and sipped on my glass of freebee wine courtesy of the Ritz-Carlton Naples. Within the private sanctum catering to their wealthiest guests, eager club lounge hostesses fluttered about with their decadent offerings of hors d'oeuvres and liquor and God knows what else. Delicate, artful desserts stood on display like rows of debutants posing on a staircase.

From the hall, the click-clacking of towering heels called our attention to the girl, Tatiana, the fifth player in this tragic production. I took advantage of her arrival, to slip onto one of several small balconies under the guise of making a call. I wasn't using my cell phone. I was watching her.

She nearly pulled it off. The pencil skirt. The blond chignon, no roots. The expensive handbag. She almost looked as though she belonged. Almost. The small details gave her away, her choice of foundation too sheer to disguise either the rainbow of bruises or the serpent tattoo running from her right ankle bone to mid-calf, the piercings obvious despite removing the studs and hoops. More than anything, however, the darting eyes, the timid mouth, that terrified I-don't-belong-here expression served as a neon road sign. Here she is, it announced, the naive young thing about to take the fall for your crime.

She looked like a child next to Sadovsky. Too innocent—as ironic as that sounded—to be in his company. Too young to be his child let alone his companion. She winced as he snatched at her wrist and pulled her close, whispering in her ear. She paled noticeably in reaction to whatever he was saying and nodded emphatically. He released her abruptly and his vicious leer followed her to her seat.

I felt eyes upon me and without glancing up, raised the phone to my ear, mouthing gibberish and gesturing in an animated fashion. Sadovsky might be considered one of the most feared men in Florida—nix that, in the whole of the U.S.—but there was only one person in this room capable of unnerving me and it wasn't him.

When at last I met Dhar's gaze, he didn't bother to look away. Instead, he narrowed his dark eyes and smiled, the wiry Indian baring his teeth like a wolf snarling at its prey. I shuddered and turned to the calming ocean view with its cathartic rolling surf. I closed my eyes and inhaled long and deep like that single breath may have to sustain me for hours.

Fire.

I'm playing with fire even occupying the same room as him.

* * *

Endangered loggerhead turtles take refuge along Florida's gulf coast where they lay their eggs in the warm sands at night. After nine p.m., the hotel clears the beach of furniture, dims landscape lighting and closes the beach bar.

More important to me, they darken the balconies.

Wearing head-to-toe beige, the sandy color of the hotel's stucco walls, I tugged on lambskin gloves and leaned over the iron railing. Vertigo played with my adrenal glands, releasing that tantalizing buzz. Below, a fountain hidden somewhere in the lush foliage babbled away and surf pounded the shoreline. Further along, traffic roamed the strip under the watchful eye of condo buildings and hotels vying for pristine beachfront. Above stars winked as though they thought this was all a joke.

Some joke.

Five floors down, a couple sat out on their own balcony enjoying the night, their words rising on the hot humid air. From here I could see the top of the woman's head. Blonde. Black tank top. If she tilted her head back she'd see me and she'd most certainly notice if I plummeted past her, a theory I had no desire to test.

Maybe four feet of air hung between my balcony and the one next door. That and a fourteen-story drop. Between them, a six-inch drain pipe ran from roof to ground. I wiggled it for the third time and once again, it gave no indication it could support anything more than a few pounds. Unfortunate.

Earlier in the evening, Sadovsky had stood on that same adjacent balcony, smoking a cigar and belittling Tatiana with vicious taunts, precursors to the real fun, the sharp commands and sharper slaps, muffled cries and banging furniture.

Such a gentleman.

I stretched my shoulders and rolled my head, feeling the grind of vertebrae. With a final look to the concrete path below, I slipped over the railing to the outside of the balcony, feet jammed between iron bars. In my head, I'd practiced the move a dozen times. My imagination had nothing on the rush of reality.

Holding on with one hand, I leaned out to a forty-five degree angle, testing my resolve as much as the strength of the railing. I flexed my bicep, pulled in flush and shoved off, leaping to Sadovsky's balcony with a nimbleness I didn't know I possessed.

A car honked and I lost my grip, flailing for a brief second in empty air before regaining my balance. I scrambled over the rail and pressed tight to the wall.

Well, that was fun.

The hardest part—other than leaping between balconies—would be convincing the girl. Much easier to take them all out: the target, the companion, the bodyguard, but I was never one for collateral damage.

Through the glass, I heard the shower running and Sadovsky yowling something I'm sure in his mind sounded like the finest of arias. Tatiana sat crumpled, a tiny island on a sea of sofa cushions, clutching a white towel around her body and sucking hard on a cigarette like she wanted to consume it all in a single drag. Her hair was piled in a messy knot on top of her head, the tips spiky with water. She'd been crying.

I stepped through the slider, held up an index finger and made a shushing sound. Wide-eyed, her mouth opened and the cigarette dangled as if glued to her bottom lip. She looked like she might run and I touched the knife in my pocket, hoping I wouldn't have to use it on her.

"I'm here to help you," I said. The soothing cadence of my words kept her in place as I approached.

"Tatiana!" Sadovsky bellowed over the running water, dragging out the name, Ta-tee-a-naaah. She flinched at his voice.

"He hurts you," I said, standing over her.

"He's a monster," she said, swiping at tears. Without makeup, she looked even younger. More vulnerable.

"I can make it so he will never do this"—I pressed a fingertip to a fresh bruise on her neck—"to you again."

"Where are you, my little suka?" Sadovsky's sing-song

voice turning to a growl, showing signs of his temper. The shower stopped and Sadovsky barked a string of curses in both English and Russian followed by a massive coughing fit. The shower door slammed.

Time to move.

"Let me save you," I said, extending a hand.

Tatiana stubbed out her cigarette. "Thank you," she said.

Fuelled by the intense mania that always followed a job, the second time over the balcony was easier than the first. I threw a flamboyant muumuu over my clothes, donned a grey wig and, after a quick call to the front desk alerting security, let myself into the hallway, head down, ostensibly searching through an enormous tote bag. Moving slow and stiff-limbed as though suffering in the angry grip of arthritis, I battled my natural inclination to sprint to the elevator, away from the body.

In a large public restroom on the ground floor, I changed, combed out my dark hair and applied makeup. I hacked the wig apart with my knife and flushed the pieces. The muumuu, tote and gloves found new homes in various garbage cans between there and the pool bar where I spent the next hour drinking some fruity concoction and exchanging flirty words with the young bartender. When the hushed gossip surrounding the sudden appearance of both police cruisers and an ambulance died down, I returned to my original suite, as far from Sadovsky's as possible.

The lotion smelled of lemon and sugar and made me think of meringue pie as I rubbed it into my skin still damp from the shower. I pawed through the closet and selected a night gown the muted pink color of the inside of a seashell. Tossed it to the bed and untied my robe.

He cleared his throat and I froze.

Rajani Dhar sat in the dim light, no longer in tropical costume but rather wearing a tight black T-shirt and dress pants. A living shadow.

"Please," he said, unfolding himself gracefully from the chair. "Do not stop on my account." His voice poured over me like liquid chocolate, rich and deep and flawless.

I retied the robe and crossed my hands over my chest, gripping the lapels as though the terrycloth could shield me. He prowled forward, holding my gaze like a cobra.

"Did you have a successful evening?" he asked, closing in. I nodded once and he grinned, white teeth against dark skin. "Did you not think to consult with me ahead of time?"

I glanced toward the hall, the door. Escape.

"Don't," he said. "There is no need to run from me." The mania returned, pouring into me like acid, the need to move, to flee, struggling in vain against the need to obey him.

He fisted a handful of my hair—hard enough, painful enough, to show he meant business—and forced me face first against the wall. He pressed his full length against mine until I could feel every hard muscle in his body.

"Yet," he hissed into my ear, planting my hands flat against the wall, fingers splayed. "Stay still," he said, the warning inherent, floating like an ice cube in the cocktail of his voice. "Are you armed?"

"No."

"We will see."

His hands skimmed over my torso, belly, hips, searching for a weapon I hadn't had the foresight to keep close, my pockets empty. I closed my eyes as he searched, his body rubbing against mine, his hands taking liberties.

"Do not move." He knelt and slid his hands down my legs one at a time. "Turn around."

"Please." I didn't even know what I was begging for. His mercy? My life? Something else entirely?

"I asked you to turn around."

I did as instructed. He laced his fingers in mine and raised them in two arcs as though painting snow angels on the wall. Crossed my wrists over my head and trapped them in one hand while he traced the neckline of my robe with an index finger, following the edge diagonally across my chest to the tie at my hip. He plucked the bow and slowly unwrapped me like a gift, eyes roaming. His fingers traced the lace of my lingerie.

Ignoring his earlier command, I dug my hands into his thick coarse hair and whimpered as he sunk his teeth into the soft spot where my neck met my shoulder.

"I have missed you, Olivia," he whispered, kissing the bite mark. "It has been far too long since I have had you under me, shaking like a scared rabbit."

Filtered by the sheer drapes, dawn light warmed the pale yellow walls. Curled on my side, he held me loosely, my back to his chest. I wasn't ready for the day but apparently Dhar's curiosity demanded the conversation we'd so aptly avoided the night before.

"Imagine my surprise when first the *police*"—he said the word with some distain—"and then the medical examiner showed up outside Mr. Sadovsky's door." I said nothing. "You have deprived me of some fun. I suppose I will need to find a new client."

"As if that's a problem for you. As if you even need the money."

"I am easily bored," he said. "Idle hands and all of that."

"I can think of something to do with your idle hands," I said, trying to distract him. I wasn't sure what he knew or the extent of his anger, an emotion always hidden beneath his cool facade. He grazed my shoulder blade with his mouth, stubble scratching my skin.

"Who hired you, if I may ask?"

Back to business.

When I didn't answer, he dug his fingers into my chin and wrenched, waiting patiently until I looked him in the eye. Still I said nothing. With breathtaking speed he moved to kneel between my legs, glaring like he might devour me. I sat up against the linen headboard, rubbing my jaw.

"Wouldn't you like to know," I said, a lame attempt at levity that came off as tense and nervous.

He spread his hands on my hips, the contrast of his darkness making graphic patterns against pale skin and white sheets. I held my breath and waited. Waited for him to press for information. Wondered how long I'd last should he decide to properly interrogate me.

Not long.

He yanked hard, dragging me flat to my back and knocking the air from my lungs.

"I am sure you will tell me when the time is right," he said, voice nonchalant, belying the ever-present threat.

He dipped his head and lavished attention to my skin, growing more aggressive the lower he moved. I once again relinquished not only my body to him but my mind, my sense of logic—*hell*—my sense of survival. The thrill of danger more arousing than any touch. It wasn't until much later as he lay still, hands clasped over his chest in a death repose, his breathing even, and I, in utter contrast, sprawled on my stomach beside him, panting, one arm dangling over the side of the bed, allowed the instinctive fear to return. My fingers crept into the tight space between mattress and box spring to touch cold metal, one of several compact knives stashed around the suite. I shimmied it closer.

"I'm not sure I'll ever be able to walk again," I said.

"You are most welcome."

"You can be an arrogant prick at times."

He chuckled and sat up swinging his legs over the side of the bed. "Clearly, you bring out the best in me."

He bent over, reaching to the floor and I palmed the knife, its razor edge threatening to shred my skin. I rolled to face him tucking my hand and the knife under a pillow.

"I suppose I must check out of the hotel," he said with a bored sigh.

"Will the bodyguard suspect you?" I asked.

"Possibly."

"Will he come after you?"

He shrugged and slipped on his shorts. "Doubtful."

"Was he on the boat last year when you questioned the Czech?"

"Yes."

"Then he won't," I said with a finality acknowledging what I knew about the deep chasm of cruelty Dhar possessed. He snorted in response. Admittedly, it was a hell of a declaration coming from someone like me.

He stood and zipped his trousers. Shoved his fingers in the pockets, jingling loose change and whatever else might be concealed. I waited. His hands came out empty and he crouched, reaching to the floor. I tightened my grip on the knife and he straightened up holding his leather belt. It slid through his long fingers and his eyes narrowed. Before I could move, the belt rippled through the air and cracked over my bare skin. It stung like hell and I muffled a cry into the mattress. Seriously considered chucking the knife at his head. He crawled onto the bed over me, soothing what felt like a serious welt with his cool hand.

"Jerk."

"I could not help myself. It was too tempting," he said, running his palm back and forth across the mark. "*You* are too tempting." He sighed again. "I must be going, though I should like to take this opportunity to thank you for the use of your body."

I laughed. "My body? And here I thought you were attracted to my mind."

"Your mind?" He wove his fingers through my hair. "Your mind is a twisted nightshade thing."

"Nightshade?"

"Dark. Exquisite." He rose. "Lethal."

"Where will you go?" I asked.

"I have rented a home down the beach."

"I see."

"You will join me, of course?"

I blinked, the invitation wholly unexpected. As I considered it though, it made sense. More privacy. Easier to dispose of a body should he find the need. My body.

"You'd like me there?" I asked.

"I must insist."

"Then I suppose I must accept."

Like walking into a den of vipers, you idiot.

"Excellent. It's settled." He pulled the black T-shirt over his head. "And, Olivia..."

"Yes?"

"You may put away your little knives," he said. "For now."

* * *

At his suggestion, Dhar drove to the beach house, my luggage amongst his things. I walked the beach. Best if no hotel staff were to notice us together, he'd said.

Best for whom?

The hot wind whipped at my gauzy tunic. The wide brimmed sun hat and dark sunglasses hid my face. I took my time strolling the waterline.

Flocks of sandpipers scattered, giving me a wide berth and wary looks. Much braver than the sandpipers, a single snowy egret with bright yellow feet stood its ground as I passed.

I knew the house as soon as Dhar had described it, one of many ostentatious monstrosities littering the beach abandoned, waiting for their wealthy owners to visit. This particular Mediterranean-style home with its terracotta roof, pale stucco, arches and Juliet balconies towered over the fringe of palm trees separating it from the expansive white beach. As I drew closer, my breathing grew more rapid, the wildness within me, the mania, hauling on the reins I held tight.

Outside the house, a large crowd swarmed the shore, their excited voices, gasps and laughter fanning the flame of curiosity. I joined them. Something slick and grey torpedoed through the water inches from my feet and I hopped back, startled. The woman beside me giggled, touched a leathery hand to my pale arm and pointed.

"Dolphin," she said. "He's corralling fish."

Close to shore, silver fish much too large for the shallow water flashed in the sunlight. The dolphin circled and with a burst of speed hydroplaned past to the delight of the crowd. I left the woman to her show, dangling at the far edge of the group, mesmerized as again and again the dolphin trapped and killed the frenzied fish.

A hand touched my lower back, knuckles grazing up and down. Dhar slipped in beside me.

"I wondered what had distracted you," he said.

"A dolphin corralling fish."

"Ahh. A beautiful hunter." He leaned close, ducking under

the brim of my hat, his mouth to my ear and whispered, "A beautiful hunter watching a beautiful hunter." His knuckles skimmed my spine and I shivered. "Shall we go?" he asked.

I looked from the killing scene before me to the house in the dunes and Dhar studied me, an amused expression on his face like he could read my mind. I shoved my hands into the pockets of my white denim shorts to still them.

"Yes, I suppose we should," I said, turning from the water to follow him.

There was no shortage of security cameras in and around the house. I couldn't help but notice their tiny red lights were dark, the cameras dead. I suspected Dhar was the one responsible.

After the heat of the beach, the air conditioning waved a frigid hand even before I'd stepped through the door. I trailed behind Dhar, my flip flops slapping against the marble floors as I absorbed the grandness of the home. The ceilings soared, the cavernous space filled with ornate furniture, gilt mirrors, huge canvasses and tapestries, and plush antique rugs, all autumn ochres and reds and sage greens.

"How big is it?" I asked.

"Eight or nine thousand square feet, I believe."

"Seems like overkill for one person."

He shrugged. "I take pleasure in the view. And technically there are two of us."

"For how long?" I asked and he stopped, turning to gape at me over his shoulder. I waited a beat then clarified: "*For how long* do you have the house?"

"A week." He continued on, his footfalls silent. "You will join me in some wine with lunch?"

"Yes, thank you."

He led me into a huge, elaborate kitchen with marble countertops, professional appliances, embellished millwork and cabinetry the color of whipped butter. Crystal chandeliers dripped from the ceiling. Dhar selected a bottle from the well-stocked fridge and uncorked it.

"I have had lunch catered for us," he said, nodding toward

the mahogany table set with two china and crystal place settings.

He held out a chair for me and poured wine. We clinked glasses, the ting of crystal as long and clear as if it had originated from some fine musical instrument. We ate in silence.

When finished, I touched the linen napkin to my lips and said, "That was delicious. Thank you."

He rested against the back of his chair, pushing it out from the table. "I feel the strange desire to spoil you."

"Why?"

"Why not?"

"I ruined your job."

Dhar made a dismissive gesture with his hand. "No one else knows what you have done. I will be paid the same as if I had carried out the contract myself."

He didn't know.

If I left now, I'd...what? Spend months running. *If* I could outrun him. Were I to tell him, would my admission buy me some mercy?

"Raj, I must—"

His phone rang. He looked at the screen and frowned. Shot me a look of such intensity I felt I might spontaneously implode.

"Excuse me," he said, taking the call to another room.

Unable to sit still, I gathered the dishes and rinsed them in the sink, staring out the window to the garden beyond. I felt rather than heard him return. He leaned against the huge kitchen island and fiddled with his cell phone.

"It would appear Mr. Sadovsky is not dead," he said after a time.

I exhaled a shaky breath. "No."

He raised an eyebrow. I fought the command of his silent question for a full minute before caving. "He wasn't my target. She was. Tatiana."

He tossed his phone to the counter and crossed his arms. "Who is your client?"

"I'd rather not say."

"Such honor."

"I'm sorry, Raj. I thought you knew," I said quietly. "When you came to my room, I thought you already knew."

He shook his head. "Mr. Sadovsky is in police custody."

I wiped my hands and folded the tea towel over a cabinet door. "I'm not surprised."

"What did you do exactly?"

"Broke her neck. Sadovsky was nice enough to cover her in bruises the size and shape of his hands. I suspect he's royally screwed."

"Did your client request the setup?"

"No. Just covering my ass."

Dhar rubbed his temples. "This will cause me some serious problems, Olivia."

"I realize. I'm sorry."

"How am I to gain access if he is in police custody?"

"He'll make bail. We could track him down. Team up together." I sounded desperate, bloody chum to a shark such as Dhar. "Like Long Beach."

At a client's insistence we had worked together once, a convention in Long Beach, California. The job had been an unmitigated success, clean, uneventful, plenty of time for recreational activities. Yet, despite our mutual respect and attraction, we could never quite get over our trust issues.

To him, the job was a game, entertainment. To me, it was nothing more than an extremely profitable outlet for my danger addiction. The same addiction that would most likely get me killed. The same addiction that drew me to Dhar.

"It would work," I said.

"Perhaps." He pushed off with his hip and stood beside me. "Do not worry," he said, brushing a strand of hair from my face. "We will think of something."

He snaked an arm around my waist and pulled me tight to his body. I choked back a whimper. His head fell to my collarbone and he scraped his teeth along my throat.

"My lovely nightshade flower," he whispered, leaning back just far enough to look at my face, his attention flicking between my eyes and my mouth. And then he did something he'd never done before, something that terrified me to the core.

He kissed me on the mouth.

Tentative at first, like he'd surprised even himself, then deeper, exploring. I swallowed his moan. He tightened his grip on me and shifted slightly to the left.

I drove my knife under his ribcage. Angled it to reach his heart. Pivoted the blade. He staggered back clutching the gaping wound, face in shock. For the briefest of seconds before he crumbled, he smirked like I'd amused him one final time.

He opened his fist and his own knife clattered to the marble tile, as clean and unsoiled as mine was bloody.

My Victim's Killer
Al Abramson

I don't have much time left. So I'm going to tell you right out that I killed the person who gave birth to me. My name is—

No—wait, you people are the jerks who like to figure out the "mystery" yourself, aren't you? Suspects revealed, clues scattered around, a lot of whiny characters you're hoping will be dead by the time the story ends...a damsel-in-distress and a thickly muscled hero—or *vice versa*, but not often.

You want to play that game? I'll play it—there are six suspects—no identical cousins, no outsider tricks! The murder weapon was a poisoned pen, of course; in the library, also of course. It was right after the Opening Ceremonies at the Long Beach Bouchercon. All clear?

The victim was one of the Bouchercon Guests of Honor. And any of you who just said "it's a start" should be ashamed of yourselves.

Here's a clue: the killer is a character created by one of the Guests. So you can guess that each of the suspects had to have a motive, right?

THE CREATORS AND THEIR SUSPECTS

JEFFREY DEAVER

Let's start with Mr. Jeffery Deaver. "Jeff" to his friends, so everybody calls him "Mr. Deaver." His character suspect, from a rich store of possibilities, is Lincoln Rhyme. Why would this seventeen-year-old, rich with book and movie money, want to kill the person who created him?

Well, Justin Bieber gets to race cars and chase felony convictions wherever he wants, and he has the talent and depth of a—Justin Bieber. Lincoln Rhyme, who admittedly does have a better haircut, is no more mature, although he is a lot smarter and better educated. But he has to lie in a bed every day and worry about Angelina Jolie in a "Ruby, Don't Take Your Love to Town" way every time she walks out the door.

But that's not the real reason—did you know that Denzel wasn't Mr. Deaver's first choice for the movie role? He wanted Whoopi Goldberg, but she had a conflict filming a "Burglar" sequel. Then he wanted Tom Cruise, until the studio stepped in and said that Lincoln was over six feet and Cruise wasn't tall enough for the role.

But the final straw was when Deaver wanted to play the role himself, right after Jolie was signed to play Amelia. At that point, Lincoln Rhyme knew that Jeffrey Deaver had to die...or did he?

J.A. JANCE

If you've met J.A. Jance, you might think nobody would want to kill her—unless you've sat next to Joanna Brady at a Boucheron event. There's no expiration date on ruined dreams, and Joanna's were the sourest milk.

"I was a young, naïve character in 1969—there was an open casting call for *The Brady Bunch*, and I knew I could get it—Florence Henderson was way too old, plus my blond hair didn't come out of a perox—let's just say they wouldn't have had to put so much into the makeup budget. And Robert Reed—wrrrooowlll!

"But Jance had other plans for me, even if she didn't know what they were then. She wouldn't let me go to the audition, and kept me in the drawer for more than twenty years while she dallied with some Seattle detective! Does that sound fair to you? Even if I'll be carded for an "R" movie long after Henderson has won the AARP "Woman of the Year Award" —my life was put on hold for twenty years; it's fair if I take a few years off hers in exchange..."

That's what Brady might have said if she is the killer.

EDWARD MARSTON

Then there's Edward Marston, or whatever name the witness protection program is using for him today—Keith Miles, Conrad Allen, Miley Cyrus—he has more pseudonyms than the widow of the Nigerian Oil Minister. And I suspect he also has seventy-four million dollars he would be interested in having you help him get out of the country; you may keep ten percent for your trouble. Just give him your account number and password.

Which of his many characters would hate him enough to kill him? You might be surprised to learn it's Nicholas Bracewell. Not your career criminal—he's a smart and resourceful stage manager in the late 1500s, and he usually leaves his ego off-stage while his actors hog the limelight. His one touch of vanity? He uses pancake makeup—in Elizabethan times this was actual pancake batter—to cover a curious lightning-bolt shaped scar on his forehead.

Only last week he learned that his "parents"—a Devon merchant and his wife—had actually adopted him, and that he had had an identical twin.

Worse, he learned that his parents had snatched him away from Jim and Lily Potter, who were also shopping at the orphanage; Lily especially was taken with Nicholas, but when Nicholas' parents gave the orphanage manager a hefty bribe, the Potters were forced to settle for his identical twin, Harry.

While Nicholas had had no regrets about the course of his life, last year Harry grossed nearly forty billion dollars. That would buy a lot of pancakes, and it has to eat at his soul...

If Marston hadn't allowed the Bracewells to bribe the orphanage, it would have been "Nicholas Potter and the..." on all those bookshelves. So when he came into the library and saw Marston standing there, would it be any wonder if Nicholas Bracewell had picked up that poisoned pen?

EOIN COLFER

Eoin Colfer's characters could be forgiven for wanting to kill him just for being forced to figure out how to pronounce his name—Owen? Ian? Didn't they have spell-check when his folks named him? At least he spelled Artemis correctly...

But still Artemis Fowl (the Second) wants him dead. Maybe it's being stuck next to a "fabulously flatulent dwarf" or threatened with a "blue rinse" in the first Fowl book, when he should clearly have had only a cut-and-perm. Or the many other insults from fairies and centaurs, trolls, goblins and lawyers...

The real reason is much more prosaic—Artemis, doomed to be a thirteen-year-old criminal genius mastermind, pines for a different life. He has always dreamed of being a certified public accountant, carefully filling out Form 13. B. Slash. 179 and filing the same each year before the deadline. After forty years, putting away four percent of his salary at a compound interest of three point one five percent, dividends reinvested, he hoped to retire to a seaside cottage, where he would cultivate vegetable marrows and—if he ever got through puberty—grow a handlebar mustache and read books about his favorite Christie character, Miss Marple.

Eoin has kept him from his dreams, flatulently so! Is it any wonder Artemis might want to retire his creator from living?

SIMON WOOD

If you've met Simon Wood, murder has crossed your mind. I'll tell you there was a lottery among his characters over who (whom?) would be allowed the chance to kill him. It raised more than three hundred grand, which will go to support education in Simon's native England—mainly teaching them that "football" is really called "soccer".

The winner was Aidy Westlake, coincidentally one of the few characters Wood created who would not automatically be on a terrorist watch list. Simon writes what he knows, so most of his characters are serial killers, cannibals, politicians or all three...except for Aidy, a rookie race car driver.

Aidy was pretty peeved when he realized his name was "Aidy." What the heck kind of name is Aidy? "Aiden," his real name, would have gotten him beaten up in school, but at least the bullies would have then forgotten him.

With "Aidy," they stopped when their knuckles were bruised, then paused to ask "What kind of name is Aidy?" and then resumed their beating, their knuckles having recovered in that time...

It's good Johnny Cash didn't record "A Boy Named Aidy." Wood had no such compunction, although thankfully he didn't insist on singing on the CD of this book. Other than the name, Wood did an acceptable job with Aidy, giving him a kick-backside job as a race driver and a promising romance. Most characters wouldn't think of killing their creators for the small embarrassment of "Aidy." But Wood's characters, as I noted, aren't what you'd call normal.

That's the list—wait, that's five suspects, and I said six, didn't I? Oh yes, the Fan Guest of Honor, Al Abramson. Easy to forget the Fan Guest of Honor, since she or he's usually just the first person to bribe the chair with five bucks or a free drink—or both in the Long Beach example.

AL ABRAMSON

That's the challenge here—Abramson isn't an author. If he did create a character, it would be one remarkably like himself. Six-foot-one, six-pack abs, flaxen locks flowing gradually—while still attached—to his shoulders like some Viking warrior of old. A face to make Brad Pitt spit with envy, and a physique to make Ah-nold spit on Brad Pitt with envy.

When he's not making millions each day with his business acumen, he's traveling with Hunky Doctors Without Boundary Issues or bringing peace to the Middle East after he succeeds there he hopes to bring some peace to the U.S. Congress, although that will be a much more difficult task.

Abramson, if I say so myself, rocks. And so must his character—so why would a character based on such a paragon want to kill such a creator? I can't think of a reason, which of course might make it likely that he's the killer...you crime fiction readers really do look for the worst in people, don't you?

IN CONCLUSION

So the real killer must be revealed. Write down your guess, and pass it, along with your bank account number and your password, to Edward Marston in the left aisle.

OPTION 1: Have you all done it? Fine, I'll tell you the name of the killer—but first I have to grab some dinner. I'm starved.

Gosh, Holsten's is mobbed. I don't see an open table. And who the heck put that Journey crap on the jukebox? Hey, there's Tony and his family. "Tony, do you mind if I join you?"

What a jerk—would it kill him to let me sit down?

OPTION 2: Have you all done it? Fine, I'll tell you that the killer is *[continued on page 433]*

Or go with your suggested language in your email. Your choice!

Honeymoon Sweet
Craig Faustus Buck

For a sweet house, right on Santa Monica Beach, it was unbelievably easy to break into. Mickey found a window he could open with a putty knife, so the double-locked doors were a joke. And Lana disabled the alarm within the forty-five-second grace period before it would have triggered. They were in and no one knew. What a great way to kick off the honeymoon.

Mickey couldn't imagine anything else they could have hijacked to bring them any closer to heaven: salt air, pounding surf, white sand, five-million dollar love nest whose owner was en route to Europe. Lana had told him she'd always dreamed of a house on the beach and he'd delivered.

She strolled out of the alarm closet, clapping her hands to beat off the dust. Mickey's heart soared at his good fortune to have married her. He loved the sway of her hips, the trill of her laugh, the smell of her skin, how her jet black bangs set off her turquoise eyes, the way she knew how to do things: clean a squid or repair a zipper or break down a Beretta. He'd known he wanted to marry her by their second date though he'd needed two months to muster the courage to ask.

He wrapped his arms around her and ran his tongue between her lips. She toyed with it for a moment, then yanked off his shirt. He pulled her sweater over her head. She slid her hand over his fly. He was already hard.

She stroked him through his pants as she backed him across the great room toward the wall of windows overlooking the moonlit Pacific. They knocked over a glass-shaded lamp but neither reacted when it shattered on the floor. She slammed him down on the couch and went straight for his belt buckle. He wrestled with her jeans. The heat was intense.

Their clothes were barely off but he could already feel her tremble. This was record time for her, which only excited him more. Her tremors were intensifying and he was along for the wild ride.

Then she froze.

Had he done something wrong? "What?" he said.

She put her finger to his lips, then whispered, "Didn't you hear that?"

He had not.

But then he did. Almost lost in the ocean's roar: *scritch scratch.* Like a mouse clawing at the inside of a wall. Someone was having trouble getting a key into one of the front-door locks.

They scrambled to pull on their clothes.

"I thought you said this place was going to be empty," said Lana.

"That's what Wally told me."

"Wally One-nut? You trusted that inbred idiot?"

Mickey knew he should have double-checked Wally's information. The guy was famous for blunders. But the deserted beach house had seemed so perfect that Mickey let romance cloud his judgment. Now, because of Wally's bad data, Mickey felt like a nitwit, a feeling he was getting to know all too well. That's what happens when you fall for a chick who's smarter than you. But did it have to happen on the first night of their honeymoon?

Scritch scratch.

Mickey crossed to the wall by the door, to be behind it when it opened. Lana rushed into the kitchen area, grabbed a chef's knife from the block and dropped out of sight behind the island.

The *scritch scratch* finally *clacked* as the key turned and shot the deadbolt.

As Mickey listened to the sound of the key moving to the second lock, the one in the door-handle that probably cost as much as his car, he felt the familiar rush of danger. That exhilaration was one of the main attractions of his line of work. He glanced toward the kitchen end of the great room and wished he could see Lana to share the anticipation. At least he knew she was there for him, knife in hand, ready to spring. *My wife has my back.* It had a nice ring to it.

The oversized door swung open, ramping up the sound of the crashing waves. A man stood framed in the doorway, stock still, as if sensing something wrong.

Behind the door, Mickey held his breath and peered through the spyhole. The fisheye gave him a funhouse-mirror view of the profile of the man. He was wearing a tuxedo and seemed off-balance as he turned to grab the huge stainless door handle. He now faced the spyhole and Mickey could see that he wore no tie or cummerbund. The waistband of his pants hung open, apparently to relieve the pressure of his slight pot belly.

The man headed back outside. *He knows we're here,* thought Mickey, *he's going for help.* Mickey was about to run after him when he heard the man throw up on the pavement in front. Mickey relaxed, flexing his hands to relieve his tension without making any noise.

The man stumbled back into the house and did a face-plant on the seagrass carpet. He lay on the floor like a sandbag, bathed in the blue moonlight reflecting off the ocean.

Mickey closed the door. Lana slowly approached the man and knelt to feel for a pulse.

"He's still breathing," she said.

"Let's get the fuck out of here," said Mickey.

"Give me a second."

She searched the man's pockets. He had a wallet, some keys, some breath mints and something that stopped her cold.

"Hello," she said and held up a glassine envelope filled with white powder.

"What is it?" he said.

Lana squeezed the sides of the envelope to pop it open. Dipping her little finger inside, she scooped a bit of the powder under her nail and touched it to her tongue. Her face scrunched up from the taste.

"Bitter," she said. "Not numbing like coke. I'm guessing smack."

She closed the packet, then grabbed a Kleenex from a nearby dispenser and wiped the glassine clean.

"What are you doing?" he asked.

"Hedging our bets."

Mickey had no idea what she was planning, but this honeymoon was clearly taking a sharp turn in a new direction.

Holding the envelope by its edges, she pressed the unconscious man's fingers onto the glassine. Then she wrapped the packet in the tissue and set it aside. Mickey was pleased that she hadn't pocketed the dope. He didn't think she did hard drugs but this was the first time he'd seen her face the temptation.

She returned to her search. Mickey felt his anxiety building.

"It's time to go," he said. "If he comes around while we're here, we're talking felonies."

"Hang tight. This guy could be our ticket."

"You don't want to do hard time. Look what State prison did to your mother. You want to end up like her?"

Lana looked up empathetically. Mickey had met her mother soon after they'd gotten engaged. They'd picked the woman up at her halfway house and taken her to Denny's. When Lana went to the ladies' room, her mother offered to sell Mickey a happy ending after lunch. It had been an unpleasant afternoon for all.

"Babe," said Lana, "I promise you I'll never be like my mother."

She shuffled through the man's credit cards.

"Just take his wallet and let's blow."

She found a business card. "Avery Blain," she read. "Esquire. Beverly Hills law firm with six names and he's one of 'em." She held up another card. "Member of the Jonathan Club. This is looking more and more like a cash cow. And we, my blushing husband, are going to suckle the teats."

"Are you talking about selling that dope on the street?" he said.

"Please," she said contemptuously. He knew it was a put-down, but he didn't get it.

She fanned the contents of Avery's wallet like a poker hand, enticing him to pick a card. He reached out and plucked a photograph from the array.

It was a snapshot of a red-haired woman with an infectious smile posing beside a carousel horse. She was tall and well-padded but shapely, about Lana's age, maybe ten years younger than Avery Blain.

"You think this is his wife?" He flipped the photo for Lana to see.

They were startled by a loud belch and looked down at Avery, still lying with his face on the floor, his visible eye an amalgam of sky blue and rummy red. He stared at Lana's feet but his expression implied no comprehension of what, much less whose, they were.

"You in or out?" asked Lana.

Mickey felt a fresh flush of excitement. He answered her question by stripping off his belt and binding Avery's hands behind his back. Their flirtation with felony had become a full-blown orgy. Life with this woman was going to be a kick.

Lana grabbed a dishtowel and tied it around Avery's eyes.

"Talk to him," said Mickey.

That was her job. Whenever they ran a scam, Lana did the talking. She was the one with the people skills.

She bent down and spoke softly in Avery's ear. "Can you hear me?"

He struggled against the restraint on his wrists.

"Relax, Avery," she said. "We're not going to hurt you. We just want to make sure you're calm before we talk. Okay?"

She patted his knee encouragingly.

"I just need to drop something off. I can't miss my flight."

She shot Mickey a glance then turned back to Avery.

"Where are you going?" she asked.

"My hands are stuck." He was still too groggy to grasp his situation.

"Doctor's orders. You've had too much to drink."

Mickey turned a chair around to watch Lana work. He straddled and crossed his arms over the back for a chin rest.

"I can't see," said Avery.

"If you want to make your flight you'll have to trust me," said Lana. "Where are you flying?"

"Aix en Province" said Avery, pronouncing it "aches."

Mickey didn't know what the correct pronunciation was but he was pretty sure this wasn't it. He asked, "Are you going alone?"

"Huh?" Avery turned toward the voice as if aware, for the first time, that a third person was in the room.

"He wants to know if you're meeting up with anyone in Aix en Province?" said Lana, pronouncing it "ex." Mickey suspected she knew. He felt a small burst of pride.

"What?" said Avery, struggling to shake off the booze.

"Maybe the woman whose picture you've got in your wallet?" she asked.

"She's divorcing me."

He let out a sob.

"Great," said Mickey. "A fucking basket case."

The disapproval in her glance irritated him.

"Why don't you do something helpful?" she said to Mickey. "Maybe find something we can use to get him upright."

She turned back to Avery and tenderly wiped his brow, chanting "It's okay" in a soothing voice, as if calming a child. A tear escaped the blindfold and dripped into Avery's ear.

As Lana tried to soothe Avery, she watched Mickey look through drawers and cabinets in the kitchen area. She felt bad about dismissing him like an underling, but he seemed unusually slow on the uptake and it annoyed her. Could it be that she'd never noticed how dense he was? Or was he folding under pressure? Apparently, she didn't know him as well as she'd thought.

They'd been together only six months, so his marriage proposal had come as a surprise. She'd been ambivalent. She couldn't decide if he was hopelessly romantic or deluded by lust. Joyfully spontaneous or dangerously impetuous. To his credit, the man's tongue was like a witching stick for her erogenous zones, discovering nerves she never knew existed, triggering feelings that turned her to jelly. And she was a sucker for the way his dark five-o'clock shadow set off his sweet baby face. Granted, he was no Rhodes Scholar, but he made her laugh and he seemed sharp enough to avoid jobs that were likely to land him in jail.

Mickey pulled a roll of duct tape out of a catchall drawer and gave her a victory grin.

"Let's get old Avery off the floor," he said.

Mickey made Avery close his eyes, then swapped the dishtowel for duct tape wrapped around his head.

"Hey!" said Avery. "Watch the hair."

"I avoided your ears, didn't I?" said Mickey.

Typical male response, thought Lana. But Mickey was still better than most. For one thing, she felt certain he would never hit her. That just wasn't his style. And taking the fear out of love was nine tenths of the battle.

Mickey dragged an armchair over from the dining room table and helped Avery up and in. Then Mickey started taping.

"What the hell is going on here?" said Avery. He tried to kick but found his ankles strapped to the chair legs. He finally fathomed his predicament as Mickey wrapped the last strip around his calf.

"Who are you?" said Avery. "What do you want?"

"We want money, asshole," said Mickey. People skills be damned.

"Just take what you want and get out." said Avery. "All my cash is in my wallet."

"We don't want your petty cash," said Lana. "We want a payday."

"A big one," said Mickey.

"I don't negotiate with terrorists."

Avery sounded confident, as if he was used to dealing with thugs. Lana suspected he might practice criminal law.

"Well we don't take crap from junkies," said Mickey and slapped Avery's head hard enough to send him tumbling over in his chair. His head hit the mat carpeting with a sickening thud. It happened so fast it was over before Lana could react. Mickey shifted his weight to deliver a follow-up kick.

"That's enough!" she said, stepping between the two men. When she put her hand on Mickey's chest to hold him back, her fingers were trembling.

Mickey gave Avery a last look of contempt, then walked across the room to stare out the window. Lana watched him brood at the roiling black Pacific. She and Mickey had run plenty of cons together, and a few had gotten physical. The worst was the time they'd been caught by a rent-a-cop in a Brentwood mansion and Mickey had been forced to knock the guy down to get away. But that had been self-defense. This was the first time she'd seen him get aggressive. She felt something like indigestion in the pit of her stomach.

Lana tried to pull Avery upright but the combined weight of the man and the chair were too much for her.

"A little help?"

Mickey came back and righted the chair. "Sorry," he said. To her, not to Avery. But she could tell Mickey's fury wasn't spent. His jaw was ticcing all over the place.

"Why don't you go downstairs," she said. "Find his investment records or bank statements. They'll either be in files or on his computer. Let me work my magic alone."

His fist clenched as he glared at Avery and she thought Mickey might try for one last shot. She was afraid she wouldn't be able to stop him. But then he turned and stomped down the stairs. Mickey was accustomed to two-bit swindles and low-risk burglaries. Kidnapping and extortion were much more serious crimes. She suspected the stakes were chafing his nerves.

Lana pulled a chair up close to Avery for an intimate conversation. She usually entered negotiations by trying to build a relationship with her mark. The blindfold made that problematic.

"How's your head?" she asked.

"Sobering fast," he said.

"Look. You're a named partner in a Beverly Hills law firm. I'm sure you've got a lot of high-powered friends and clients. You have a beautiful home on the beach in Santa Monica. You have a lot to lose. My husband and I understand it's in our interest to make this relatively painless for you. We're reasonable people. We don't want to take so much that you think it's worth a risk to try to get it back. We want your upside to be greater than your downside so you're motivated to cooperate. We need your payout to be small enough that your lifestyle doesn't change because if anyone else finds out about your heroin hobby or our little agreement, who knows where that might lead? So the idea is to make everybody happy, including you."

"I don't negotiate with terrorists," he repeated, but this time his voice lacked conviction. It was encouraging that the threat of exposure seemed to be weighing on him.

"We're not terrorists, Avery. Terrorists destroy things. We don't want to destroy you. We just want enough money to make us feel like our risk has been rewarded. If we go away happy, we'll go away forever. That's not terrorism. We don't want to destabilize anything. We're not anarchists, we're business people. You give us what we want and you'll never see us again. Wouldn't that be the best solution all around?"

"The best solution would be for you to cut me loose and leave," he said.

She smiled. "If our relationship is going to work out, you need to be face the truth about the situation you're in and be smart about getting out of it. Doesn't that make sense? Be honest with me."

"Honesty is a two-way street," he said. "You expect me to believe that lowlife husband of yours will just leave and not come back?"

Avery fidgeted against his bindings.

"Let me lay it out for you," she said. "You're a junkie. Which, I might add, is much more pathetic than being a lowlife."

"I'm no junkie. I'm an occasional recreational user."

"Spare me. What I have that you want is the incriminating evidence with your fingerprints all over it. What you have that I want is money—a fair price to make this all go away. Once I sell you the evidence, we'll have no leverage to come back at you with. You can shoot up your occasional recreation to your heart's content."

Lana was uneasy with the thought of abetting Avery's drug

use, but if withdrawal was an unspoken bargaining chip, she wanted to make sure he understood that his dope was in the pot.

"That heroin isn't evidence of anything," said Avery. "If you call the cops I'll just claim you brought it with you and forced me to put my prints on it. The D.A. won't even open a case."

"I'm not going to call the cops; I'll let some reporter do that. I'll send the dope to the *L.A. Times* as an unnamed addict who wants to come clean. I'll tell them my dealer is prominent Beverly Hills lawyer Avery Blain whose prints are all over the dope. They may be skeptical, but you can bet they'll follow up with the cops, the D.A., the State Bar, your partners, your friends and your neighbors. The publicity alone will kill your reputation. You can kiss your career goodbye, along with this house and your friends at the Jonathan Club. And if the cops find your dealer, you know he'll roll over and you'll go to prison."

They heard the crackling pop of splintering wood downstairs as if Mickey had crowbarred a locked drawer.

"He's looking for your financial records, Avery. That's step one in the simple resolution of this thing. I need you to show me how much you've got so we can settle on a figure and wrap this up quietly."

"My accountant has all my financials," he said.

Again, she felt hamstrung by the blindfold. Men lied easily with their words, but their eyes always gave them away.

"You're a lawyer, Avery. You're going through a divorce. That means you've been hiding assets. You're too smart to trust that to some accountant who might be called to testify under oath."

"There's nothing to hide. It's all tied up in the divorce."

Could he be telling the truth? Her bullshit meter was useless without seeing his eyes.

"Should I be worried about your wife walking in unannounced, Avery? It's better that I know. I'd hate for her to surprise us and wind up getting beaten up. You've seen how impetuous my husband can be."

"You don't have to worry about her," said Avery. "She

wouldn't set foot in this house without a hazmat suit."

His lips quivered and she sensed his pain. Did they really need to blindfold him? She was certain she'd convinced Avery that they had him over a barrel.

Lana made a unilateral decision. She grabbed a pair of scissors from a pencil cup on the kitchen counter.

"Don't move," she said, and slipped a blade under the duct tape to cut through the band around his head. When she peeled it off his skin he winced.

She'd had a glimpse of his eyes before, but this was the first time she got a good look. The peek of blue she'd seen before was now revealed to be a dazzling multitude of shades, shimmering with the allure of a tropical lagoon. He returned her gaze and she felt him assessing her, like a jeweler examining a diamond through a loupe.

She tried to yank the tape off his hair and he cried out in pain.

"My husband didn't give your blindfold a lot of forethought," she said.

"Forethought doesn't seem to be his long suit."

She had to cut through his hair to free it from the tape.

"I'm afraid you're going to need a buzz cut to fix this. Maybe shave your head."

The rhythmic white noise of the surf was suddenly pierced by the sound of a siren in the distance. Mickey came bounding up the stairs, looking frightened.

"Nobody knows we're here," she said. "Relax."

But he didn't. The siren grew louder.

And then it passed.

But relief was fleeting. "What the hell are you doing?" asked Mickey as he registered Avery's unmasking.

Lana's scissors were back under the duct tape, snipping at Avery's hair.

"What difference does it make?" she said. "He's not going to call the cops."

"He's a fucking witness!"

She didn't like being criticized, especially not by him. "He's got way more to lose from the cops than we do," she said. "Use your head."

"*You* use your head. What if his dealer finds out we hassled his customer? Avery can describe us. People can find us."

"You think I want anyone to find out about this?" said Avery. "You should listen to her."

Mickey's neck flushed crimson and he brandished his fist. "Listen to *this*, you lawyer fuck!"

Lana grabbed Mickey's arm to prevent him from swinging. He turned on her and she saw a feral rage in his eyes that chilled her. He was losing control under pressure. She'd had bad luck with men like this in the past. The kind of luck that required hospitalization.

She felt something snap deep down inside and knew her trust in him had died. Her love for Mickey vaporized like a drop of water on a hot skillet.

Mickey went back downstairs to pick up where he'd left off—sweeping books off the wall-to-ceiling shelves in Avery's office, looking for a hidden safe.

Use your head. Was that supposed to be some sort of putdown? Because this whole snakepit was her idea. Mickey tried to brush a set of law books off a shelf, but they were too heavy so he had to toss them on the floor one by one. One more pain in the ass to add to the list.

Use your head. This marriage thing was beginning to feel like a mistake. Maybe he'd been too hasty. He'd been so intoxicated by Lana that he'd wanted to strike while the iron was hot, before some other guy got his hooks into her. And then the honeymoon had started off with a bang. Even when Avery came along, they still seemed like they were riding high.

But now he wasn't so sure. He couldn't believe she'd cut off the blindfold.

Could she have a soft spot for Avery? The thought had been gnawing at Mickey since he'd seen her touch the guy. The only reason to touch someone you've got hogtied is to make them talk. And that entails pain. Yet she'd stroked his brow like a fucking nursemaid. She'd patted his knee. Did she think Mickey was blind?

He gritted his teeth and used all his strength to send thirty pounds of law books flying off the shelf.

Lana's mouth was dry from the adrenaline rush of Mickey's assault on Avery. She went into the kitchen to find something to drink. She was surprised when she opened the fridge. She'd expected a guy's fridge: beer, leftover pizza, bologna, ketchup, maybe something moldy and unidentifiable. But Avery's fridge was stocked with vegetables, fresh herbs, fancy stuff in jars. A guy who liked to cook. She'd never met one of those before. Mickey couldn't even open a can.

She walked back into the living room area with a Perrier, imagining Avery tipping a steak pan, letting the flames lick cognac fumes to light up a flambé. He wasn't a classically handsome man but there was something about him she found attractive. Fortyish, full head of silky black hair framed by graying temples, Grecian nose, and those eyes—kaleidoscopic blue and radiating intelligence, now that he'd sobered up a bit.

She cracked open the Perrier and took a sip.

She wondered what he'd be like in bed. She'd never been with a man who made his money legally. And never with one who made the kind of money you'd need to live right on the beach. She'd never known a life without the constant worry of being caught for one thing or another. Life with Avery would be a whole other ballgame.

"You must be thirsty," she said.

"A bit."

She held the bottle to his lips. He parted them and she poured slowly enough for him to drink. When he'd finished, she wiped an errant drop off his lip with her fingertip, then absently licked it off her finger. She watched his eyes follow her tongue.

"You really know how to pick 'em," he said. "What do you see in that jackass anyway?"

"He's just being cautious," said Lana. "Maybe too cautious. But we're newlyweds. He thinks he's supposed to protect me."

She could feel Avery's keen gaze boring into her innermost thoughts.

"You seem like the kind of woman who can take care of herself. Why would a woman like you want to haul around baggage like him?"

"You don't know anything about me," she said.

"Oh, but I do," said Avery. "I know you're already disillusioned with this marriage. I know your husband is already starting to irritate you. I know you think you could have done a lot better. And I know you still can."

She wondered how he could be so perceptive. He was a man, after all. Weren't all men emotional dolts?

She snipped the last of the tape away from his head. His hair looked like it had been vandalized.

"What about you?" she asked. "You say your wife hates you but you cried when I asked about her."

"Booze tears don't count. I'm ready for a new beginning."

"You should take her out of your wallet," she said. "She's wasting space."

Mickey had looked everywhere downstairs for a safe. He'd checked for places where the carpet wasn't tacked down. He'd rapped his knuckles between the studs of every wall to make sure they were hollow. He'd scanned the ceiling for attic hatches. He'd pulled down every book and some pretty heavy art. He was frustrated and he was tired. Where the hell else would someone keep financial records? As far as Mickey could see, Avery didn't have a computer and he didn't have a safe and he didn't have any files for investments or bank accounts. Could he be totally dependent on his smart phone? Mickey didn't think the financial dealings of a rich guy like Avery could be managed on a three-inch screen, but what did he know?

He stepped into Avery's office and flopped into the fancy mesh desk chair to regroup. He ran his finger across the hand-crafted bird's-eye maple trim that edged Avery's desk and felt something above the top of the right wall of the kneehole. It was a barely-visible slit that he hadn't noticed when he'd first searched the room. He saw a matching slit on the left side. He reached between them and pulled on the trim. A hidden drawer slid out on glides, less than an inch deep, just big enough for Avery's MacBook.

Mickey smiled. Maybe he wasn't so stupid after all. He opened the notebook and watched it wake up. Avery's desktop resolved; no password required. The shmuck had assumed he was safe in his own home. Mickey felt a thrill of accomplishment in having shattered that complacency.

He clicked on a Wells Fargo icon and found himself staring at a login screen.

Lana watched Mickey top the stairs with a MacBook Air, grinning at her like a gladiator presenting his opponent's severed head to the Queen.

"Lookee what I found," he said. "Just need a few passwords from my buddy Avery."

"Change of plans," she said. Mickey's face morphed from confusion to suspicion and back as she raised her arm. She was holding a gun—Avery's Glock—aimed at Mickey's heart.

"What the hell?" said Mickey.

"Surprise," said Avery. He lifted his hands. They were no longer taped to the chair. He swung his legs forward. She had cut him free.

"You conned me into marrying you, Mickey," she said. "You pretended to be someone you're not."

"Baby, I love you."

"Honeymoon's over," she said. "I'm moving on."

"With him?" He shot Avery a sneer.

"Only losers slap people around for no reason," said Avery. "Smart women don't find that attractive."

Mickey's jaw was working overtime again. He looked at Lana. "You're dumping me for a fucking lawyer?"

She was enjoying Mickey's humiliation more than she'd thought she would. She gave Avery a lusty grin.

"I like a man who thinks things through," she said. "It makes me want to do dirty things."

Mickey erupted. "You fucking bitch!" He launched himself at her.

Lana fired a shot into his chest.

Mickey went down. He took a labored breath and sucked air through his wound. She'd hit a lung. Mickey stared at her disbelievingly. His lips moved but he couldn't muster the strength to speak.

She felt unsettled. She'd never shot anyone before. She looked at Avery to make sure he'd caught it all on video. He gave her an assuring nod, then held the iPhone up for Mickey to see.

"You shouldn't have gotten violent," said Avery. "Now it's self-defense."

"See, Mickey?" She kissed her fingertips and touched them to Avery's lips. "He thinks things through."

"Go ahead," said Avery. "Finish the thought."

Lana pointed the Glock at Mickey's forehead and fired again.

She stared at Mickey's corpse as the relentless pounding of the ocean slowly washed the gunshot's echo from her ears.

"Till death do us part," she said.

Avery wiped his own prints off the packet of heroin, knelt beside Mickey and pressed the dead man's fingerprints onto the glassine. Then he slipped the envelope into Mickey's pocket.

"Here's what we tell the police," said Avery. "You were unhappy in your new marriage so you went for a walk on the beach to think about it. I saw you and struck up a conversation. When you found out I was a lawyer you asked if I knew anything about annulments. I invited you up to discuss it. Your husband must have been following you. He barged in, raving like a lunatic. I tried to get the gun I keep in the sideboard, but he jumped me and it fell. He knocked me down and dove for the gun but you grabbed it first. He threatened to kill you and I started a phone video in case you wanted to press charges. That's when he attacked you. You were afraid for your life. You had to shoot him."

"So much to remember."

"I'll do the talking. As your attorney, I'll advise you not to speak."

They heard the wail of an approaching siren. Someone must have heard the shots.

Lana stared out at the crashing waves reflecting the moonlight like small explosions of neon white. A tear rolled down her cheek. She'd always dreamed of a life on the beach.

On the Pacific Beach
Patricia Abbott

That's my mother sitting on the discolored red bench outside Von's Market. She's pushing her shopping cart back and forth as if a fretful baby lay inside. Luckily, it's one of the small ones so shoppers can circumnavigate it without being inconvenienced. I wonder if she ever rocked me so lovingly.

Even if I didn't recognize Mom, which I sometimes don't, I'd recognize her hair, a long, reddish-gray braid that's beginning to look skimpy. She must be what—fifty-eight—now? She's taken to wearing a baseball cap—an item easy to find on the beach. Today it's a Padres cap, and her braid, mostly reddish in the sun, erupts from the hole in back like a dragon's tongue.

Her cart looks a little lighter than when I saw her four months ago, just five blocks from here at a Rubios Taco Shop. It's the 1970s era TV she pushed around for a year or more that's gone. It's hard to imagine pinching a useless TV from a homeless woman.

Why is she on the street? I'm told there's no facility that can keep my mother off the street for long. San Diego's Health and Human Services office has tried many times.

"I'm so sorry, Ms. Delaney," the woman in a lavender pants suit told me a long time ago, thumbing through Mom's chart when I went in to ask . That was probably a decade ago—back when I still hoped Mom's problems could be solved.

"Andrea. Call me Andrea," I told the woman, hoping to create camaraderie at that point.

"Andrea, right. Well, your mom outfoxes us every time. She can pick any lock, disarm guards with her smile, and shimmy down the wobbliest gutter." Ms. Gutierrez chuckled, then covered her mouth. "She's very inventive. And so affable."

"I know." There was a time when I thought of Mom's resourcefulness as a good thing, too—when it got us the food we needed to survive, when it got the rent paid or the school authorities off my back for missing classes.

"Since Audrey's so affable (there's that word again) we let her be. Not confrontational like she's when confined—so we mostly leave her alone. She's managed to accumulate a group of local residents who feed and look after her in a fashion. One called a month or two ago to say she was sick. Nice, wasn't it?"

Nice in its way, but living on the street, a woman's so vulnerable. I thought of that flying into San Diego today when my eyes hit a headline in the local paper.

"Girl Found Strangled on the Beach."

I picked the newspaper up long enough to read the story. It reminded me for a minute of those deaths on Long Island, but it's too early to know if this girl's associated with the sex trade. Is it something about beaches that make women so defenseless there?

Does Mom remember the names of these folks who look out for her any better than she does mine? I still remember the first time she forgot it. Introducing me to someone on the street, she was tongue-tied for a minute, and then called me Suzie. Was Suzie a name she came up with on the spot? I searched for some meaning in it and find none.

I used to get angry when people questioned me—when an EMS technician, a doctor on the phone, or a cop on the street said, "Can't you do something about this?"

If a two hundred fifty pound cop couldn't wrestle her into a van, what chance did I have?

I want to say tell them—all of those people employed some government service—not to judge me. None of you know about the days there was no food in the fridge; the nights she set fire to her bed with a cigarette; the occasions she showed up at school wearing a foil hat to protect her from "the forces;" the stuff of mine she hocked to buy her booze or

Kools. There is no one to tell these stories to.

The items in my mother's cart are different from those in a northern state. No need for heavy winter coats, boots, or an ice scraper. The guy who's staked out my entrance to 1-94 in Chicago has built the kind of tent city I used to make as a kid. Blanket after blanket connected in some jerry-rigged system to keep him warm, to protect his stuff. Even a shovel to dig his way out pokes out a hole. When I stopped to slip him a five last month, several cars behind me beeped.

"You're part of the problem, lady," someone yelled. I gave him the finger, which shut him right up. The possibility I suffer from road rage douses any follow-up remarks. Oh, yes, I have some of my mother coursing through my veins.

"Know me?" I ask Mom now when I finally ratchet up my nerve today. "It's Andrea." When she doesn't blink, I add, "Andy?" Still nothing. "Your daughter?" And finally, "Suzie," which gets a small smile.

Though she doesn't usually seem to know me, I think I must represent possible captivity. Or maybe my face or actual name—Andrea not Suzie—summons up some vestige of remorse. But in the swirling eddy inside her head, my face does not bode well for hand-outs or a Subway Sub. So I rarely get a smile.

Today, she shakes her head and begins to rearrange her cart. She's gotten her hands on a bright blue boogie board, which she strokes possessively. She's a vessel of maternal gestures she never expends in the usual ways. The boogie board's in good shape so it won't last long. But she makes no attempt to hide it under her dirty beach towels, her copies of *La Jolla Light*, her pile of T-shirts.

"Going surfing?" I ask, trying for a little humor. She considers my remark, her bright blue eyes sizing me up. She's a big thinner than the last time I saw her—four months ago now. Handouts for the homeless must have an ebb and flow.

These trips to the coast three or four times a year stretch my paltry salary as an EMS dispatcher to the breaking point. They also raise my level of stress for weeks before and after each visit.

"Why don't you just move back there?" my friend Rachel

asks me every so often.

Why indeed?

A full half-minute passes before Mom laughs, showing me another tooth is missing. The reason for this is simple: homeless people sift through trash cans, and the most common item in that trash can is a sugary drink. Mom's chief diet staple is a Slurpee. That's why both her health and her teeth suffer.

"How about getting some lunch?" I say.

There are several possibilities for a healthy lunch on the street, but since I can't take her inside, we walk to a taco stand where I order the healthiest items on the menu: a tossed salad, a chicken taco, and a carton of milk. She carefully removes the beans and lettuce from the taco, the cucumber and avocado from the salad, then eats it eagerly without saying a word. The milk carton is hard for her to open, and she executes a nice hook shot into the trash can before I can intervene.

"Do you know who I am?" I ask again. "Remember me, Mom?"

She gives me her brightest smile, the one she probably offers to anyone who buys her a meal. "Of course, I do," she says, getting up. In a second, she pushes off.

She stops at a trash can half a block away to retrieve a Big Gulp drink, thirsty I'm sure.

I see her again the next day and the day after, doing what I can each time to clean her up, feed her, and finally, fumbling with her behind a vacant auto parts store to change her clothes. She hates me touching her; hates me making her step into a new pair of pants; shudders when I momentarily expose her bare breasts to the dark windows above us; wiggles her feet when I try to trim her toenails before putting on a new pair of sneakers. It's frustrating, but there is something curative for me at least in the feel of her flesh under my hand.

I used to smuggle her into the showers on the beach or the one in my motel, but no one, including Mom, liked that idea. So any washing or a change of clothes must be done on the street. Over time I have learned how to do this discreetly.

Before I take off, I call the social service agency to talk to

Ms. Gutierrez, who still takes an interest in my mother. A harried-sounding man tells me she's on vacation—won't return until the next Monday. Where does someone who lives at a resort go for a vacation, I wonder?

In my childhood in the Encanto section of San Diego, I never heard of anyone taking a vacation. A trip to the amusement park at Mission Beach was a big deal, a weekend at a grandparents' place in Rosarita even bigger. I left home at seventeen, searching for an entirely different view to look at from my window. At that time, Mom was neither a street person nor homeless. Just a woman living on food stamps and handouts from men she picked up. Odd, forgetful, but not completely daft. She sometimes even took the occasional job until her list of deficits became clear to a potential employer.

"Now, keep in touch," she said as I headed out the door that last day. "Send a postcard when you get there."

Did she imagine I was going to Hollywood to become a movie star? Did she think I was off to see the Queen?

I keep up with Mom, or at least the city where she lives, through an online subscription to *U-T San Diego*, the local newspaper. Pacific Beach's the northernmost section of San Diego. I have never been clear on how Mom found her way there from Encanto. Probably a date drove her up there one night and she liked what she saw and stayed. It's a good place for the homeless, not too toney but fairly safe. I often wonder if the homeless migrate to the southwest for the better climate. Like birds finding a more hospitable roost as their former one become unwelcoming.

As I click through stories about the mayoral race, the rise in housing prices, a new film being shot in the Hillside area, the price of guavas and exotic chilies at Whole Foods a few days later, I find a story that makes me sit up. It's about that dead girl found on the beach—Mission Beach it turns out—just down the Boulevard from Pacific Beach. She was dressed in a wetsuit and found strangled on the sand by a sunrise class in Tai Chi. It still gives no name—five days later now—which may mean they haven't been able to ID her.

I don't think about this news story much over the next few days—people who've lived in Chicago any length of time aren't surprised by such things. But when another girl turns up strangled a week later, I begin to feel some dread.

This time it's Carlsbad, thirty minutes up the coast. I'm not actually afraid for my mother—these were both girls after all. The first woman has now been named Rebecca Sweet. And it turns out she's not a surfer at all—but a twenty-five-year-old day-tripper who must have wanted to try her hand at surfing. Or maybe not. There's speculation she wasn't surfing, but had been dressed in the wetsuit by her assailant—something about the size of it being wrong. I follow the story closely in the days ahead, hoping for more information about either case. Is the murderer looking for day-trippers, young girls, surfers, or none of the above?

Maya Velasquez, the second victim, was not a surfer, not dressed in a wetsuit, not a day-tripper, and not under thirty, I find this out three days later. She was a thirty-five-year-old tax accountant from L.A., down in Carlsbad for a meeting. She'd been expected back by eight o'clock but never turned up. There's a photo online. She looks attractive even though the lighting isn't good and her hair is yanked back—it's probably a picture from a driver's license.

With the third murder, three weeks later, I go into alarm mode. They post pictures of the three victims side by side—large photos now—and the third woman's said to be a hooker found on Imperial Beach. Felicity Brown serviced the servicemen and was probably abducted from her usual post and taken, still alive, to the beach. She was found under an abutment of rocks, had probably been there for several days. An unusual period of rain had kept the beach empty.

They have a better photo of Maya Velasquez in this edition, too, and it's easy to see the one object the three victims have in common. It's not surfing accoutrements, nor an age similarity, nor the location of their bodies. It's that all three women wear their hair in a braid, and apparently these braids were used to strangle them. Or suffocate them rather: the hair was stuffed down their throats. Pushed so far down, in fact, that strands of hair were found in the lower esophagus of all three women. Did he use an instrument to do this, I wonder? Some sort of barbecue skewer perhaps.

My mother wears her hair in a braid and has her entire life. I used to ask her why, back in the days when she could still answer a question.

"Hair on my face makes my skin itch," she explained, "and a braid it easy to do."

I've tried giving my mother a phone, but each time it was gone before I even left San Diego. She cannot learn to use one either. People, far more sentient than Mom, struggle with such devices.

I call Ms. Gutierrez's number as soon as it's nine a.m. on the West Coast.

"I'm sorry," a woman says, "She doesn't work her anymore."

"Is she in another office?"

"No. With the government cuts, she was laid off."

Laid off? She had to have spent at least ten years in that office. I try to remember the first time I called her. How deep were these cuts?

"Has someone taken over her caseload," I ask, realizing as I say this that Mom is not part of anyone's caseload. At best, she's someone who pops up on the radar from time to time. Because she was affable, no one really paid much attention to her. Could anyone in the State of California ID her in a morgue? How would anyone know where to call me should such a thing happen? I am stunned at my own negligence. Stunned at my inability to foresee such a large hole in my flight plan.

"We're sorting it out now," the woman said. She sounds exhausted and it is only 9:02 in the morning. "What was her name again?"

"Audrey Delaney."

"And her address?"

I sighed inwardly. "She's homeless. That's why I can't get in touch with her."

"We give cell phones to the homeless now. Especially the women. It's a new program. So they can call in for help."

"She's not that kind of homeless person. She wouldn't be able to hold onto a phone." When the woman didn't say anything, I add, "I've given her at least three phones in the last five years. And even if she could keep one, she'd never use it." Why am I explaining this to her?

Pause. "God helps those who help themselves."

I am speechless after that *bon mot* from a servant of the state so it is she who speaks again.

A huge sigh and then, "Well, I'll see what I can do. Might take a few days. Can you give me your name and number?"

Without a shred of hope that I'll hear from her again, I give it to her and she promises to get back to me, adding, "Did you ever consider coming out here to help her out. Your mother, I mean."

I hang up the phone.

But that's what I do—fly west.

I can ill afford this trip, and have to use my last three vacation days. If I can't resolve whatever it is I want resolved, I will probably have to quit my job or take an unpaid leave. And our office has no unpaid leaves as far as I know.

My little purple Fiesta rental gets me in Pacific Beach around one o'clock. The streets look as benign as ever—certainly not the locale for a serial killer. I don't see a single woman wearing a braid, not that this is a common hair style. Perhaps it's more popular on the beach than elsewhere though—a way to deal with wet hair. But I imagine any woman with a braid has changed her hairdo after those newspaper photos. Except, of course, for the sort of women who don't follow the news. Like my mother.

The street in P.B. that Mom favors is Garnet, where restaurants, several supermarkets, and a Trader Joe's offer the opportunity to pick up food, rest on a bench, and watch the foot traffic. She's usually too out of it to pan-handle, and if she does, the money probably ends up in another person's pocket. Most of the time, she will be somewhere on this stretch that runs from I-5 to the Pacific. Other times, I can find her down on the boardwalk that runs along the beach. The nest of benches there is usually occupied by her cronies, and like the birds that badger outdoor diners, the homeless sweep in for discarded food, too.

Today she's in neither place. I stop a few of the sort of people who look like they might know her and ask, "Have you seen Audrey? Audrey Delaney?"

I try to describe her but my words sounds vague. I approach people on benches, the ones shuffling down the street, a guy lying comatose in an alcove, several on the beach, two propped up against the back wall of Vons. Head shakes, frowns, shrugs. Obviously it's not a name they know. But do they know her face?

For God's sake, why don't I have a picture of her? Why has this never occurred to me before—the idea that I might need such a thing? Do I want to leave her behind—or at least her image—when I fly back east? Or is it her face, after years of living rough, is just too disheartening to hang on to?

"Check out the food bank," someone advises. He looks like a man who's spent decades on the street, too—so tanned that the hue looks like mud on his face, so whip-thin that no size pants will fit him. I offer him one of sandwiches I bought, but he waves it away.

"I'm on disability now," he says. "Save it for—what's her name—Audrey?"

I begin to describe her. "A reddish braid, a San Diego Padres cap, skinny, about five-five, a shopping cart?" I pause, thinking. "Although it might not be a Padres cap by now."

"Lots of places she could be," he says, "but probably out on the street. Supposed to get a shelter here but it never happened."

I nod, having read about this in the local newspaper.

"She could be in a thrift shop, or a church, a donation center or a recycling place, a food kitchen, going through the trash somewhere. The cops could've picked her up. There's a guy comes by couple times a week and gives people a lift to a food bank. Try there." His eyes light up. "Maybe she has a boyfriend."

I run across a couple—maybe twenty years old—with a sign that says, "Help send us back to Houston."

"How long you been here?" I ask, nearly tripping over the tambourine they're using to collect cash. I add a buck. Then another.

"'Bout a week," the guy says, looking at his girlfriend. "Right?"

"Yeah, our break started about then," she says, nodding. They are too attractive to have been here long. Did they set out knowing they'd have to pan-handle their way back to Texas or did some bad stuff happen? I don't ask.

When I finally get to the boardwalk, I find an artist doing caricatures nestled between a burger place and a surfboard shop. He's seated on a high stool with an umbrella attached to it, his long legs dangling.

"Think you could do a picture—the way a police sketch artist does."

"I can give it a try." He picks up a pencil. It takes me an inordinate amount of time to summon up my mother's nose, the shape of her eyes, her chin. I have a poor facial memory I decide. Perhaps my mom does, too and that's why she calls me Suzie.

But after ten minutes or so, it's a reasonably close facsimile. At least the accessories are right.

"This is your mom then?" he asks as we trade ten bucks for the portrait. "Wasn't till I got the eyes right that I recognized her."

"You know her?"

"Seen her around. Folks call her Brady." He looks down at the drawing. "The braid, I guess. Never thought about it 'till now."

"Have you seen her lately?"

He thinks about it. "Wish I could tell you exactly when. One day pretty much blends into the next around here. Every day—the same blue sky, the same seventy degrees." We both look up. "It hasn't been very long though. She and her boyfriend..."

"Boyfriend?"

I don't know why it strikes me as so improbable. Just because she can't hold onto a cell phone or a TV doesn't mean she can't hold onto a man. "Do you know his name—or where I can find him?"

The artist purses his lips. I am waiting for the "one day blends into the next" sentiment again when he suddenly comes up with it. "Name's George. He's usually at that recycling center over on Lamont Street. People that run it are pretty cool about lettin' a few of the homeless drop in. Folks like it better than the shelters downtown where their junk gets stolen and they catch head lice. Center is just back-up place— for when someone's hasslin' them. Or if the cops are givin' them a hard time. You know. You can usually just hang on the street."

I thank the artist and drive to the recycling center on Lamont, where an employee in a tiny office at the far end of the huge facility says she doesn't know anyone named Brady but thinks she might know George. "Big guy with a tat on the top of his head?" she asks, and then laughs. "That tat makes me chuckle every time I think of it."

Now why didn't the sketch artist mention this tattoo? Maybe George wears a hat outside? "Why does it make you laugh?"

"You never seen it then, honey?" I shake my head. "It looks like steam—like steam coming out of his head. Don't know how they did it, but that's what it looks like. Like ole George is blowing his top."

"Is George the kind of guy who does that—the sort who gets angry?"

"Just the opposite. Nicest guy in the world."

"Do you know where he might be?"

"Geez, no. I'm stuck in here all day. I don't know where folks go when they leave here. Don't know where they come from either." She laughs harder. "They're kinda like those zombies that just turn up—coming across the warehouse floor real slow."

In the years I've come to check up on Mom, I've never had this much trouble finding her. Is it because of the murders that she's keeping out of sight? Is it because she has a boyfriend? I am halfway to the Olney Street Police Station when it occurs to me. Usually when I arrive in Pacific Beach, I sit down on a bench and wait until Mom turns up. I read a book, have some iced coffee, take in some of the sun that's scarce in Chicago a lot of the year, watch the street action, watch the sun set over the ocean. And sooner or later, Mom strolls by. Always. She favors that stretch near Trader Joe's. It's like her home. Why did I approach it differently today?

So that is what I do. I park the car, buy myself a cappuccino, pull out a paperback, and sit down on a bench. It takes about forty minutes. In fact, I am pulling out my map to consider other destinations when I catch a glimpse of her turning, a corner. Her cart is fuller than ever. The boogie board is gone, but she seems to have picked up a number of other goodies. As she grows closer something unusual happens: she spots me and cries out, "Suzie!"

I rise smiling and wave. As she grows close, I pull out the article I bought in an airport shop as soon as my plane landed. I was so relieved to find it—had worried about its availability the entire flight. As soon as she's near enough to me, near enough to put my hands on, I reach out for her. Scissors in hand, I cut off that braid.

Marlowe's Wake
Phillip DePoy

Christopher Marlowe held his dead father's hand. Dressed in black, Marlowe was beyond mourning, body numb, brain silent. His father had been in perfect health that morning, had even spent an extra hour in his favorite tavern that afternoon, celebrating the fact that sixteen-year-old son Christopher was shortly bound for scholarship at Cambridge. He had staggered home, more drunk than usual.

By dark his body lay on the kitchen table of their family home in Canterbury.

Later friends and relatives would gather, dancing, singing, making all the noise they could in the hope they might somehow call back the departed from beyond the grave.

More often than not, the dead remained dead and were buried. Christopher had been born in 1564, the year after the worst plague in England's history. The Black Death claimed the lives of eighty thousand people. There had been so little room to bury the dead that coffins were frequently dug up, older bones taken elsewhere, and graves reused. A grisly discovery had been made: one in twenty coffins had fierce scratch marks on the inside. Five percent of the people buried in plague times in England had been put in their graves alive.

So in an effort to avoid that horror, the Marlowe family dutifully waited, leaving the body of the beloved sire out for all to see, with no real hope of recovery in so obvious a corpse.

As Marlowe sat, eyes closed, dressed all in black, mumbling a confused prayer, the door swung open.

Instinctively Marlowe stood, dagger already in hand, as his father had taught him to do. In the doorway stood a thin man in a blood-red cape, rapier drawn.

The two men stared at each other for a moment.

"Dr. Lopez," Marlowe finally muttered. "You're too late, as you can see."

Rodrigo Lopez, a Portuguese Jew converted to Church of England, was the most renowned physician in Europe. An old friend to the Marlowe family, he had achieved lofty status when he had twice saved the life of Queen Elizabeth. Rumor in London had it that Lopez was shortly to be named the Royal Physician, a notion that enraged half the court. A Jew and a Portuguese tending to the world's greatest monarch!

"Hello, Chris," Lopez whispered, putting away his rapier. "Sorry. I saw someone sitting over the body and I was afraid—how long has he been like this?"

"Since late this afternoon," Marlowe answered hopelessly.

"Good," Lopez said crisply. "If you'll allow me, I think I might have something that would help matters."

Lopez moved to the dead man's side, withdrawing a small leather pouch from beneath his arcane cloak.

"What are you doing?" Marlowe demanded.

"I'll tell you later," Lopez answered vaguely "if it works."

With that Lopez opened the pouch, took out a small silver vial and a bag the size of an apple. Lopez lifted John Marlowe's lifeless head carefully, setting the bag on the table. The contents of the vial were poured into the dead man's mouth.

"Now hand me the bag," Lopez commanded.

Marlowe blinked, then handed Lopez the bag in question. Lopez opened it and held it under the corpse's nose.

"What are you *doing*?" Marlowe insisted again.

"Sh!" Lopez snapped.

Suddenly the deceased eyes opened wide and the dead man drew in a tremendous breath. As he did, he breathed in the dusty white contents of the bag that Lopez held under his nose. A second later John Marlowe gasped, coughed, and sat up on his own.

"Christ in heaven!" he hollered.

Marlowe, mouth wide, could only utter, "Father?"

In the blink of an eye John Marlowe recognized Lopez, nodded, and struggled to get off the table.

"They've done it, then," he said to Lopez.

Lopez only nodded.

The father, still dressed in his best suit of clothes, purple doublet, tall boots, took a deep breath.

"Chris, you know Dr. Lopez," he said as if he were making a casual introduction in the street.

"Do I know Doctor—what the hell just *happened?*"

"First, a brief explanation of the science behind your father's recent, though impermanent, demise," Lopez interjected pedantically. "The combination of a lead cup and any ale may sometimes induce a death-like trance. Full many a man presumed dead from the plague has merely suffered this lead poisoning, hence our newly minted custom of *the wake*. Someone knew this, and accelerated the effect by somehow corroding a cup with a potion or a powder so that massive amounts of lead would find their way into your father's blood and render him dead or near it."

Believing that to be a sufficient explanation, Lopez began packing his pouch.

"No." Marlowe gaped. "There's more—there's more to it than that. How do you know that's what happened?"

"The cure for such a malady worked," Lopez answered, "ergo my guess was correct."

He shrugged.

Marlowe stared. "Father. You were dead."

"I was not, in fact," John said. "Obviously. Clever of you to send for Dr. Lopez."

Lopez and the younger Marlowe looked at each other.

"I didn't send for this man," Christopher said softly. "I—you're alive! I have to tell Mother."

"Chris," Lopez said as his mysterious pouch disappeared, "you should probably sit down."

"Son," John said, "there's more to this than—yes, you should probably sit down."

Marlowe sat. Only then did he realize he still had his dagger in his hand.

"Someone has nearly murdered your father," Lopez began. "We should let them believe they have succeeded."

"Murdered my father?" Marlowe looked between the

other two men. "Why would anyone want to kill him? He makes boots!"

"If it were possible," Lopez answered, "I would find that out for myself. But I am officially in London at this moment. I am not here. Your father won't have the strength to do anything like this for days, and by then it will be too late. And as I've said, there is an advantage in allowing the murderers to believe that they have succeeded."

Marlowe's head swam.

"The Pope's men have been in Canterbury for years now," the father began. "Because of our family's Catholic history, they continue to believe we might help them restore England to the Pope, and even take away our Queen. Nothing could be further from the truth, of course, but I have been convinced— I have been persuaded—to feign an interest in their cause, and to report their activities to—to the Queen's officials. From time to time."

"What?" Marlowe said, straining to believe his ears.

"Dr. Lopez and I have been training you to similar effect since you were ten," John Marlowe went on, "though you did not know it. Now I'm afraid, a bit before your time, you must use these subtle skills we've taught you and take matters in hand. Tonight, I'm afraid. It is imperative you discover the identity of the head of their organization. They're bold enough, now, to resort to murder. So now is the time to stop them. You must find out who killed me."

"No." Marlowe shook his head.

"You can do it," his father said. "I have faith in you."

"I—I wouldn't know where to begin," he stammered.

"If I were in your place," Lopez said, drawing his cloak around his neck, "I would start in the tavern where your father was last drinking. The place where he was killed."

"He's right," John Marlowe agreed. "When I announced I was celebrating your Cambridge scholarship, two men bought me a drink. One was all in green and the other had a face like an otter. Look for them. One of them is very likely our man."

"They won't still be there," Marlowe snapped, "after they've killed a man."

John Marlowe smiled. "They will, in fact. In the first place, they believe they did their work surreptitiously, and were not detected. And in the second place, they were drunk beyond belief, with the apparent intention of drinking even more. They'll be there because they're idiots."

Even after dark the Parrot Inn was crowded, a riot of color and noise. Men in torn black tunics, boys in soiled red doublets, old drunkards in brown rags all crowded around the long tables. The floor, hard-packed soil of England, was covered with straw, old food, and mangy curs. The low ceiling was held aloft by six columns of rough timber.

At the bar, a small oak barricade against the onslaught of customers, stood the woman of the house, Nell Whatley. Beside her: husband Pinch. It was widely imagined he acquired the name because he was a thief; Nell insisted it had more to do with the gesture which had first brought them together.

Three younger women in nearly identical ginger dresses danced and weaved their way through the glut of men, setting cups here, plates there, enduring the occasional rude suggestion.

Ordinarily in a place like this the serving women might have entertained or even made profit by rude suggestions. Serving women in public houses were very often public women as well. But it was known far and wide that these three girls were the dark-eyed daughters of Nell and Pinch, and the all had a different response to such behavior. A man named Leyden had once accosted the youngest, Jenny, with carnal invitations. As a testament to that moment in history, a withered leathery disc was affixed to the column closest to the fire. It was a warning, there for all to see. Jenny had cut off Leyden's right ear and nailed it to the wood.

No one bothered the girls at the Parrot Inn.

Jenny excused herself when she nudged past the two men who were leaning against Leyden's Post, staring at Marlowe as he entered the Parrot and slipped behind his father's usual table.

"Sorry, boys," her voice lilted. "Do you want a bench?

There's one by the bar."

She always had a kind word for a stranger.

"Skiv off, you," the taller man hissed without even looking at her. "We're trying to work."

That man was dressed in dark green from head to foot, so tall he had to stoop. Still his soiled red hair brushed the roof beams.

The other man was shorter, and did, indeed, look a little like an otter. He was wrapped all in dirty grey. He kept his silent gaze on Marlowe.

"All right." She smiled.

A moment later Jenny brought ale and a cut of brown bread to Marlowe's table. He had already taken out a piece of paper and a pen and begun writing, as he often did.

"Kit, sorry to hear about your father," she whispered in his ear, her black hair brushing across his cheek. "Listen, I wouldn't look now, but there's two boys at Leyden's Post who's staring you down."

He kept writing, his eyes glued to the paper. "Hello, Jen."

"Should I tell Papa?"

Marlowe reached into his doublet and pulled out two coins. "Thank you, sweet, I saw them when I came in. They've been in here since this afternoon?"

She nodded.

"I see." Marlowe continued writing. "I think they may be the ones who—who killed my father, as a matter of fact."

"Killed?" she asked breathlessly.

"Soft, Jen," Marlowe said, still not looking up. "I'll take care of it."

"You don't need help with them?" she asked, alarmed. "They've both got knives."

He looked up. His smile dazzled, his words were drawn out.

"I am more afraid of your lips," he murmured, "than I am of any man's blade. I know how to fight a dagger, but there is no defense against the taste of your mouth. Or so I have imagined."

"Oh." She tried to steady herself, but she appeared unused to the ordinary poetry of public seduction. For a heartbeat or two, it seemed she had forgotten how to breathe.

Still, she did her best to return to herself. "Well, at least let me get out of your way before you go carving up them boys."

She straightened up, managed a wink, and was off in a ginger blur toward the bar.

Marlowe kept writing with his left hand, but under the table, in the darkness, his right hand found the knife he had tucked into his boot. Out of the corner of his eye, he saw the two men by the post. They were making the appearance of warming themselves by the fire, but it was ridiculously clear that they were, in fact, studying Marlowe.

Jenny whispered a few well-chosen words to her father as she set down empty cups. Pinch nodded once, and put his hand under the bar.

The rest of the crowd of twenty or more—a large number for the size of the room—seemed oblivious to any impending danger.

Marlowe finished what he was writing. He nodded, satisfied, it seemed, with what was on the page. He calmly leaned back in his chair. His face and body were then obscured by the shadows in his corner.

In a blur of black shadow, his arm shot forward.

In the next instant he leaned forward again, took up the quill, and began, calmly and steadily, to write more on his page, as if nothing had changed.

But the weasel-man in grey began to bleed. Marlowe's knife was stuck in his shoulder. The man beside him, dressed in green, didn't notice until the littler man grabbed his companion's arm and spilled blood on it.

The taller man let out a shriek, but it was barely heard above the din of the room. No one seemed to notice that anything was amiss.

Pinch's hand relaxed on the thick wooden club behind the bar.

"Help!" the tall man in green cried out at last, a bit of panic in his eyes as he scanned the room for the owner of the knife that was stuck in his companion's shoulder.

Several men permitted themselves a glance then.

Marlowe stood. "My God," he said theatrically, "I think

that man's been stabbed."

He bounded across the room, deliberately provoking laughter at his choreography. One man even applauded.

Marlowe grabbed the taller man's esophagus.

"Why have you stabbed this man?" Marlowe demanded.

"I never," the man rasped, eyes wide.

Marlowe leaned in close to the man's ear.

"Then tell me this," Marlowe whispered so that only the man could hear, "why did you kill my father?"

The man shook his head, gasping for breath.

"I want to know why you're here," Marlowe went on. "I'll skin your flesh from your face if I don't get an answer. And your friend, here, is in no condition to help you. Do you understand me?"

The man did his best to nod. The shorter man in grey had sunk to his knees and was trying to pull the knife from the blood at his drooping lace collar.

"Are you certain?" Marlowe went on, pressing deeper into the man's gullet.

The man's eyes began to roll back into his head.

"I'll take that as a yes."

Marlowe's hand darted for a second, and pulled his knife free from the otter's shoulder. Blood gushed onto the boots of the man in green.

Marlowe released that man's esophagus, and shot his gaze to the man on the floor. "Pinch?" Marlowe called without looking up. "Would you give me a hand with these two? They've had a quarrel and I think they should leave. See? One's stabbed the other."

"None of that in my place!" Pinch roared, rounding the bar.

Marlowe wiped his knife on the green jacket, and returned the blade to his boot. He grabbed the short man by the hair and started dragging him toward the door.

Pinch lurched forward and took the taller man under the armpits.

All four were out in the street in the blink of an eye.

"Thank you, Pinch," Marlowe said pleasantly, "I'll handle it from here out."

Pinch nodded silently and vanished.

The little man was about to pass out and the one in green was still coughing, holding his throat.

Marlowe took away their blades, tossed the weapons down the street, clattering on the stones. Then he withdrew his own dagger again and addressed the man in green.

"I'll cut your friend's throat in a minute," Marlowe told him calmly, "and then I'll start to carve you up. Or I can stop his wound from bleeding and you can talk to me. I can tell you, though, that I'm not in a receptive mood, and I'd really rather just kill you."

"Let's talk," the man croaked.

Marlowe hesitated for a moment, then leaned over, ripped a bit of grey cloth from the otter's shirt, and wrapped it around the bleeding wound.

"That should hold for a while." Marlowe then placed the point of his dagger at the green man's gullet. "Now. You bought a drink for a man in there earlier today, this afternoon."

The man nodded. "Your father, Mr. Marlowe."

Marlowe hesitated. "You know who I am?"

"You're Christopher Marlowe," the man said. "You're actually the man we wanted to get at, you see. And we never meant to kill your old dad, we—this idiot here used too much of the powder."

He kicked the otter. The otter was too weak to respond.

"Explain that to me," Marlowe snapped. "What do you mean you *wanted to get at me*?"

"The plan was," the man went on, attempting to sound conversational, "to make your dad sick. He'd pass out here at the old Parrot. You'd be called. We'd—well, truth be told, we'd do you."

"Kill me?"

"That's right."

"Why?" Marlowe asked, a bit of the energy drained from his voice.

"Two gold crowns!" the man answered. "Each!"

"No," Marlowe pressed the point of his dagger into the man's Adam's apple, "I mean why did someone want you to kill me?"

"Oh, right," the man nodded. "No idea."

"Who hired you?"

"Don't know," the man said.

The point of Marlowe's dagger drew blood.

"Don't know his name!" the man said desperately. "That's I meant to say."

"Is he in the pub now?"

"No."

"What did he look like?"

"Look like?" the man asked. "He was dark. Wore a red cape. Had an accent. Said he was a doctor."

Marlowe nearly dropped his blade.

"Jesus," he whispered.

The man in green began to bleed a little, and the otter passed out in the street.

Racing back home, Marlowe tried to calm himself. If Lopez had actually been the architect of these strange events, there was no telling what he might find in his house.

He did not expect to discover his mother sitting all alone at the barren kitchen table, sobbing.

"Mother?" Marlowe asked as he stood in the door way. "Where is my father—where is my father's body?"

"I couldn't bear to have him just lying here like that," she managed to say. "So when Dr. Lopez suggested moving him to the church, I breathed a sigh of relief, I can tell you."

"Lopez suggested?" Marlowe's heart was pounding. "You saw the body moved?"

"No, I couldn't watch that," she sniffed. "The good doctor took charge. Thank God for that man."

"Yes," Marlowe mumbled. "What church?"

"Sorry, dear?" His mother looked up.

"Where exactly was the body taken?"

"Oh." She sighed. "He's in St. George's, of course, where you were baptized."

Without another word, Marlowe was off. Lopez might have lied to his mother, Marlowe knew that, and there was certainly no telling what strange plans were at work. But at least the church of St. George the Martyr was just around the corner from the Marlowe home, a very short dash.

Bursting in through the front door, Marlowe's eyes searched the candle-lit sanctuary. Nothing moved. There was no sound; no sign of his father, or Lopez. High columns ascended into darkness, the stained glass window was lifeless. Candles flickered here and there, but did little to illuminate. In a few hours someone would come and ring the four a.m. bell, but at that moment the place seemed empty.

Then, a whispered footstep close to a side door broke the silence.

Marlowe stuck to the shadows, working his way around the outer walls, dagger in his hand. There it was again: the shuffling footfalls of another human being, someone close to the altar.

Marlowe bent low, crept soundlessly, and rounded a column just in time to catch sight of a fleeting figure wrapped in a floor-length cloak. It had moved to the other side of the altar and was crouched, waiting.

Marlowe drew in a silent breath, steadied himself, and then dropped slowly to his knees. Crawling between the front two pews, he made his way carefully to the center aisle. As far as he could tell, the figure was still hiding just beyond the altar.

It wasn't like Lopez to hide and wait. He had taught Marlowe to be bold. In fact, Lopez had taught him nearly everything he knew about fighting with dagger and rapier. So what was Lopez doing?

If he doesn't know I'm here, I might surprise him.

With no further thought, Marlowe leapt from between the pews out into the center aisle, roaring like a wild beast.

The figure hidden in the shadows jumped wildly and clattered backward, letting out a high-pitched shriek.

In the next second, Marlowe was there, dagger in hand. Dressed all in black he was nearly impossible to see in the sputtering light from the altar candles.

Then up from the stones the figure flew at Marlowe, landing on top of him, knocking him backward. The two bodies thumped on the hard floor, and Marlowe was momentarily immobilized.

The figure above him threw back the shoulders of the cape and raised a silver dagger high in the air. Marlowe rallied when he saw the blade plunging toward his face, and rolled hard to his left. The figure lost balance, and toppled.

Marlowe got to his feet, gasping for breath. His opponent rolled twice and was standing, snarling.

Suddenly Marlowe realized that his opponent's cape was not scarlet. It was ginger-colored. In the next second the hood was thrown back and the identity of his attacker revealed.

"Jenny!" Marlowe shouted.

She responded by flying forward, blade first.

Marlowe jumped sideways, kicked out, and hobbled the girl. She fell, skidding on the floor, but she was up again in the next second.

"What are you doing?" Marlowe demanded.

"Finishing the job those two idiots couldn't," she panted. "I was certain they'd kill you in the street. You seem to be better trained than we thought."

She tossed her cloak behind her back and somehow gained a pistol from a belt at her waist. Dagger in one hand, pistol in the other, she planted her feet.

"This is a Catholic country!" she snarled. "Your father used to tell us he was helping the cause, but we know now that he was lying!"

There was such rage in her voice, Marlowe feared she had lost her mind.

"I—I really don't know what you're talking about, Jen," Marlowe said, hoping for a reasonable tone of voice. "Why would you want to get rid of me?"

"Shut it," she demanded. "Your father told you everything!"

"Honestly, sweet," Marlowe implored, "he told me nothing before he died. I truly don't know what this is about."

Jen seemed to lose a small portion of her madness. The pistol stayed trained on Marlowe's midsection, but the dagger hand dropped to her side.

"You're leaving, Kit," she said, softer. "You're the greater threat, you see. Your father, he was in the way, but he would never have left Canterbury. You're about to go off into the bigger world. College. London. You'll do real damage to the cause. I'm sorry. *Sweet.* We can't let you do that. We can't let you leave."

She cocked the pistol.

Without thinking, Marlowe flipped his knife with direct precision. It hit the barrel of the gun perfectly. The gun went off, but the ball went sideways, dusting a bit of stone from the nearest column.

Marlowe's rapier was in his hand.

"I don't want to hurt you, Jen," he told her genuinely.

She nodded, looking down.

He took a step closer.

She sighed, or sobbed.

"Jenny," he murmured.

Jenny nodded.

Then, giving no warning, she screamed and slashed. Marlowe had forgotten about the blade in her other hand. It cut Marlowe's hand deeply, and he dropped the rapier.

She whirled, turned, and lunged again, aiming to strike him in the heart.

Marlowe dropped down just in time, and her blade plunged into the pew nearest Marlowe's leg.

Marlowe kicked Jenny's right ankle and she fell forward, her head glancing against another pew. Marlowe grabbed her arm, twisted it, and took the dagger away from her as they both plummeted to the floor of the church once more.

Marlowe sat astride her as Jenny blinked, trying to recover from the blow to her head.

"I have no idea why you're doing this, Jenny," Marlowe gasped, trying to get his breath, "but I can tell you that this is *not* the circumstance I imagined when I dreamt of being on top of you."

"Well." She smiled, and seemed to relax. "Get off me and perhaps we can discuss this in a more civil manner."

"Good," Marlowe said, still trying to catch his breath.

He backed away a little, secure in the fact that he had her

knife in his hand.

She sat up.

"So, my sweet," she began, "I shall tell you—"

From behind Marlowe, someone plunged a rapier into her heart. She didn't have time to scream. She didn't even close her eyes. She could only fall backward, dead.

Marlowe jumped up, spinning around, dagger at the ready.

Lopez stood, bloody rapier in hand, and behind him: Marlowe's father.

"What in—in Christ's name have you done?" Marlowe stammered.

"Look at her left hand, son," Marlowe's father said softly.

He did. Jenny held another pistol, cocked and ready to fire.

"She would have shot you," Lopez said, returning his rapier to its sheath.

Marlowe could only stare.

"Jenny is, or was, the head of Catholic Intelligence in this part of England," Marlowe's father said. "Or at least that's our theory now."

"We didn't suspect until tonight," Lopez added. "You got her to admit her affiliation. We've been trying to find that out for some time now."

"She was most likely the one who approached me several years ago," his father said, "though she was in disguise. She was dressed as a man, but I knew something was amiss."

"You did tell me you thought it might have been a woman," Lopez agreed, conversationally. "You were right."

"Approached you about what?" Marlowe asked, hopelessly lost.

"As I've said, owing to our family's previous Catholic allegiances," his father began, "this person wanted me to— how shall I say it?"

"Betray your country," Lopez said simply. "She wanted you to spy on your Queen."

"Well, yes," the father admitted. "But I became something of a—what did you call it?"

"A double agent," Lopez said indulgently.

"Yes, a double agent." Marlowe's father sighed. "As you've just heard her admit, however, you were the greater threat, at least in her mind. She apparently discovered my true nature, and believed that you were spying with me, so you had to be killed. I was a decoy. You were the target."

"But," Marlowe began, "the—the man in green, one of the men who poisoned your cup, or so I was persuaded to believe—that man told me that Dr. Lopez had hired him."

"Ah." Lopez smiled. "Brilliant."

"Yes," Marlowe's father agreed. "And savage."

"That's why you came here to St. George's, not to see your father," Lopez went on. "You were after me."

"Yes," Marlowe concurred. "Why did you tell my mother that you were moving the body to this church?"

"To keep the rest of your family out of harm's way," Lopez answered. "I knew they could come for you. I assumed you'd follow us here, which would draw them away from your home. I just didn't know you'd be coming here to kill me."

"It really was a perfect strategy on their part," Marlowe's father mused. "If you happened to somehow kill Dr. Lopez, the Queen's favorite physician, you'd be in prison and out of their way. In the more likely event that Lopez killed you, their problem would be even better solved."

"But how did Jenny know I would be here, in St. George's?" Marlowe asked.

"She didn't," Lopez said. "Probably followed you from the pub."

"Obviously," the father agreed. "She said that she knew those two men hadn't killed you in the street. She was probably watching."

"How is it that you've never told me any of this?" Marlowe asked his father, doing his best to take it all in. "Spies. Secrets."

"Perhaps we should discuss the meaning of the word *secrets*," his father suggested. "I was sworn to *secrecy*."

"By the Queen," Lopez added in attempt to help.

Beginning to piece things together, Marlowe said slowly, "Then the man in green, he was just—he was just lying to me."

"Yes," Lopez affirmed patiently.

"Everybody lies, son," his father said. "That's the spy game."

"The spy game?" Marlowe stared down at Jenny.

"Yes, and you're good at it," Lopez said brightly. "I knew you would be. You brought out Jenny, gave her time to confess her role in this. You did good work tonight. I hope you'll continue to work for—"

"No," Marlowe insisted, wondering how he could explain to his father and Dr. Lopez that the so-called *good work* he'd done that night had all been a matter of luck. "I'm not working for—I'm going to college. Next week I'm going to Cambridge!"

Lopez looked away. Marlowe's father was silent.

"I'm telling you, Doctor, I don't want any part of this!" Marlowe insisted softly.

"Wake up, Chris," Lopez said, staring idly at the crucifix on the altar, "you're already in."

KE Nave

The Gumshoe Actor
Krista Nave

The new office—my new office—was as devoid of ornaments and fixings as the boss that came with it. Melanie Katsaros seemed pretty dull if you didn't know where to look. With other women, you looked to the clothes, tailored and colorful. She restricted herself to plain trousers and men's button-down shirts. Her hair hung limply, framing an odd-looking face with exaggerated features: a wide forehead, high cheekbones, thick teeth peeking out behind soft lips, and big eyes. It was those eyes you needed to pay attention to. They made you pay attention. And it wasn't just the way they kind of bugged out; it was the intelligence behind them. It was looks like those, not ugly, but not conventional either, that made her impossible to categorize.

She had commanded my respect the moment I met her—sitting behind this desk like I was now, the room bare except for a lamp and a rotary phone, with those eyes assessing me. It was more intimidating than any audition I had done before. I should've run then and there.

I chastised myself for being gullible enough to answer a newspaper ad looking for actors. I thought the worst I might have to do was a silly song-and-dance for some local business. Instead I got Melanie Katsaros, a female private detective looking for a respectable face. The idea was ridiculous but I was desperate for money, desperate enough to stay as she explained her situation. She had started her agency three years ago, but found no one would take her seriously without a male partner. After the last guy, Adam Hawk, had fallen through, she wasn't looking for an equal. She wanted a mouthpiece. I still wasn't completely sure this whole thing wasn't an elaborate joke.

The woman, who was the first to grace our doorstep since I had begun this whole dog and pony show, was Melanie's foil. Stylishly coifed and garbed, she had the smell, taste, and inviting golden color to go with her honey. It was enough to grab any man's attention as their eyes slid past the austere Melanie. For me, it just left a pit in my stomach.

The door between my office and the reception was wide open. The woman made a beeline to me, bypassing Melanie without even a glance. She slid into the chair. Peering into my eyes, she told me, "My colleague has been missing for the past three days."

I was embarrassed to admit that my mind went blank—I had forgotten what I was supposed to say, to do. What actually came out of my mouth was idiotic.

"Then why haven't you gone to the police?"

She raised a thin, perfectly penciled eyebrow, clearly sharing my internal opinion. "Because I thought that, being a private investigator, you would be able to do the job. Was I mistaken?"

Melanie had entered the office by this point, tense and holding a pen and notepad. She gave me a warning glance.

"The police are free, doll. I'm not," I managed to salvage.

"Money isn't an object. I can pay more than your retainer if you find him before the end of the week."

"That's quite the hassle for you to go through, for your boss."

"I said colleague, not boss," she sharply corrected. "We run an accounting firm together. Not every woman is content to be a secretary." She cut her eyes dismissively at Melanie.

"My apologies," I was flustered at her rebuff, and at the way Melanie was grinding her teeth together.

"Welcome to 1946, Mr. Kendrick, the world is changing," she said with a sarcastic sigh. The woman waited a beat, and then when sensing there would be no further interruption, continued with purpose but the animation of someone reciting a grocery list, "My colleague's name is James Bennett. He's thirty-four years old, and we've worked together for the past two years. The last time I saw him was four days ago, when he left work at five o'clock. He didn't come in the next day, and he didn't call. He's the reliable type, so I'm worried."

"Did you swing by his house to check if he was there?" I interjected.

"Yes, and he wasn't. There were a few newspapers piled up at the door, so I was thinking he hadn't been home in a few days," she shifted in her seat. Her skirt bunched up, revealing a little of her thigh. My eyes glanced there involuntarily, and she seemed to notice. Her mouth tightened for a moment before smoothing out into a smirk. She adjusted her skirt on purpose this time, revealing more leg.

"Look, Mr. Kendrick," she lowered her eyes and voice to a more vulnerable presentation. "Mr. Bennett might not be my boss, but I do need his help to run my business. If I had the time, I would look for him myself. But I need your help."

"And you got it," I said. "We'll take the case. Right, Melanie?"

"Sure," my impotent boss ground out.

The woman reached into her purse and pulled out a business card. "This is my number," she told him. "Do you have a pen?"

Melanie handed her one. The woman flipped over the card and began to write on the back. When no ink came out, she raised the fountain pen to her lips and licked the tip of it. Melanie and I both shivered at her smile. She put the pen back to the paper.

"This is Mr. Bennett's address," she handed me the business card and stood up. "Call me when you find him."

As she reached the door, she paused and turned back. "My name is Tamsin, since you didn't ask. Tamsin Saxa."

"You fat-head," Melanie told me, minutes later. I couldn't disagree.

We took the time out of our not-so-busy workday to drive over to Mr. Bennett's house. He lived in a nondescript suburb. The houses looked like an extended family, slight differences but the same peach-colored faces. Melanie parked the car and we walked up to the man's front porch. The pathway was bordered with yellow rose bushes.

"There aren't any newspapers," Melanie mumbled, scuffing the toe of her shoe on the polished wood. The way she had been glaring at me in the car, I knew she was talking to herself rather than me.

"Cover me," Melanie ordered me, pulling a lock-picking kit out of her pocket. I casually blocked her from the eye line of nosy windows. Apparently displeased, the house across the street spit out its occupant: a young housewife. She waved cheerfully at me and made her way over. Melanie continued to scratch away at the doorknob.

"Hello there. I'm Josephine Bradley," she introduced herself.

"Arthur Kendrick and this is my secretary Melanie. Did we disturb you?" I intercepted her before she could see what Melanie was doing.

"Not at all! I was just wondering what you were doing here over at James and Barbara's house!"

"We work with James," I lied—or as I preferred to call it, acted. "We need to drop off some important papers. He told us he'd be out of town, and to just drop by."

The door clicked open as Melanie succeeded. She surreptitiously slipped the kit back into her pocket.

"He gave us a key," I continued. I dialed up my most charming smile to nuclear.

"Oh, what a shame!" Josephine exclaimed. "James got back from his trip earlier today. You just missed him."

Melanie and I faltered.

"Oh? I wasn't aware..."

"I don't blame you! Unexpected departure, unexpected return, you know. He really rushed out a few days ago."

"I'll just be a few minutes," Melanie whispered, slipping inside the house. Josephine didn't seem to notice her close the door. I was struck by the contrast Melanie presented. One moment she seemed as conspicuous as an Axis alliance tank rolling into your living room, the next moment she was a ghost, slipping through walls unseen.

"Yeah, he didn't really give any details about where he was going. Do you know?" I asked her, pegging the woman for a gossip. I was right.

"It's quite a personal matter. He probably didn't want it getting around. Barbara, his wife, left him two weeks ago. Just packed up and moved back in with her parents. They live in Nevada, now," Josephine giggled.

"Wow! Do you know why she left?" I prodded her.

"Probably because he was carrying on with some woman he worked with."

"Tamsin Saxa?" I asked on a hunch.

"Exactly! She's stacked, but she's bad news. You met her?"

"Once. It left an impression."

"That woman thinks she's better than everyone because she knows how to add some numbers together. She was always coming over here, staying late into the night. Barbara was so upset that he wouldn't leave his work at the office. And Saxa would use any excuse to get fresh with him, even in another woman's living room!"

"So he went to Nevada?"

"To get Barbara back, I think. A week is enough to make any man realize how much his wife does for him. To make him see what he'll be missing. James came to his senses," Josephine huffed.

"But he came back early. I guess things didn't go over well," I said.

"I wouldn't know. He was in and out before I could ask him. I called Barbara, but she couldn't come to the phone."

"Where?"

"In Nevada, silly. At her parent's house!"

"No. I mean, where did James go?" Worrying about how abrupt that sounded, I angled my body closer to hers. She bloomed under the attention.

"Oh, on his morning run. He goes every day before work to the Santa Monica Pier and runs a mile. I don't see the appeal, but men tend to bring home quirks after serving in the military. He left about thirty minutes before you got here."

I felt a spark of triumph run up my spine. I might not have been the great detective Melanie was, but I had figured out where Mr. Bennett was with my own talents. But Melanie was still inside the house, and I couldn't have Josephine getting suspicious.

"I never saw the appeal of a woman like Ms. Saxa. A man needs a stable home, not a sharp tongue. I'm sure she couldn't be half the wife you are, Mrs. Bradley. Your husband's a lucky man," I began to flirt more overtly.

Josephine flushed. "You're much too handsome for your own good, Mr. Kendrick. You're making me talk too much."

"I could say the same thing about you, Mrs. Bradley. You make me want to listen to you all day," I winked.

Melanie slammed the door shut. "I got what I need. Let's go."

I waved goodbye to Josephine, who looked confused as to why I was taking orders from such a short, severe-looking woman. I kept in character until we were safely seated inside the car, but Melanie had a harder time containing her amusement. "So you can talk to women."

I chose not to respond and instead relayed to her what I had learned. "Tamsin's having an affair with Mr. Bennett."

"Oh really?" Melanie raised an eyebrow, which was far thicker than trend called for.

"Yes. His wife left him—"

"Two weeks ago, I know. To live with her parents in Nevada."

"You heard Josephine from inside the house?" I was a bit disappointed.

"I didn't need to," Melanie rolled her eyes condescendingly. "I use these things called detecting skills. I looked around Mr. Bennett's house, found he had pictures of him and his wife, but most of her closet was cleared out. I also found out some interesting things about his accounting work that Mrs. Josephine Bradley couldn't have possibly known about. I don't need to talk to some unreliable busybody to find these things out."

"That is what you hired me to do. Talk to people." I was a little offended. Melanie seemed to notice, so her next words were softer but still teasing.

"Yes, but I was having my doubts after this morning."

"That was an extraordinary circumstance," I huffed indignantly. "Ms. Saxa is not a normal woman. That's like comparing apples to diamonds."

"Excuses, excuses," she laughed.

"I happen to be very good at charming people. Better than you, I'd bet," I challenged.

"Excuse you," she scoffed, "I happen to be ace at charming women. She's just not one of my people."

"One of your people?" I was confused, but there was a thought itching at the back of my brain. I didn't voice it in fear of being wrong.

"I'm queer, Arthur," she stated bluntly. It was no shameful, vulnerable confession. She spoke like she was firmly correcting a rude child. There was a slight twist of humor on her lips, like she knew how uncomfortable she made people, and she took pleasure in it. "Are you surprised?"

"That's just not something you usually admit in polite company."

"Once you get past that grandstand exterior you use," she paused and bared her teeth in preparation for attack, "I don't think you're very polite."

"Probably not," I laughed it off. I didn't want her to see how hard that had hit. I had spent too many years perfecting my outward nature. I changed the subject quickly, "Where are you driving?"

"Saxa and Bennett's office. I figured that's where he would be going."

"No, he'll be at Santa Monica beach," I smirked. Melanie's hands twitched on the wheel.

"According to Josephine, he goes running every morning."

"Why didn't you mention that earlier?" She said crossly, but my response was prompt and smug.

"You interrupted me."

Melanie assessed me for a moment before nodding in satisfaction and turning the car around. The drive to Santa Monica was long but quiet and almost peaceful. We drove through the winding streets, past the electric trolley shuttling people to and from Venice Beach. I felt a childish glee when we passed under the iconic blue-and-white "Santa Monica Yacht Harbor" sign.

As we reached the Pier and the beach, we noticed there

were a few police cars. Crowds of people gathered around, dressed in their bathing suits and carrying colorful paddle boards. I muttered, "I got a bad feeling about this."

"I'm not really surprised," Melanie sighed. "Let's see who the detectives are."

A couple of uniforms sneered at Melanie, clearly recognizing her, but let her pass through anyway. They gave me a few curious and confused glances. Melanie relaxed a bit as she saw one of the detectives, an older and slightly hairy man in a suit. He smiled back at her as the man beside him scowled.

"Arthur, this is Detective Katsaros and Detective Jeffries. One of them is useless, but the other is my uncle. He'll let us see the body, won't he?" Melanie smiled disarmingly at them. It was surprisingly effective.

"Melanie, I've never doubted your ability to sniff out a murder like a bloodhound, but this is ridiculous. His body isn't even cold yet," her uncle, Detective Katsaros, spoke with fondness brushed against every word.

"James Bennett. I was looking for him, but it seems like someone found him first. I want to examine his body."

"Absolutely not," Detective Jeffries protested. Katsaros shifted uncomfortably. "Melanie, I can't just let you into a crime scene..."

As Melanie argued with her uncle about why she should be allowed past, Jeffries sidled up next to me. "So you're the guy who bought Pallas Investigations from Adam Hawk, right?"

I nodded cautiously. During my interview, Melanie had mentioned her former partner had been a real detective, someone who knew as many tricks to the trade as she did. She had been vague about why he had left, but the scowl on her mouth spoke more loudly than words.

"You have some big shoes to fill. Adam solved a few big murders and extortions that had some of my superiors scratching their heads."

"I have faith he'll do just fine. Melanie doesn't work with fools," Katsaros interjected, apparently defeated by his niece. "That's why we're going to let them pass."

Detective Jeffries glared, but he didn't protest again. The

men led us alongside the Pier; I glanced upwards at the La Monica Ballroom. The air was salty and smelled a little like sewage. Sand shifted under every footstep, hitching a new ride on the inside of my shoe.

Underneath the pier, where tides pushed and pulled shells and starfish, James Bennett's body was laying face down on the sand. The back of his head caved in, blood and brains still sluggishly oozing out. His clothes were wet from the waves. Most of the blood had been washed from the sand, but it was still tinged pink.

"We think it was blunt force trauma," Jeffries explained. "Someone came up from behind him and hit him in the head hard enough to cave it in. Then he threw the weapon into the water—probably a piece of wood."

Melanie kneeled down to examine the body, and I self-consciously followed her after a beat. The gore was making me woozy. It didn't seem to affect her much as she leaned in for a closer look. She even prodded at the wound with gloved fingers.

"Can we roll the body over?" she asked.

"Sure," Katsaros shrugged. I helped her carefully rearrange him. The blood was uncomfortably sticky as it congealed with the sand.

"Who found the body?" I asked. Melanie nodded absently, so I supposed she approved of my question.

"Some dog walker found him a few minutes after. He's been dead less than an hour. Probably less than thirty minutes."

Melanie unbuttoned the man's shirt and pushed it back. Blood had run down the front of his neck as well, covering his chest and shoulders. She rubbed it away, making a small noise of triumph when she found a pair of hand-shaped bruises on the area below his collarbone, on his shoulders.

"You know, Uncle, I'm surprised you didn't recognize him," Melanie said casually.

"Why would I?"

"Bennett Saxa and Associates Accounting Firm manages your money, don't they? I thought maybe you would have met the boss before."

Detective Katsaros scratched the back of his neck and laughed, "No, I was never important enough to meet with the big bosses. I only got underlings."

Melanie stood up and walked up to one of the pillars covered in barnacles and mussels. Standing on his tiptoes to reach the area where the back of Mr. Bennett's head would be, she rubbed her fingers against the hard shells. They came back bloody.

"He was facing his murderer. They were arguing. The man shoved him backwards, and Mr. Bennett hit his head on the pillar. The barnacles cut through his skull. He stumbled forward and fell on his stomach."

"It wasn't planned," It suddenly came to me, inspired by Melanie's description. "This place is too populated to hide the body. It was spur of the moment, a mistake."

Katsaros and Jeffries hunched together, considering the idea. I ambled over to Melanie and whispered, "It's a wonder you need me to be your new face; yours is transparent."

"If I'm that obvious, Jeffries really is useless," she said loudly enough for the man to hear. Katsaros was quick to keep his partner from responding.

"Who would have motive?" Katsaros asked. "Tell me everything you've learned in your investigation."

Melanie clammed up, her eyes tense as she thought. I took over describing the information we had learned earlier today.

"So he had an established schedule. I bet this Tamsin Saxa would know that. She hires someone to find her lover, but when he returns home, she finds him first. He tells her he's reconciling with his wife. She flips her wig, and he ends up dead," Katsaros grinned triumphantly. "Not bad, kid."

"You sure about that theory? Completely?" Melanie asked with a dangerous look in her eyes. I gulped. Despite the sun burning down on us, the breeze cut through my jacket chilled my bones.

"Stop worrying, Melanie," Katsaros laughed. "I'm sure you'll still get your money out of her. Don't try and complicate things."

That was a dismissal if I ever heard one, and I'd heard a lot. Melanie was surly as we went back to the car. Nervous energy bubbled under my skin, causing me to ramble. "I have to say, I'm surprised. Ms. Saxa didn't look the crime of passion type; she didn't seem to really care that much about Mr. Bennett. Though I guess I wouldn't have a lot of experience. But she just seemed so put together and...deliberate. This whole thing is sloppy and easily tied to her."

I stopped as it hit me. "She's like you."

"What's that supposed to mean?" Melanie grouched.

"She plays to people's misconceptions about her. It offends her, but she likes being underestimated at the same time. She let people think she was having an affair with Bennett because they were going to believe it anyway. But she doesn't actually have a motive for killing him. Tamsin didn't do it."

"Forget it, Arthur."

"We need to tell the police."

"I said forget it!"

I stared at Melanie, disbelieving. She elaborated, "If she didn't do it, she'll have an alibi. Let the police handle it. I don't care about the money. I don't want to deal with this case anymore."

"What is wrong with you? I don't understand how your brain works!"

"Better than yours," Melanie growled. "We're going back to the office."

The rest of the day was spent in awkward silence as I struggled to understand what was going on. Once I thought I had wrapped my head around it, Melanie changed the entire game. It was mistake to take this job, and I was beginning to think it was a mistake to come to Los Angeles at all. I'd been a successful theater actor in New York, but I just couldn't resist the allure of being in pictures. I was in way over my head, in a world I didn't belong in. The most shameful part was that I wanted to be a part of it desperately. What was wrong with me?

Just as it was getting late in the day and I was itching to go home, the phone rang. Melanie and I answered our separate lines. The clear voice of Tamsin Saxa sounded through the receiver.

"Mr. Kendrick, it looks like I have to hire you for yet another service."

"Mr. Bennett is dead, Ms. Saxa," I told her bluntly.

"I know. I've been arrested for his murder. I'd like you to come to the police station."

That was quick. "Shouldn't you be calling a lawyer?"

"I already have. My lawyer can easily prove I'm innocent, but I'd like for you to actually find out who did it."

"Why should we help you again?" Melanie asked coolly.

Tamsin was smug as she played her trump card: "It was blackmail, wasn't it?"

Melanie hung up the phone abruptly and rushed into my office, doing the same with mine. "We need to go."

"Where?"

"Bennett Saxa and Associates Accounting Firm. Come on, before it gets too dark out," she ushered me outside the door. The drive was a quick seven minutes before we pulled in front of an unfamiliar office building. Right outside the entrance was the enigmatic Tamsin Saxa. I noticed her jacket and skirt were the same shade of pink as the bloody sand.

"You're late," she greeted me.

"Did you call from here? Weren't you in jail?"

"Oh, that. My lawyer already got the charges dropped and is filing a lawsuit against the department. And, well, I didn't actually expect you to pick me up at the police station. Not when you're covering for someone and making me the patsy."

"I have no idea what you're talking about," I scoffed.

"I might be smart, but even I make mistakes. After I left, I realized that when you went to James' house you would probably find all the files he idiotically keeps—kept lying around. And if you looked closely enough, you would notice the same discrepancies I did."

"You're saying you didn't notice your colleague was managing money for the mob?" Melanie raised an eyebrow.

Tamsin burst out laughing. "Of course I knew about that. I'm the one who oversees that aspect of our little business. No, I'm talking about how he's been blackmailing certain parties of interest. You know: the business men, politicians, and policemen that line their pockets with bribes. Not with my approval, I will tell you. Can you imagine how bad for business that would be if the news got out? I'd end up like James, except no one would find my body."

My jaw slackened in momentary surprise. I wasn't covering for anyone, but Melanie was. She had figured all this out at Bennett's house. I pushed past Tamsin and Melanie and rushed inside the accounting office.

The rooms were dark except for the file room. A light flickered overhead, almost in tandem with the waste bin fire in the middle of the room. Detective Katsaros fed papers to the hungry flame. I could feel the two women enter behind me.

Katsaros looked up and only had eyes for one of us, "Melanie."

Melanie, looking uncharacteristically childish, turned her back to him. She covered her face with her hands. Her voice came out muffled, "there must be some mistake."

"Melanie," he began again, "it was never supposed to turn out like this."

"Like what?" I snorted angrily. "Taking bribes from criminals or killing an innocent man?"

"Bennett was not innocent! He was shaking me down for practically every cent I got from those guys. I didn't mean to kill him, but he wasn't a good guy!"

"I could say the same about you," Tamsin looked unfairly unruffled. "Regular transactions at the beginning of the month, every month. Four hundred dollars is a little much just to keep your mouth shut and look the other way. You must have been doing my client's dirty work."

"Melanie, Melanie," his voice became a desperate litany. "It's more complicated than that. It used to be the only way you could survive as a cop was if you were dirty. Now they're going to destroy me for playing the game. You need to understand. That's why you do it, right, hide behind some guy? We all play the game."

"I could've joined the police," Melanie turned around to face him. "It was corrupt creeps like you that convinced me I could do better on my own. So, no, I don't understand."

Melanie lunged toward him, on a seemingly unstoppable trajectory, only to halt at the sight of her uncle's gun drawn on her. She looked both sad and challenging, "Are you going to shoot me?"

There was hesitation in Katsaros' eyes. I took the opportunity and grabbed his arm, shoving it away from Melanie. The gun went off when he clenched his hand in surprise. The bullet missed hitting Tamsin by a few inches, imbedding itself in the wall. She let out a yelp and ran from the room.

The gun clattered to the other side of the room. Katsaros head-butted me in the face, sending me reeling back as stars burst in front of me. Uncle and niece raced for the gun at the same time. The scrambled in the dark of the room. Melanie gained the advantage when she elbowed him in the solar plexus. She turned the gun on the gasping detective.

"Arthur, call the police," she ordered me, not taking her unforgiving eyes off of Katsaros.

The tell-tale sign of a gun being cocked made me think she was going to shoot Katsaros. But then Melanie whipped around, a shocked look on her face, and I realized the noise had come from behind me. I glanced back to see Tamsin holding a revolver to my head.

"I'd rather keep the police out of this," she frowned. The fire was still the only light in the room. Shadows danced across her face. Suddenly she was more frightening than beautiful.

"Why? He killed your colleague!" I exclaimed.

"James was an idiot. Someone would have gotten to him eventually. I just wanted to know if it was someone who was working alone, or if my client had found out about his shakedown. He hasn't, so I'm going to keep this from his attention."

"Are you really that loyal to a bunch of criminals?" Melanie asked.

"Not at all. But once the police follow the money trail from my firm, they'll realize there are dozens of other identical trails. I have to protect my own interests," Tamsin lowered the gun. "I'm going to let you all go now. Return home and never speak of this again."

"That's it?" Katsaros seemed a little disbelieving.

"No. Now I own all of you," Tamsin smirked.

"Excuse me?" Melanie was outraged, I was just shocked.

"I'll come asking for a favor one day. Neither of you will refuse, if you want to keep the dear detective out of prison. I'll enjoy being your puppeteer. Now, Mr. Katsaros, if we may discuss a few things..."

As she ushered Katsaros to a more private corner, Melanie and I huddled together.

"I know I made a mistake," Melanie admitted quietly.

"You figured this whole thing out hours ago, didn't you? But you didn't want to believe it—that your uncle might be dirty. So you tried to ignore it and let me pin the blame on Saxa. I don't think I really knew what I was getting into when I accepted this job. I certainly didn't think I would be covering up crimes and being beholden to some megalomaniac accountant."

"I won't begrudge you if you run. Saxa doesn't have anything to hold over you. This is my problem."

"I don't know," I sighed.

"I don't think you'll leave, Arthur," Tamsin said, coming up behind him. "People get into this business for two reasons: the money and the thrills. You've gotten a taste, and it's addictive, isn't it?"

Part of me wanted to prove her wrong, but my silence told more than any answer would. Melanie let out a sigh of relief.

"Even so, I think you've had enough thrills for the night," Tamsin pulled out a wad of cash from her purse and turned to Melanie, "It's been a pleasure working with you..."

"Melanie Katsaros, since you didn't ask."

"Ah, yes," Tamsin had a delighted expression as she slid the money into Melanie's hand. Her fingers lingered for a moment. "I'll be calling. Now, if you'll excuse me, I have a few fires to put out."

She brushed past Melanie, deliberately sliding their shoulders against one another, and not breaking eye contact until the last possible moment.

"She's trouble," Melanie was flustered and flushed.

"Yeah," I chuckled. "But it looks like she's your trouble now."

The Sand Fairies
Sharon Fiffer

"How did you build that castle?" I asked the little girl who had trudged up from the water's edge to stand at the foot of my blanket.

"The sand fairies helped me," she said.

"Ah...do they help everyone or just you?" I asked.

"They help everyone they like," she said, brushing some of the sand from her bathing suit.

"I see. How do I get them to like me?"

"If I like you, they will like you," she said.

The girl scanned the beach, turning slowly away in a half circle. Turning back, she trained her gray eyes on me.

"Can I have one of your sandwiches?" she asked.

"If it's all right with your mother," I answered, removing my carefully wrapped sandwiches from the basket.

"It's all right. My mother says I am in charge of what I eat and don't eat," she said, plopping down on the blanket as if there wasn't a rigid bone in her body.

"Peanut butter or roast beef?" I asked, admiring her effortless perfect posture.

"Is it rare?" she asked.

If she were an average child I would have made a joke. *No, just ordinary peanut butter.*

"Yes, it's rare. With mustard," I answered.

"I'll have that, please."

She sat down on my blanket and ate the sandwich. I always brought a full picnic with me to the beach, even though I came alone. I packed a basket as if children and a husband would be joining me, ravenous after a morning of jumping in the waves.

"This sandwich is a little dry," she said.

I told her I had ginger ale and fizzy water.

"In bottles?" she asked.

I nodded.

"Straws?"

"Yes," I said.

I had sturdy plastic reusable straws. Red, white and blue striped, they came with the plastic picnic set that fit neatly inside the basket.

For the first time she smiled.

"The sand fairies like straws."

"Do they drink soda?" I asked.

Her smile vanished.

As I said, she wasn't an ordinary child.

The beach wasn't crowded. Most of the people were townies like me. We closed our stores and offices on Mondays and Tuesdays so we could take back our beach from the summer people who claimed it on the weekends. Only a few families played down by the water. Two teenagers tossed a plastic disc. Apart from the crowd, under the shade of the big rocks that formed a horseshoe around them, an amorous couple fondled each other as if they were invisible. Or as if the rest of us were. The lifeguard, perched on his chair, looked like he might be asleep under the brim of his hat.

"To whom do you belong?" I asked the girl.

"My mother says I belong to myself. As does she."

"As does she?" I repeated it because I loved the way she said the phrase, like a haughty English princess. She heard my echo as a question.

"Yes. She says if she has a friend, it's her business. She doesn't belong to Daddy. She belongs to herself," said the little girl, sipping the last of her ginger ale.

Steer away, steer away. Sounds like summer indiscretion and we witness these dramas every season. Dish is not my dish. I am not a gossip and I've found avoiding the juicy bits altogether is the best way not to become one.

"How old are you?" I asked.

"Eleven in September," she answered.

"And your name?" I asked.

"You can call me Lake," she said, her eyes never leaving

my face.

"Ah, but is it your name?" I asked

"It's my middle name and I like it better than my first. What shall I call you?"

"Ann is my middle name, so why don't you call me Ann? We'll be a middle name club," I offered.

"I don't like clubs."

"Then we'll just be friends," I said.

Lake held out her hand and allowed me to shake it. Even though she began the gesture, she had no interest in a firm grip. Instead, she let her hand lie limp inside mine for a moment, then pushed herself up off of my blanket.

"Thank you for the sandwich."

"You're welcome," I said.

"May I keep the straw?" she asked.

I nodded.

Lake ran back down to the water where her castle stood. The waves had filled in the moats and even from several yards away, I could see that the meticulously crafted towers and turrets remained. I studied the families who by this time were eating their own lunches. I wanted to see what adult welcomed her back or scolded her for going off alone.

The girl was ignored by everyone until she spoke to a boy, four or five inches taller than she, who nodded enthusiastically at something she said. He grabbed a smaller version of himself, a mopey younger brother I guessed, and both boys came with shovels and buckets in hand and began kicking at her castle. I started to rise, to defend her, but saw she was kicking with them. She had invited the demolition crew.

I pulled my hat lower down over my face so I could continue to study my new friend, Lake, but I dozed off. Even though I stay under my umbrella, the sun works its sleepy magic and I always end up napping after lunch.

When I woke, Lake was almost finished burying someone in the sand. She was as careful shoveling and digging and patting and watering as she had been with her castle. The man, I could see it was a man, had stretched out his arms and Lake patted piles of sand over each one. She worked quickly and the man was soon outlined in mounded sand. Legs, arms belly, all molded and shaped as he was underneath. I was watching the work, so didn't see the woman who approached them as an entire person. I only saw a long pair of female legs enter the frame of the semi-moving picture I was enjoying. Semi-moving, since the man remained inert. Only Lake danced around, packing the heavy wet sand around him.

The woman, now fully in frame, her long hair in waves around her shoulders, gestured toward the parking lot. She was barefoot in the sand, but I could picture her wearing high heels, tap, tap, tapping them on a wooden floor.

The buried man shook his head from side to side. He had some trouble disengaging his legs and arms. The woman laughed and refused to help. Lake stood to one side, studying him as he struggled. When he stood up, he wobbled unsteadily and the woman reached into the compact cooler she was carrying and handed him a bottle of beer that she twisted open for him. He downed it quickly, dropped the bottle on the sand and started toward the parking lot, the woman following.

It was the man and woman who had been cavorting on the blanket earlier.

Lake stood still, watching them for several seconds. Then the woman turned and called out.

Lake shrugged, picked up pail and shovel and blanket and followed them. She didn't turn to wave goodbye to me. I didn't expect her to.

Tuesday was nearly identical to Monday. A few minutes before noon, Lake appeared on my blanket and accepted a sandwich. Ham with pickle and mustard on rye bread.

"The sand fairies helped me build that tunnel," she said.

"I see," I said, unpacking two bunches of grapes, green and red.

"It's big. People can fit in the hole that I dug," she said.

"Yes. Chips?" I offered.

"Not good for you. My mother says they are highly caloric and with no nutritional value."

I could see Lake's mother. At this moment she was once again rolling around with her friend on a blanket in the semiprivate horseshoe annex of the beach

Lake watched me eat a chip, then nodded. "You don't care about such things because you're so much older than my mother."

True enough.

"I needn't offer you a cookie, then?" I asked holding out a raisin oatmeal bar.

Lake took the cookie and bit into it with her small pointed teeth.

"Mother says we all deserve something sweet now and then," she said.

I could see over the rocks to the horseshoe, and observed that mother and friend had untangled themselves from each other and he was drinking a beer. Judging from the two empty bottles next to mother's friend, he appeared to be a liquid lunch man.

Lake finished her cookie and once again asked if she could keep her straw.

"For the sand fairies?" I asked.

She nodded and ran back to her spot next to the water where she resumed digging. Her tunnel was large enough to hold at least two adults.

As usual, I dozed off and when I woke, I saw the beer drinker hurrying Lake away from her work. As they got closer to my blanket, the man spoke, slightly slurring, something about Aubrey's audition. He loomed over Lake and snapped the strap on the right shoulder of her bathing suit. The gesture was both crude and cruel. Lake stared straight ahead.

On Wednesday, I brought layered salads in jars, vegetable chips and chocolate drop cookies. Lake poked a fork into the jar and mixed the ingredients slowly, holding the jar up to her eyes and smiling.

"I like this," she said.

"I thought you might," I said.

After a bite of her salad, Lake asked me," Do you have trouble sleeping?"

"Sometimes," I answered. "Why do you ask?"

"I've heard old people can't sleep."

Lake twirled her fork into her salad, stirring lentils and

lettuce and cucumbers. Placing the jar on the blanket, she reached into the small canvas backpack she carried.

"Here's one of my mommy's pills. She uses them to sleep."

She placed a large serious-looking capsule in my hand. I shook my head.

"I don't need it and you should never take your mommy's pills," I said.

"I don't *take* them. I would never *take* them. I got it for you," she said, jumping up. "It's a present. You can throw it away if you don't want it."

I slipped the pill into a small coin purse in my bag thinking that I might be able to identify it later. It seemed important to hold on to it.

"Thank you. But no more pills, Lake. Nothing like that. I sleep fine."

"May I keep my jar?" she asked, holding it up and turning it in her hand.

She waited until I nodded and then tucked the half-full jar into her bag.

On Saturday, I shopped for groceries, choosing food I thought Lake might like. Gouda cheese, marinated artichokes, pitted ripe olives she could stick on her fingers like rings. I bought an extravagant pound of dark cherries. Would she hold the stem, chew off the cherry and ask if she could keep the stone?

On my way home from the market, I saw Lake in the village. She was with a man who was not her mother's beach friend. I assumed this was her father, down from the city for the weekend. They were sitting at the counter in Piggy's Snack Shop, Lake licking an ice cream cone while the man sipped a cup of coffee and nodded, although neither of them seemed to be speaking. I didn't remain watching at the window long. If Lake swiveled on her stool and saw me staring, she might think it odd. I taught school long enough to know that when children see you outside of the place where they think you belong, they are startled and suspicious.

On Sunday, our small village newspaper announced a cost cutting measure. Lifeguards would no longer be on duty on Mondays, Tuesdays, or Wednesdays. SWIM AT YOUR

OWN RISK shouted the headline. Since the beach would remain open and I don't swim, this shouldn't have bothered me, but I felt a chill. What if Lake and her mother no longer came to the beach?

I needn't have worried. On Monday, as soon as I planted my umbrella and spread my blanket, I saw Lake close to the water digging. I only saw her when she moved from side to side, since the mountain of sand she had removed from her tunnel obstructed my direct view.

She appeared at my blanket earlier than usual. Why did I never see her until she stood at the edge of my blanket? I felt as if I never averted my eyes from her and yet it always surprised me when she arrived.

"Could we have lunch a little later today?" she asked

I nodded, amused at how much she sounded like a co-worker, someone who had the cubicle next to mine.

Although I assumed she would head back to her giant tunnel, putting some finishing touch that the sand fairies demanded, I was surprised to see her climb over one of the rocks that led to the horseshoe.

Her mother and the *friend*, who was certainly not the man I had seen Lake with over the weekend, were sitting close together on the blanket, but thankfully not engaged in any behavior that might upset the child. I watched Lake open the large tote bag next to the cooler and spread out lunch for the two adults.

It was like watching a pantomime or silent film. I didn't even need to see the dialogue cards on the screen. Lake's mother was surprised and pleased. I watched Lake set out small layered salads in jars. She pointed to the man's salad and shook her head at her mother and waggled her index finger. I could read her lips clearly. *Fish.* Her mother must be allergic and Lake had been careful to make separate salads. The male friend opened a beer, unscrewed the jar, and sniffed its contents. While Lake set out grapes and cookies, her mother elbowed the man and nodded at the food. He shrugged and began to eat. Lake stood up quickly, blew them an extravagant kiss and scampered back across the rocks.

I watched her return to her tunnel and lay down her shovel

and pail and place her canvas bag on her towel. She then ran up to me and sank down next to my picnic basket.

"Mother has a callback this afternoon," Lake announced. "It's for a national spot."

"So you made her a special lunch?" I said, smiling at her authoritative use of *national spot.*

"Yes. Lunch for her and Freddy," said Lake.

Although I always gave Lake my undivided attention, I glanced over at the couple in the horseshoe. Freddy was on his third beer. I could see him pointing to the almost empty jar and thought he was saying something about being thirsty. *Tunafish,* I thought. *Always too salty.*

"Your mother's an actress?" I asked.

Lake nodded. She was eating the cherries, slowly and carefully, just as I imagined she would. She spit the pits carefully into her hand and made a pile of them in the sand.

"She's catching the train to the city right after lunch and then turning right around. If she's not back by four, Freddy's going to take me home."

I was careful not to ask anything. What I didn't know wouldn't hurt me.

"You like the cherries?" I asked.

"Especially the stones," said Lake.

She didn't ask if she could have them, but I noticed after we'd eaten our macaroons and she'd hopped up to go back to her tunnel that the little pile of cherry pits was gone.

I was still packing away the lunch supplies when I saw Lake's mother leave the beach. She was a beautiful woman, all legs and long hair. I wondered what the national spot was for. What did it matter? Beautiful young women could sell anything, couldn't they?

Freddy stood up on wobbly legs and walked out toward the water. Walking through the waves was the only way to get out of the horseshoe without climbing a few rocks and Freddy looked in no condition to climb. He didn't seem to notice he was dragging his towel through the water as he made his way toward Lake and her tunnel. When he reached her, he sat down on the edge of the hole and swung his legs over the side where they disappeared.

I wanted to keep an eye on Freddy and the child and so I struggled to stay awake, but the sun and waves never failed to knock me out. What Lake had guessed about old ladies and sleep was true. I didn't rest well at night and this summer, the beach had become the only place where I could sleep for an hour or more at a time.

When I did open my eyes again and adjusted to the light, I could tell right away by the long shadows across the sand that I had dozed longer than usual. There were a few more people on the beach now. A family was playing paddleball near the shore and a gaggle of teenaged girls huddled together on their towels, their heads bent, plotting.

Lake was next to what had been her tunnel but was now a man-sized mound of earth. I assumed that she had once again buried Freddy. That hole had been deep. I had seen her stand in it. Hadn't I seen Freddy sit on the side, dangling his legs in the space?

My thoughts came together more clearly. Freddy's unsteady walk, his disorientation as he sat down next to Lake. What had she put in the salad to make it salty? To make sure that only Freddy ate it and not her mother?

Lake stood up and began jumping the waves as they came closer and closer to shore, closer and closer to where buried Freddy lay under the sand. No lifeguard. SWIM AT YOUR OWN RISK. I checked my watch. It was 3:30.

I folded my chair and packed up my things. I piled them on the edge of my blanket. I was going to go. Leave. Mind my own business. But when I stood up, I found myself making my own unsteady way down to the water. When I got to Lake's blanket, I saw her canvas bag, her pail and shovel. I saw the giant mound of sand, a crumbling sarcophagus. Two straws, my straws, stuck out of the sand in the place where the head would be. A pile of cherry pits mixed in with the smooth round beach stones sat on top of where Freddy's midsection would be. A cairn marking what?

"Lake," I called out scanning the water. She was no longer skipping waves. She was nowhere in sight.

"Lake, what have you done?"

I dropped down to my knees, no easy task. I heard the

bones rub in my ankles, in my hips. I wasn't sure I'd be able to get up again, but it didn't matter. There was a man buried alive and I was the only one who knew he was there. I wasn't able to dig through the packed wet sand as quickly as I thought I could. I reached for Lake's tin shovel and scraped away sand at where I thought Freddy's face would be. Were the straws sticking out of his mouth allowing him to breathe? Would I be in time to save him?

I dug frantically, calling out Lake's name. I could hear people rushing up behind me. "Help me, there's a man buried here," I said. I heard my own voice, creaky and raspy.

"Lake," I yelled.

When I turned around they were all standing there, a respectful distance from the crazy old lady shouting at the lake.

The family who had been playing paddleball stared openly at me, their hands holding paddles, dangling by their sides. The coven of teenaged girls, a few of them with fingers flying on their phones mid-text or tweet or whatever they were doing as I caught them staring at me. Their faces were identical to the haughty ones I stared down year after year, the girls who ignored me as I tried to pour social studies facts into their vacant skulls.

Directly behind me stood Lake's mother. Her makeup perfectly applied, she was wearing an expensive looking sundress and carrying her high-heeled sandals in one hand and holding Lake's hand with the other.

"Lake," I said, "we have to dig up Freddy. The straws." I said, holding them out to her, "They're filled with sand."

"Why is she looking at you that way?" her mother asked. "Why is she calling you Lake? And who in the world is Freddy?"

Lake shrugged. "I don't know," said Lake. "Mommy, Bill went home because he didn't feel so good," said Lake. "I want to go home now."

I couldn't speak. As confused as I was, I knew that Freddy or Bill or whoever the man was under the sand was buried deeply enough that it would take more than my weak scratching to uncover him. I held the straws in my hand and once again reached them out to Lake.

"Lake, the sand fairies," I said. "They'd want you to uncover him."

Lake began to whimper and hide behind her mother. The teenagers snickered at the mention of sand fairies and the paddleball mother began whispering rapidly to her husband in a language I didn't immediately recognize.

Lake's mother began backing away from me, Lake in tow. "We'll get you some help," she said to me, then turned toward the parking lot, pulling Lake behind her. "The woman's confused, Christine, let's go."

"Lake," I called, my voice now weak.

"Why does she keep calling you that?" asked her mother. The girl shook her head, making a face both sad and frightened.

"I don't know," said the girl.

"We're done with Bill, leaving you alone like that." The breeze carried her mother's words down to me as I stayed on my knees, unable to move the packed sand with my gnarled hands.

"Daddy drove me back here. I got the commercial and we're going back to the city tonight."

My knees were locked. I knew I needed help to get up. The father from the paddleball family offered me his arm and I took it and slowly struggled into a standing position.

"Can I call someone for you?" he offered. "Should we call the police, or an ambulance from the next village?" He spoke with a slight accent and I knew they must be the German family staying in the Meyer beach house for the month. I slowly turned around in time to see the little girl I knew as Lake skipping alongside her mother as they reached the parking lot.

I shook my head. "I was confused," I said. "It must have been a bad dream."

The teenagers, bored by my confession, began to drift off to their spot down the beach and the family looked relieved that I had quieted. "I'm just an old woman," I said to them. "I get confused."

I could no longer see Lake or her mother. They were

probably already on the road, driving to their summer rental to pack. The girl I now knew was Christine and her mother would be swallowed up into the city by tomorrow morning, by the time the water uncovered the body, if there was a body, wave by wave by wave.

The Haunted Room
Gigi Pandian

"There's no such thing as ghosts," I said.

I believed what I said. At the time. But what Nadia was about to tell me made me question what I thought I knew.

"Jaya," my landlady said to me with a shake of her head. "Though your experience in Scotland had rational explanation, that does not mean it is always so."

I eyed Nadia skeptically. "I didn't know you were superstitious."

We were sitting together on a park bench across the street from the "haunted" house Nadia had brought me to see, a San Francisco mansion from the post-Gold Rush boom in the late 1800s. Because I'd recently solved a mystery that involved folklore and a legendary Scottish fairy, Nadia wanted to tell me about her own unsolved mystery.

Nadia shrugged. *"There are more things in heaven and earth, Horatio, than are dreamt of in your philosophy."*

Nadia had come to California from Russia as a young woman and had lived in San Francisco for decades. She spoke perfect English, but with a strong accent. And she loved being dramatic. Which included quoting Shakespeare.

"Your ghost story has to have a rational explanation," I insisted. A swath of fog descended around us as I spoke, making my statement less convincing. I shook off the feeling. It was summer in San Francisco. Chilly weather was to be expected, especially on the hilltop that gave the Pacific Heights neighborhood its name.

After leaving India as a child, I grew up in the Bay Area, but on the other side of the bay. My father raised my brother and me in Berkeley, which, while only ten miles from San Francisco, has a completely different climate. After spending

my childhood in scorching Goa and sunny Berkeley, I still
wasn't used to San Francisco weather.

"I will tell you the whole story," Nadia said, wrapping her
black stole more closely around her elegant shoulders. "You
can be the judge of whether or not you believe it."

I nodded, not taking my eyes from the building. A gust of
wind blew my bob of thick black hair around my face.

"It was in October," Nadia continued, "nearly two years
ago, before you moved here for your teaching job. I have
always thought of Halloween as a holiday for children, but
Jack made it sound exciting. Plus, the profits from this
haunted house go to charity."

"I remember hearing about this place." It sounded like the
kind of thing Nadia's on-again off-again paramour would
like.

"It is still a popular attraction," Nadia said, "but I will
never again step inside. Not after what happened there." She
shivered as she looked at the dark windows of the house.

The effect was contagious. Nadia was not a woman who
scared easily. The haunted house was in a part of the city I
rarely passed by, and based on Nadia's reaction to it, I found
myself wondering if this imposing Victorian structure had
unconsciously caused me to avoid the neighborhood, in spite
of its gorgeous views of bridges and beaches. This house was
one of the oldest in the area, having survived the Great
Earthquake of 1906.

"I wore a gown from that thrift store down the street," she
continued. "Cream-colored satin, reminiscent of Countess
Volkonskaya. A brocade, matching satin gloves, and a
crimson silk hat."

That was more like Nadia. She noticed my amused
reaction and shrugged.

"Even though the holiday is childish," she said, leaning
forward conspiratorially, "if one chooses to participate, one
should do so in the spirit of the occasion. Jack did not mind
my smoking that evening—I was playing the part of a
countess, you see, with an elegant cigarette holder—"

"Nadia," I cut in.

"Yes, yes. You young people are so impatient. You must

allow an old woman an excuse to ramble."

I had never learned Nadia's exact age. She looked like she was barely old enough to have retired, but I had a suspicion she wore her years well and may have been much older. And I wasn't so young. I'd recently turned thirty. I've been told I look younger, which I attribute to the fact that I'm only five feet tall. It's an image I've had to fight against. As an assistant professor of history, it's rather embarrassing to be mistaken for a college student.

"Jack said it would be a romantic evening to go to a haunted house," Nadia continued, "for there was a full moon that night. He said we could go on a moonlit walk afterward."

"So you went to the haunted house and it was *spooky?*"

Nadia ignored my sarcastic remark. "You will not be able to dispute what I experienced. After waiting in line, we were placed into groups to walk through the rooms of the house. The darkness was nearly complete. The brightest lights were the dim 'EXIT' signs above the doors. Only the light of electric candle chandeliers lit up the displays—dry ice around tombstones in a cemetery room, animated skeletons in caskets in a morgue room, mannequin figures masked with beaked bird masks in a plague room...It was the plague room where it occurred."

Nadia paused, and in spite of myself I waited in rapt anticipation for what she would say next.

"This room, it was not like the others. As soon as I entered, I knew this. A strong sensation of cold washed over us. You may be aware that cold spots in a house can indicate the presence of a ghost."

I was tempted to think Nadia was re-imagining the past, since she had a dramatic personality. A more rational explanation was that cold air was piped into the room for exactly the effect Nadia described.

"One of the plague figures in this cold room was not a mannequin, but a teenage boy working at the haunted house. He was very still at first—then reached out and grabbed a woman in front of me. I was not frightened, but it was a shock, you understand. That is why I dropped what I was holding in my hands: my gloves—which I had taken off in the heat of the stifling rooms—and a large ring that slipped off when I removed the gloves. It was not a ring that was especially valuable, but it was meaningful to me. Blue sapphire costume jewelry. As soon as my gloves and ring fell, I alerted Jack. He found a light switch hidden next to the exit door. The other six visitors in the room complained of ruining the atmosphere, but they did not stop him. My gloves were where they had fallen, *but the ring was gone.*"

"It must have rolled away," I said.

"Jaya, do you think us stupid? We searched everywhere. The others moved on, but Jack and I searched the entire room. The ring was gone. And before you say that one of the others must have stolen it, remember this was *not* a valuable ring. Nor did it look like one. Even if someone had thought it to be valuable, none of the people we were with crouched down to the ground. They did not have an opportunity to pick it up.

"It was then," she continued, "that I learned the history of this haunted room. There was a crime committed there almost three-quarters of a century ago. A crime that was never solved. Because it was committed by a ghost—a ghost who is still there."

As if on cue, a light rain began to fall.

"Come on," I said, "let's get out of here."

Nadia lingered a moment longer before following.

"Tell me the rest of the story," I said, ducking into the awning of a nearby café as the rain began falling harder.

We grabbed a table at the front of the café. With the rain pelting against the window, I ordered hot coffee and a piece of the thick, gooey apple pie I saw another patron eating. There was sure to be enough butter and sugar in that pie to solve any problem.

"The house," Nadia said, "was built by a man with money from the Gold Rush. Several workmen died during its construction, which explains the ghost."

"Naturally."

"You mock me, but you should not. In the early 1900s, he lavishly entertained many wealthy people who would visit.

On this famous visit, a portly scholar was visiting from his East Coast university. They shared a good meal with wine, and the owner saw his guest to his bedchamber. It was no ordinary night. The scholar locked himself into the room, and put a chair under the door handle. You see, he was traveling with something very valuable to the academic community. This is why he wished to stay with his friend rather than at a hotel. But his precautions were for naught.

"The good professor reported a strange, ghostly noise shortly after lying down to sleep. He would not have thought much of it, for his girth made most beds squeak with all manner of sounds under his weight, except that this noise came from *the other side* of the room."

I had to hand it to Nadia. She was a great storyteller. "You sound like you were there," I said.

"After I experienced it myself, I read a history book. May I continue?"

I nodded and took a sip of the coffee that had been set in front of me without my noticing.

"When the scholar rose from the bed," Nadia said, "he saw that the historical scroll he had discovered was *gone.*"

"That sounds like a strange thing for a *ghost* to steal," I commented.

"It was the reason he was visiting San Francisco. The ghost must have sensed its importance and wished to be malicious."

"Or someone in the house stole it because it was valuable."

"The room," Nadia said with a raised eyebrow, "and the *whole house* was searched. But that was unnecessary, since he had secured his room *from the inside.*"

"There must have been a false panel in the room."

"The room was carefully inspected by a police officer, and then a private detective. There were no false panels. Even if you do not believe that, you must believe what has happened in the decades since then. The man who owned the house was long dead when Alan Marcus bought the house and opened it up for a Halloween charity.

"Yet," she continued, "whenever people go into that room...*something disappears.* It began with children's toys.

The ghost stole marbles from a child. This was decades ago when marbles were popular. The ghost has continued to steal, most frequently from children. It can only be a matter of time before the ghost takes not only crayons, but a *child.*"

This time my shiver wasn't from the cold. I didn't feel nearly as warm and cozy as I should have sitting across from Nadia with a steaming coffee in my hands.

"I know that expression of yours," Nadia said. "I have convinced you."

"You've got me curious. I admit that much."

Two hours later, I sat surrounded by books and printouts from the newspaper archive at the library. As a professor of history, piecing through history is what I do, and I do it well. Absorbed in research, I was in my element—but I failed to come up with answers. Instead, I was more intrigued than ever. Much like Sarah Winchester's desire to build new rooms onto her sprawling San Jose mansion until she died, the wealthy man who built this house wanted to renovate his home until his death. Unfortunately, he didn't care much for the safety of his workers. At least two men had died in construction accidents while working on the house.

I didn't blame Nadia and countless others for assigning supernatural significance to the events that had taken place in the mansion. Though Nadia had exaggerated—it wasn't every time someone entered the haunted room that something went missing—the disappearances had happened enough times that *something* was going on.

Had the new owner Alan Marcus figured out the secret of the room and decided to use it to rob people? Initially that seemed like the easiest explanation, but none of the facts supported it. Not only was Mr. Marcus a wealthy man with no financial troubles, but the things that went missing were very rarely valuable.

Another strike against that theory: When I called Mr. Marcus, the retired gentleman wasn't the slightest bit evasive. He said he'd be happy to meet with us and show us the peculiar room.

On my way downstairs to tell Nadia of my plan to visit the inside of the house, I ran into my neighbor, Miles, a poet who was stopping by to invite me to a poetry open mic night that evening. When I told him what I was busy doing, he asked if he could come.

"I thought you had to practice reading your poem," I said.

"You're going *now*?" he asked. "Aren't you supposed to be working on a course syllabus or something?"

"Don't remind me."

I wished Miles good luck preparing for his poetry reading, then found Nadia, who wasn't any more helpful. True to her word, she refused to go back to the house. Was I the only one who cared about the baffling mystery of the haunted room?

"What if we could get your ring back," I said.

"Tempting," Nadia said. "Very tempting."

That's how I found myself heading back to the mansion with Nadia that afternoon. At least the rain had let up.

"I've been thinking," I said as we approached the house. "What if Mr. Marcus wanted to throw the police off the scent by stealing seemingly random items to disguise the theft of a few valuable ones?"

"You found a historic treasure, Jaya, and now you think you are an expert at all types of crime-solving?"

Nadia's sarcasm be dammed, I was feeling quite pleased with my deductive abilities until Mr. Marcus opened the door. I liked him at once. The octogenarian greeted us with a hearty handshake and a mischievous smile as he asked us if we were going to be the ones to solve his mystery. Most importantly, he also offered us coffee and cookies before we got to work. A man after my own heart.

He explained that he only used part of the house during most of the year. The haunted house section wasn't currently in use, its sparse furniture covered in sheets for ten months of the year. "After my wife passed away," he said, "I no longer entertained. There wasn't much point in keeping up the whole house."

I ate several cookies while listening to stories about his wife, who threw a wicked party in her day. Nadia sat stiffly, barely touching her coffee. I, on the other hand, was quite comfortable. Mr. Marcus kept the heat turned up, leaving me contentedly cozy on the plush couch. If it hadn't been for my curiosity, I would have been happy to spend the afternoon looking out the sweeping bay windows with views of the Golden Gate Bridge.

Once I declared I couldn't possibly eat another cookie, Mr. Marcus led us across the sprawling house to the room. We walked on beautiful Persian rugs in the hallways and passed original oil paintings that looked vaguely familiar, plus a series of impressionist paintings of San Francisco beaches. The perspective of the scenes suggested they might have been painted from the main room of the house, long before the city had grown up around it.

Inside the supposedly haunted room, Mr. Marcus tossed the sheets aside and stood back, letting me have a closer look. The thick floorboards creaked beneath my feet.

I had learned a thing or two about false panels from my best friend, Sanjay. He's a magician, so I would have called him except I knew he was out of town preparing for a show. Even though he didn't trust me with all his secrets, I had a good understanding of how many of his illusions worked. The same principles stage magicians used could be applied to situations like this. But that knowledge wasn't helping me here. I was fairly confident I wasn't missing any secret panels. But I had to be missing *something.*

"Intriguing, isn't it?" Mr. Marcus said. "The unsolved theft was one of the reasons that initially drew me to this place. My wife was a history buff. She loved the idea of living in a piece of history."

"So you two looked into the construction of the room."

"Oh yes," he said, "most certainly. But we never found any hidden entrances to the room."

"The walls—" I began.

"That," Mr. Marcus said, "is the strangest part. Even if we missed a false panel, there's no extra space between these walls. An electrician did some poking around years ago. There's nothing there—and no room for anything to be hidden."

* * *

After eating another cookie—it would have been rude to turn down his hospitality—Nadia and I departed, and I headed back to the library. This time I paid attention not to the sensationalism surrounding the original crime or the construction of the house, but to the pictures of the room itself.

The layout of the room struck me as strange. The nightstand had been placed across the room from the bed. That was odd...

I stepped outside and pulled out my cell phone.

"Mr. Marcus," I said, "I know you checked the walls, but did you ever check the floor for any false panels?"

"We certainly did. The floorboards were all connected to each other. There were no false panels there either."

"But did you check *the space* underneath the floor?"

There was silence on the other end of the line.

"You know," he said, "I don't believe we did. But without a teleportation device, I don't see how anything could have fallen through that solid floor."

"Do you mind if I come back?"

"It's rather late."

"I promise it won't take long."

This time I returned to the mansion with back-up. Not because I was afraid of a ghost, but because I needed to replicate the girth of the man who had once stayed there and been robbed of his valuable discovery.

Nadia pursed her lips when I insisted on grabbing Miles from the poetry open mic night that was wrapping up at a coffee house in our neighborhood, but she said nothing. She didn't like Miles, but she was at least as curious as I was.

Twenty minutes later, the three of us piled into the corner of the room where the bed once stood.

"Mr. Marcus, we need you, too, if this is going to work."

As he crossed the room and stepped within a foot of me, the floor began to shift.

It wasn't the movement of a single floorboard; the whole floor was subtly tilting. The floor was ever-so-slightly pivoting around a fulcrum in the center of the room. The tilt of the floor around the central hinge resulted in the edges of the wooden flooring being lower than the bottom of the wall. It was only a couple of inches—a small enough shift that in the dark it would have felt like stepping on a loose floorboard—but it was enough for anything small and circular to slip out of the room to the space beneath the floor.

I took a pen out of my bag and dropped it. It rolled away and disappeared into the darkness.

Everyone began to move at once.

"Stop!" I said. "If any of us moves from this spot, the floor will go back to normal. "It was only because we have enough weight here that it activated the mechanism that was put in place to rob the professor who stayed here."

"Ingenious!" Mr. Marcus said, clapping his hands together. "Ingenious, but nasty. He altered this room and set it up to rob his friend."

"Let me see if I can see what's going on under there." Without moving away from the others, I crouched down on the floor and pulled a flashlight and a magnifying glass from my messenger bag.

Sure enough, I could see an assortment of dusty items, mostly children's toys like matchbox cars—anything that *rolled.*

In the midst of the treasures, my flashlight shone across a blue stone ring. Nadia had said it was a piece of blue sapphire costume jewelry she'd lost.

"Miles," I said. "Can I borrow a pen?" He handed me a pen, and I used it to snag the large ring in the midst of the hidden treasures. Standing up, I handed Miles his pen and Nadia her ring.

"After all this time," Nadia said, shaking her head. "Thank you, Jaya."

"You can all move now if you want to," I said. "I've seen what I needed to. Nobody has been stealing things in this house—not a ghost, not even a person. At least not for around eighty years. It was this mechanism."

I stepped away from the group. The floor slowly straightened out from its central pivot point. Because the floorboards were thick and uneven in this section of the old house, the small amount of space between the floorboards in the center of the room hadn't raised any suspicions.

"A hinge," Nadia murmured.

"I'm *so* writing a poem about this," Miles said, scribbling a few lines in his beaten-up notebook he kept in the pocket of his cargo pants. "A theft from long ago," he murmured to himself, "high above the Pacific Ocean's beaches where the wind doth blow...Jaya Jones is the insightful professor, who's more than a good guesser..."

"Only when all the forces align," I said, ignoring the clunky rhymes of Miles' poem, "does something go missing. The floor was rigged to steal one particular thing—a valuable scroll from a very large man. The thief who owned this house was able to set things up with precision for that one-time event. He got his 'friend' inebriated, and saw him to bed with his valued possession safely in the corner of a room locked from the inside, with the bedside table and lamp across the room from the bed. When the large man went to bed, it would necessarily be dark. He would feel himself lower down into what he thought was an uneven mattress, but wouldn't see the shift in the floor."

"When I opened my haunted house," Mr. Marcus said, grinning excitedly, "people would huddle closely together because they were having fun being frightened. Acting as a group, they replicated the weight necessary to activate the lever. That's when the disappearances began."

"Exactly," I said. "In the darkness and commotion, people felt that something was happening, but couldn't identify exactly what it was. They were already discombobulated from walking through dark rooms that played with their senses. And as soon as they moved to turn on the lights, the floor was again completely flat. It was *the house itself* collecting treasures all these years."

"What a wonderful haunted house!" Nadia said. "I cannot wait until next Halloween."

The Hit-Man
Roger Angle

You don't know me. You never heard of me before. Let's keep it that way. The less you know about me, the better. Let's hope we never meet in real life. At least, not in my line of work.

It's been so long since I used my real name, I can't hardly remember it. Call me Sonny Owen Black. Sounds real, don't it?

That's me, Sonny Owen Black—S.O.B.

Get it? Son of a bitch. Har-har-har. Ain't that a kick in the ass?

This story is about Amanda. That's my grown daughter. She got herself into some trouble, and I had to pull her bacon outta the fire.

Amanda owned this cute little shop near the beach, in Venice, California. Hand-made soaps and perfumes. Called her store *SMELL THIS*. Funny, huh?

I thought the name was a little too much, if you catch my drift. She made her own soaps and oils and perfumes. Fragrances. People would stop in on their way to and from the beach and buy sunscreen and shampoo and girly stuff. One best seller was Red Hot Mama soap. Had peppers in it. Another was Stud Bud—soap for certain guys.

Amanda has a head on her shoulders, and business was booming. People in and out, little events on weekends, repeat business. Online sales, too.

One day, this tall skinny Latino dude drives up in a brand-new Lincoln SUV, gets out and walks in. The Lincoln is black and he is wearing all black. Amanda has a security camera that records video and audio, and she showed me. Guy looked Mexican, six-one, one-seventy-five, thirty, lean. Moves his head back and forth, steps a little to one side like a boxer when he walks. Goatee, moustache. Black suit, white shirt, bolo tie, big silver and turquoise bob on it. New Mexico or Texas. Flat-brim hat low over his eyes, you can't really see his face.

Guy walks in and the first thing he does is lock the door. Then he turns the sign around, so it says CLOSED, and pulls down the shade.

"Now we are all alone," he says, in a soft whisper. "Anybody in the back room?"

She's getting nervous. You can imagine. "No," she says.

He pulls a knife. Flicks it and the blade pops out. *Click.*

"Come here," he says.

"Not in this lifetime," she says.

"Well, maybe in the next." He dances toward her in that boxer step.

I'm proud of my Amanda for what she does next. She comes out with a baseball bat and takes a big swing at Mr. Bolo who ducks, and the bat hits some plastic shampoo bottles. They tumble to the terracotta tile and one splits open. Shampoo oozes out across the floor.

She takes another swing and the dude slips and falls. Right on his ass. I'm laughin' while I watch this whole thing. Amanda swings again, and Mr. Bolo rolls away. The bat cracks his knee. He screams bloody murder and starts to crawl toward the door. I guess he's had enough. I am cheering.

Amanda picks up the phone and dials 9-1-1. "There's a man with a knife trying to rob my store."

Mr. Bolo gets to the door and manages to stand up. He looks at her. His hat is off now and you can see his face. "I'll be back," he says, in a pretty good imitation of the Terminator.

"You do that, tough guy," she says. "I got your picture."

Oh-oh, I'm thinkin'.

"Oh really?" the guy says and splits.

The cops come and Amanda shows them the video and gives them a copy. They call her back later. They tried to I.D. him but they can't. Amanda didn't think to get the license number on his SUV and it isn't clear on the video.

Next day, a guy on a motorcycle shows up. All in black. Black helmet, black face shield, full leathers and gloves. No license plate on the bike, so there's no way to I.D. the guy. He hands her a big brown envelope. She has to sign for it. He bugs out. Inside is a stack of legal papers from some outfit called Day One Properties. The return address is in downtown L.A.

She reads through the stuff, and it basically signs over her business and the building, which she owns, to Day One Properties for about one-tenth market value.

She calls the cops and they say there is no way to connect the papers to Mr. Bolo. She shows them to her lawyer, who is also one of her customers, a lady named Kim Browne. She says it looks like a binding offer. Maybe not fair, but legal.

Kim Browne does some research and finds out that Day One has bought the entire block across the street and filed plans with the city to construct a giant mall, with a Parisian theme, called Hot Couture. It would specialize in upscale shopping. I hate that word—*upscale*. Why is nothing ever down-scale, or normal-scale, or just plain middle-class?

The next day, an old friend of hers, another shop owner, Derrick "Daddy" Crane, a barber, doesn't show up for work. Couple days later, he does show up. On the beach, in shallow water, face down, seaweed all over him. Cold as a fish. Naked. No swim suit in sight.

Cops say it's an accident. Trouble is, Daddy Crane never went swimmin' in his life. Not for fun anyway.

Amanda goes around to talk to the other shop owners, finds out three other shop owners have disappeared. One by one, over the next week, they also turn up in the shallow water. Dead, naked, food for the fishes. None of them were regular ocean swimmers. Two of them couldn't even swim, according to their relatives.

So now Amanda visits all the shop owners on both sides of the block. Most have sold out to Day One, for ten cents on the dollar.

"What're ya gonna do?" one says. "It's progress."

Amanda goes to the police station and talks to a detective. Nothing he can do, he says, without forensic evidence. "We do not have magical powers," he says.

So then Amanda asks my help. She calls me. Very unusual. She never calls. And I never heard any of this stuff before. She says she got a lowball offer on the place and she's gonna get some pressure to sell. She doesn't bother to mention the Mexican or the knife or the dead barber or her other neighbors who died and those who sold out for a slow gentle hump against the wall.

I don't realize how serious it is. "I'll come over next week."

She says, "No, Dad, I'm hurtin' right now."

But I'm livin' the good life on my *ranchito* outside Flagstaff, up in the Arizona hills. Got a little *chiquita* livin' there with me, you know. I call her *Salsa*, 'cause she's so hot. Some horses, couple dogs. A good life. Ever' body up there has guns, so it don't seem strange when I carry a six-gun or I front a stranger with a twelve-gauge pointed at his belt buckle.

Next day, Amanda calls again. Extremely unusual, two days in a row. The Mexican came back. Two other guys with him. They tied her up in the back room and he cut off her blouse and her bra, then he pricked her bazookas with the blade. Got excited by the sight of blood.

Steam comes outta my ears. You can imagine.

I load up some hardware in the trunk of my old Cadillac—two shotguns, two assault rifles, a handgun, a blowgun, which used to be my specialty, one of my own handmade knives, some grenades, and three or four teargas canisters. You know, the works.

That convertible Caddy's trunk is big enough to carry a football team all suited up, and it has the biggest V8 they ever made. I leave my little *Salsa* and my *ranchito* behind, and I hit the road.

On the drive to L.A., I make plans. I'm gonna track down

Mr. Bolo and tie him up and tickle his talking points with my knife. Draw a little blood. See how he likes it.

These guys think they're tough. They don't know tough.

I'll show them my old moves. The leg takedown. The mastoid punch. The neck cracker. The spinal jerk. The kneecapper. They'll wish they'd never seen daylight.

I show up at Amanda's shop and she says, "Dad! What happened to you? You can hardly walk!"

"Well, baby girl, I am a little crippled up. Rattlesnake bit me on the foot the other night. I went outside to use the outhouse and stepped on a big diamondback in the dark. I was barefoot. Thought it was a pile of cow dung at first, then it squirmed. Heard the buzzin' but I was half asleep, so I paid it no mind. I grabbed it by the tail, but it was hard to get off me."

"Jesus, Dad, you should take better care of yourself."

"What? Say it again."

"Do I have to yell in your ear?"

"Pretty much."

"Oh, Dad, you shouldn't have come. Here, let me help you."

So she is helping me over to a chair and I trip over a display of soaps, knocking some to the floor.

"You can't see too well, either, can you?"

"Well, the light's a little dim in here, that's all."

"How did you drive all the way over here?"

"Followed a big truck. I could see him just fine."

"Jesus Christ."

"Jesus won't help you, child."

"No, you're right about that." Then she says, under her breath, "I doubt if you will either."

She thinks I don't hear that, but I do.

I try to figure out what the bad guys will do next. I'd bring in some new talent. In other words, I'd send in somebody who looked completely innocent. You know, like the mailman.

Amanda showed me how to work the cash register and the computer. I'm pretty good at that tech stuff, so I got hip right away to the whole smartphone thing. She let me handle two regular customers who came in together.

"This is my dad," she told the two guys. I could see Amanda squirm, like she wasn't too proud of me or somethin'. But those two guys hung in there with me while I screwed up their order three times.

"It's nice to see a father who gives a damn," one guy said. "Mine never did." He put his arm around Amanda and said, "You are such a good person, Amanda, I don't know *how* you do it."

Amanda just laughed, for some reason. Then she went to see the cops while I minded the store.

The whole time she was gone, I sat in a rocking chair by the front window with that baseball bat in my hands. For some reason, no one came in. I don't know why. She was gone about three hours.

I wondered why she was gone so long.

When she came back, Amanda leaned over and said, into my good ear, "I went to that address, Dad."

"You what? Holy Christ, that could be dangerous. You shoulda taken me with you."

"Sag your muscles, Dad. I was fine. The place is an old warehouse. Looks deserted. Windows covered with dirt. All boarded up. Weeds everywhere. Looks like it's been a hundred years since anyone went in there."

"What do you think?"

"Some kinda shell game," she said.

"Okay," I tell her. "Let me handle it."

"Not likely," she said.

"Hey, honey," I said, "I need a place to stay. I was kinda hopin' you'd...you know...invite me." I grinned at her, or at the place I thought she was.

"Hey, Dad, I'm over here."

"About that place to stay...."

"Oh, yeah. Sorry, Dad. My place is way-way-way too

small."

I checked into a motel down the street, half a block away, where I could see her place, if I used my binoculars.

The next morning I got up early and sat by the window, with a handgun in my lap, and watched her place until about noon.

Ah-ha, just as I expected, there came the mailman.

Nothing could be more innocent, right?

Maybe, but I saw that movie, years ago, where the postman is a killer. You know the one? The mailman comes in, dressed in his blue uniform and his regulation hat. He pulls a machine gun with a silencer on it. Rat-a-tat-tat. Kills *everyone*.

So I *knew* this dude was up to no good.

I hobbled out the door with my cane. And my gun.

It was hard gettin' down the stairs, with my foot botherin' me. I wasn't walkin' too good, but I needed to get there, so I jumped in my car and roared over there.

The mailman was already tryin' to get away. I intercepted him, though. Just lucky, I guess. Knocked him down with the fender of my car and tried to run over him, but he jumped up and ran down the street screamin' like a little girl. Such a coward for a tough guy.

I headed him off with my car and jumped out with my roscoe. That's what we used to call it back in the old days—a roscoe. I get him down in the street with my roscoe pressed against his forehead. Like in the movies. I yell, "Do ya feel lucky, punk?! Do ya?!"

Amanda comes runnin' down the street. "Dad! Dad! That's the mailman! Stop it! Stop it! Damn it! You old fool!"

That makes me sad. No one ever called me an old fool before.

While I'm tryin' to deal with her, the mailman grabs for my gun and we start to wrestle. Holy Moses, do we have a time, Amanda and me and the mailman rollin' around in the street.

A crowd gathers. These two guys, the ones I waited on, come runnin' up and dive into the tussle.

One guy grabs me and screams, "No! No! Stop that! Be

nice!" The other guy grabs the mailman and pulls him off me. Amanda is yellin', the mailman is gruntin'.

Down the block, I see three guys step out of a black Lincoln SUV. They are laughin' so hard they are bumpin' into each other and fallin' down, like the Three Stooges. I look closer and the tall one looks like the Mexican from the video.

The next day, there I was in the motel, laid up pretty good. Bumps and bruises and my leg really hurt. Amanda and the two guys brought me some chicken soup.

I am lyin' there in bed, and the three of them are standin' around. It's all very sad. I say, "And you let the 'mailman' get away?"

One of the guys says, "Sonny, I know you mean well."

The other one starts to speak and then thinks better of it. Amanda puts her arm around him, and he bursts into tears.

After they leave, I'm layin' there with my binoculars and feelin' guilty. I have not done much good so far—those three guys are still out there somewhere, and so is the "mailman." I wish I could be more help.

I see Amanda go into the shop and the two guys leave.

I think about what I'm gonna do. I don't want to disappoint Amanda again two days in a row, so I decide to lay off awhile. Give things a chance to cool down, ya know? And I'm really tired, for some reason. My whole leg is swollen.

So I close the drapes—you know how they are at these motels. You can close out the noonday sun and it's so dark you can't even see your dreams.

I go to sleep. Haven't slept much lately, so I'm out like last year's Christmas turkey.

Apparently, that's when the poop hits the fan.

I wake up. I hear what I think is Amanda screamin'. I look out the window and there are these same three guys carryin' Amanda out the front door of the shop. She's all tied up, kickin' and screamin', and they throw her in the back of the black Lincoln SUV.

I go runnin' out the door, hobblin', with my cane and my

bad leg, yellin', loud as I can, "Stop! Let my Amanda go!"

They go tearin' off, and I jump in my car, that big old Caddy.

Then I remember two things: One, I lost my handgun. Have no idea where it is. Two, I forgot to put gas in the car. That sucker only gets about nine miles to the gallon. But away I go, by God, no time to dither now.

The black SUV goes around a corner on two wheels, tires screechin' and traffic all around. The Mexican dude, Mr. Bolo, is drivin' too fast and he almost loses it.

I floor the Caddy and then I remember one more thing: I took all the hardware out of the trunk. It's all back in the motel, all those guns and hand grenades and tear-gas canisters. Never mind, I tell myself. I still got my trusty blowgun, which I left behind the seat on the floorboards.

As I'm drivin', I reach around the seat and down. Yeah, the blowgun is there—a long thin metal tube with cork mouthpiece and wooden handle—but now I remember, the darts and the poison are in the trunk.

The blowgun has a strap on it and the strap gets caught behind the seat, so I'm not payin' much attention to my drivin', and I'm goin' really fast, that Caddy with the big engine and all.

Suddenly, I look up to see loomin' in front of me a red and white postal truck. I jam on the brakes, but it's too late, and everything goes KA-BOOM! I hit that sucker like a ton of bricks, and it jumps a curb and knocks over a fire hydrant and WHOOSH, a geyser of water shoots sky-high. Water everywhere.

The postal truck driver gets out, and guess who it is? It's that same mailman from yesterday. He's got one arm in a sling and he's on crutches, limpin' and hobblin', all crippled up. Almost as bad as me.

He takes one look at me and his face turns red and he yells at me and waves one of his crutches in the air.

I slam the Caddy in reverse and hit the gas. My bumper hooks the mail truck and there I go, draggin' that mail truck down the street, the mailman hobblin' after us, screamin' and cursin' all the time.

I wrench the wheel back and forth two or three times and finally get loose from the mail truck and I floor it and roar off down the street.

Just then, the Caddy runs out of gas. It coughs and sputters and stops dead in the street. I find the darts and the poison canister in the trunk, inside their shoulder pouch, and there I am, blowgun in hand, trying to flag down a passing car.

A pretty blonde drives up in a red convertible and I wave my blowgun in the air and she looks scared and speeds off.

Time's a wastin', so I see a guy ride a BMX bicycle up to a burrito joint across the street and he gets off and just leaves it there.

I strap the blowgun over my shoulder and run for the bike. It's small, but I hop on. It's been a long time since I rode a bike, especially one this small, so I wobble along and a couple of young people, tattoos all over, come strollin' out of a Starbucks, lookin' down at their phones, and wham, I hit 'em smack on. Their coffee cups go flyin', and they are screamin' at me, but I got no time to waste, and I keep on a goin'.

Up ahead, I see that black Lincoln SUV stuck in traffic. I zoom between the cars and pretty soon I am almost there.

The light changes and the traffic breaks and they take off, but I am only two car lengths behind. A guy leans his head out the window and aims two fingers at me and pulls the "trigger."

Ha-ha-ha, I say and shoot him with my finger, too.

I almost catch up several times at stop lights but they pull ahead, and it's cat and mouse like that.

We get close to the Marina, and I remember the dead bodies on the beach. They must have used a boat. I peddle even harder. I'm in pretty good shape for an old geezer.

I don't see too well, so I almost follow the wrong SUV, which turns left, but then I hear Amanda scream and I see a tussle in the SUV up ahead and I see an arm wavin' out the window.

They pull away, but by this time we are in the Marina, in one of those loopend streets. I round a curve and see them, a hundred yards away in a parking lot, pullin' Amanda out of the SUV and draggin' her toward the docks.

I pedal like a fiend and get to the dock just as they are motoring away, in a green and white boat about thirty feet long with an inboard motor and a small cabin. It's flying a pirate flag, a Jolly Roger, a grinning skull with two crossed swords. I unsling the blowgun, pull out a dart, dip it into the poison and lift it to my lips.

It's a long shot, maybe sixty yards, but I take a deep breath and blow. The dart flies through the air. Just when I think it might hit Amanda, the dart drops into the water. The boat motors away, picking up speed toward the breakwater, about half a mile away.

Then I remember, we've got lakes in Arizona, and hell, I've been boating a couple times. I run to the docks, fast as I can, hobbling, and pick out a boat, about twenty feet long, with a huge outboard motor.

I jump in, and it has the keys in it. It cranks right up, and I see Amanda and the three guys, far away, headed toward the open sea.

I push that throttle all the way, full speed ahead. That big motor roars, the stern squats in the water, the bow lifts up, and I take off like a goosed duck.

Then I remember, I forgot to untie the stern line.

RIP-POW! The transom rips out, and the whole back end of the boat is left behind. The motor roars for a minute, back there clamped to a piece of wood, and then it coughs and sputters and goes down, glub-glub-glub. Steam rises from the water, and the motor and the transom sink out of sight.

I feel the boat settling under me.

As the boat sinks, the wreckage and I drift out into the main channel, and the current pulls us toward the sea. The wreckage slowly goes under, with me in it, until just the nose of the boat is sticking up, with me hanging on.

Guess what? I can't swim. Not a stroke.

Just then, luck. A life preserver pops up from the boat—one of those old-fashioned ones they called a Mae West, 'cause they look like big hooters. I grab it and try to put it on but I can't, flailin' around in the water like that. So I hold onto the boat with one hand and the Mae West with the other.

The boat sinks outta sight, and I am left with just the Mae West. I pass the breakwater and the current pulls me out to sea.

A few boats cruise by. I wave and yell and the people wave back, laughing, as though this is all some kind of joke.

I think I am done for, and Amanda is even worse off.

About that time, a Coast Guard boat comes along. About twenty-five feet long, red and black, two guys in dark blue uniforms. Life preservers, too, blood-red, like the boat.

I wave at them and they cut their engine and drift up next to me, upwind, so the breeze pushes them toward me. I am grateful for that. These guys know how to handle a boat.

"What the hell?" one of them says.

One grabs my arm, the other grabs my belt, and they hoist me into the boat. I tell 'em everything. The dead shopkeepers. The kidnapping. The race for the sea. Leavin' out my guns, a course.

I describe the bad guys' boat, and they radio for a chopper.

"They'll take you with 'em," he says.

The chopper comes and it hovers over us and they lower a basket and I climb into it and they hoist me up.

Inside the chopper, they put a headset on me, and I tell them about the kidnapping while we are zooming out over the ocean. We got two pilots, an engineer, and a rescue swimmer. Machine gun mounted by the door. Maybe .30 caliber.

In the distance, we see a boat runnin' fast.

"That's them," I say.

Soon we catch up to the boat, but it looks different somehow.

This boat is a different color. Blue and white. The bad guys' boat is green and white. This one has no flag, no Jolly Roger.

"Wait," I say, but just then the two guys on the boat come up with assault rifles, AK-47s, and start snipin' at us. I hear bullets zinging past the chopper.

"Engage," the pilot says, and they aim that machine gun out the door and BLAM, BLAM, BLAM. Spouts of water lead up to the boat and across it. The two guys dive into the water and their boat lists to one side and starts to sink.

"Drug dealers," the pilot says. He banks the chopper and we fly out over the sea. We pass several other boats. Finally, I see the green and white boat with the Jolly Roger flag flappin' in the breeze.

We do several slow circles over the boat and I see Amanda on deck with the three guys. She is wrapped ankles to armpits in chains, with an anchor the size of a suitcase attached to the chains.

She looks up and sees the chopper. So do the guys.

I get excited, seein' my daughter like that. I gotta do somethin', so I lean out the door, wavin' at her, tryin' to tell her it's gonna be all right. I lose my footing, and I fall. Holy crap, that is a long way down. I hit the water like a ton of bricks, get the wind knocked outta me, and I am underwater a long time. I feel someone grab me and pull me up to the surface. It's the rescue swimmer from the chopper.

He hands me the Mae West, and I hang onto that.

I see the guys on the boat with Amanda. One of the guys aims his rifle at us and Amanda bumps into him, knocking him overboard. Splash.

The other two guys on the boat start shooting at the chopper.

"They can't shoot back," the swimmer says. "They might hit your daughter."

Amanda looks up at the chopper and then looks at us in the water. I see her make a decision. She rolls over the side of the boat, chains and all. SPLASH. Down she goes.

"Wait here," the rescue swimmer says.

"I ain't goin' nowhere," I say.

He takes a deep breath and disappears under the water.

The chopper cuts loose with that machine gun, BLAM, BLAM, BLAM, and the bullets go THUD, THUD, THUD, and the two guys dive off as the boat starts to sink.

There I am, splashing around, wondering what the hell is happening to my daughter. I picture her sinking like a stone.

About that time a Coast Guard cutter shows up. It's white with a big red stripe, about a hundred feet long, and there are crew members along the rail aiming guns at the three guys in the water.

It seems to take forever.

Then the rescue swimmer pops up, and at first I think Amanda is gone. But then she pops up beside him, and there she is, my daughter, alive and coughing and spewing water into the air and yelling bloody murder.

"Son of a bitch!" she yells.

"Over here," I say. "Over here!"

"Hi, Dad," she says and smiles real big.

Boy, am I glad to see that.

Two weeks later, she holds a meeting in her store for the shop owners. Her lawyer, Kim Browne, gives a little speech. The upshot is, they all get their properties back, the two guys from the boat are going to jail for a very long time, and the tall Mexican is going to be deported. The man behind Day One Properties, Dick Wheeler, has disappeared. He's on the lam, probably outta the country.

Half a dozen of us walk down the block and around the corner to a fancy restaurant to celebrate. Amanda stands up and raises her glass. "To my dad. The old son of a bitch *is* good for something, after all." Everybody laughs. She adds, "I wouldn't be here without him."

It brings tears to my eyes.

They give her a bottle of champagne, and later she is carrying that bottle as we walk back toward the shop, me with my cane.

It's dark out, and it's foggy.

Up ahead, a shadow separates from the alley.

It's the tall Mexican, knife in his hand.

"I'll handle this," I say.

"That'll be the day," Amanda says.

The Mexican rushes at me with the knife. I sidestep and trip him with my cane. He falls and does a quick shoulder roll and comes up just as Amanda raises the champagne bottle high in the air.

THUD! She hits him square on top the head, and he drops like a sack of potatoes and doesn't move.

We call the cops, and they take him away.

Back at the shop, she says, "You know, Dad, I could use a partner in the business."

"Really?" I said.

"Really," she says.

I don't have any trouble hearing that.

The Writers' Conference
Jeffery Deaver

"Got a plum for you, Jim. A round and ripe plum."

"That right, Stan? The Bennett case? Tell me it's so."

Friday noon in the Santa Rosa Sheriff's Department, in beautiful and some said historic Ocean Shore, California.

Perched on a hill crowned by scrub oak, succulents and pine and dusted with fine sand, the Spanish-style ranch building dated to the '60s and indeed featured a view of both ocean and shore. That is, Chief of Detective's Stan Mellers's office did, where the two men now sat. Deputy Jim Handle's desk was on the other side of the structure and his scenery was parking lot, deer-trimmed shrubbery and, for occasional variation, deer.

"Aw, Jim. Again? You don't want that case. I keep telling you."

Handle settled his lanky frame into Mellers's chair. It was a beige scene, all around. The rattan chair, Handle's uniform, and his hair. Complexion would've been part of it too, if the detective's face and arms weren't so sun ruddy.

"You know what, Stan? I *do* want that case. Want it a lot."

"I'm sorry, Jim. But—"

"I know. I'm only on the force three years, not that long. But I've run homicides. Corpse to conviction."

"Gangbangers, using each other for target practice. Not *CSI* grade, Jim. Those're what you could call Hondas. The Bennett case's your Lexus. Or even higher ticket than that."

Handle wasn't sure Mellers should be making light of a twenty-five-year-old woman abused and murdered, her body weighted down in the bay. But he wanted onto the case bad, so he kept mum on the taste issue.

Mellers, too, shifted in his chair, also rattan but a swivel model. The chief was six four and outweighed Handle by sixty or more; the furniture protested.

Handle: "I've told you, I've read every psych book and forensic text on serial killers they've got in the county library and on the internet. Most of them, anyway. I—"

"Well, I know, Jim. I'm impressed. Really am. But, see, that's a problem. Sally Bennett was one victim. Solo. *Nada* serial."

"There was that other missing girl. A year ago."

"She run off. Everybody says so."

"But Sally," Jim persisted, "her death fits a profile. The pattern of the cuts, the sexual assault, the—"

"Jury's still out on both of them. Body was a mess and a half, y'know."

Sally had been in the ocean a week before she floated to the surface. The fact that her parents had something to bury and the SCSD had proof of a murder was close to a miracle. She might never have been found but for some sea creatures chewing on the ropes binding her to the concrete blocks sixty feet down.

Though, as Handle had told his boss, at least the cold water of the Pacific had had a preservative effect. Corpses dumped into the balmy Caribbean, for instance, were often reduced to an indistinct food group in a few days. This fact was from his homework. Jim Handle frequently thought: I truly intend to get my head around this serial killer thing. I'm going places.

"Just give me a *piece* of the case, Stan."

Mellers himself was running the homicide, as he did all important cases, but he could, and did, dole out portions of the investigation from time to time.

The chief, it seemed, was genuinely troubled he couldn't help out. "Staffing, and everything...Wilkins gone with that heart attack, the budget. The Squid Festival, the car race. I just don't have the manpower I'd like."

This was true. Everybody knew it.

Handle had debated asking their ultimate boss, Sheriff Joaquin Del Rio, if he could get onto the Bennett case. But

Mellers had run the Detective Division for twenty years, longer than Del Rio had been in office, and he was a good cop. Handle didn't have either the ground or enough bad judgment to go around Mellers.

Handle gave up on Bennett and asked, "Plum assignment, you were saying?"

"Yesiree, Jim. You're going to like this one."

"What is it?"

"A do at the convention center. And you, yes, you, my friend, get to head up security." As in most cities nowadays, the convention center and attached hotel in Ocean Shore was considered a potential terrorist target, and a Santa Rosa deputy was frequently assigned to meetings there, supplementing the center's security staff.

In reaction, Handle gave a tiny nod like the bobble of a bobble head dog on the dash of a smooth-riding car, a Caddie—or, okay, a *Lexus*—idling at a stoplight.

"Security."

"Don't look so hangdog, Jim. It'll be like a vacation. You won't have anything to do, but stroll around the air conditioned halls and sip soda and eat funnel cakes. The convention? It's a bunch of writers. How much trouble can they get themselves into?"

At two p.m. Jim Handle parked his squad car in the convention center lot and made his way through the hot Santa Anna wind toward the front door, over a path beside the half-mile mile gray-sand beach, presently being caressed by waves from a Pacific Ocean living up to its name, which it didn't always do.

As a detective, Handle usually dressed down—jeans, collared shirt and sports coat. But the rule for security detail was to be obvious. There was some debate about the wisdom of this requirement. One theory was that seeing a uniformed officer would discourage a terrorist before even starting an attack.

The other theory was that they'd know who to shoot first.

He found the director of the facility, a harried man

juggling the typical issues of events of this sort. He didn't have much time for Handle, which was fine with the detective. He'd been concerned the man might micromanage and that was one thing that didn't sit well with Detective James Handle.

Then there was a fast meeting with the security staff in their office and, after that, the detective wandered off to check out the writers' meeting.

The convention center in Ocean Shore could hold only twenty thousand souls, give or take, which meant the big conferences went elsewhere; there'd never been an AMA or high-tech get-together here. The organizers of a cosplay anime event gave it a shot but there were too many Sailor Moons and Pokémons per square foot and the county fire marshal had to close the gathering down.

But a bunch of authors? They didn't but fill up a quarter of the center. This was largely due, Jim Handle supposed, to the fact that the attendees were part of a specialized group: they were all *crime* writers.

Handle didn't read much. Didn't have the time, for one thing. He tended to put in long hours on the job and he had a family, which kept him plenty busy. Becky was taking a few years off her job as a nurse to raise their boy and girl, five and three, but Handle spelled her when he could. He also spent time out on his fishing boat, Pacific-worthy, pursuing his favorite hobby.

And when he did read, it was usually for his own edification—like the criminal profiling and forensic books he'd reminded his boss about, trying again to talk his way onto the Bennett homicide.

Still, even if he didn't know much about the world of fiction, he enjoyed walking around the writers' conference, looking at the exhibits and bookseller stalls and sticking his head in some of the sessions.

He got a kick out of the titles of some of them. "Killing Your Baby," for instance, which wasn't, as he thought about infanticide, but a panel of writers griping about how Hollywood had made bad movies of their good books. He was going to ask a question—"How many of you sent your

checks back in protest?"—but, being an outsider, decided not
to.

Another was "What *Fifty Shades of Grey* Can Teach
Mystery Writers About Sex Scenes."

He passed on that one.

Handle did, however, make a bee-line to "Serial Killing
Update," which presented the latest forensic and profiling
trends on the subject. The lecture was by a former FBI agent
from the Bureau's behavioral profiling division, and he was
well informed and a gifted speaker. Even though the
presentation was for lay persons, Handle learned a few things,
jotting notes on a pad provided by the organization hosting
the event.

Then back to work, cruising the hallways, looking for
potential terrorists or robbers, noting that the concession
stand was closed, no soda, no funnel cakes.

Around five p.m. Handle noticed many attendees
gravitating to a large room off the main corridor. Inside, he
saw people queuing in front of a lengthy table at which sat
three men and two women. He turned to the attractive
brunette he found himself standing beside and asked, "Excuse
me, you connected with the convention?"

"Me? I'm just attending. I'm a literary agent."

"Scouting out new talent?"

"And meeting some of my existing clients. Deborah
Tailor."

"Jim Handle."

"As in the composer?"

"As in the drawer pull."

She eyed the uniform. "Anything I should be concerned
about."

"Just routine."

"Sergeant Joe Friday said that just after the body
appeared."

He smiled. "What's going on here? This's a book signing?"

"That's right. This's the nominees' session. Those five'll all
been nominated for the Tombstone. See, on the table there?"

Handle looked where she was pointing and noted a black
ceramic gravestone mounted to a wooden base.

"That's an award? That people win?"

"The biggest writer's award of the year."

"It comes with any money?"

"Nope. All about prestige. But you win, you'll usually sell more books. Use it for publicity."

"When's the winner announced?"

"The banquet tomorrow night."

"And those folks, the nominees, I'm curious, they famous?"

"Not like movie stars or athletes. But they're pretty well known in our world."

Tailor identified them and gave a little bio of each.

Joe Devereux, early sixties, wrote a popular series of thrillers about a blind forensic detective in New York City. Seemed a little farfetched to Handle. But who was he to talk about credibility in entertainment? He and Becky enjoyed *Phineas and Ferb* with the kids.

"He's got the longest line. He the best writer?"

"No. But he plays the game the best."

"The game?"

"Sure," she said. "The game. All the same. Writing fiction, art, movies, business, Washington. And probably the cop world."

Handle understood. "You got that right."

The game....

Beside Devereux was middle-aged Jeffery Starr, a former journalist, best known for a historical thriller about a plot to murder one of Hitler's henchmen in 1930's Germany.

"Good book," Tailor said. "Sold well overseas but didn't last long on the charts here in America. I heard a story: When he was touring, he said, a bunch of readers in their teens and twenties would come up to him and asked him how he'd thought up that guy Hitler. 'Epic bad guy, man,' one had said. 'Better than Freddy and Jason.'"

"Not a joke?"

"Sadly, no."

Sharp hadn't written anything historical since.

The next author at the table was Joan Wilson, a sexy, but twitchy, thirty-something with a centipede tattoo on her arm.

She was a native Californian. She spent as much time blogging as she did writing fiction, sharing her vehemently anti-gluten, anti-fracking, anti-Keystone pipeline views with the world. In her novels she wrote a series about woman cop on the Central Coast, who was a kinesic—body language—expert. Rumors were she inundated popular TV crime show producers with emails and Tweets, accusing them of stealing her plot ideas. No lawsuits ensued, however.

Next to her was Frederick James, a dapper man of about forty-five in suit and tie. Tailor explained to Handle that he wrote a series of espionage thrillers about a British superspy. His most recent book nearly went to the top of the *Times* of London bestseller list, but it was beaten by Joe Devereux's latest by a mere eighty-seven copies.

The last author was Edith Billingsley. She was in her late sixties or early seventies, slim, with carefully coifed white hair. She wrote a popular series of murder mysteries featuring a quirky young woman who lived in Manhattan, named Ruth Ursula Nancy Evans.

"Her books're in the cozy category. No explicit sex or violence. Her bad guys swear by saying, 'Heavens!' And they don't kill people. They 'dispatch' them."

Handle nodded. "'Dispatch.' I like that. I should use it in a report. 'A witness stated he saw Hector Gomez, of the M-13 gang, *dispatch* Alonzo Sanchez at three-thirty a.m. on Alvarado Street by firing ten .40 caliber rounds into his head."

Tailor smiled, an expression that faded as she regarded the older woman author, signing a devoted fan's book. "Edith's been nominated for the Tombstone seven times. Never won it."

Handle, who hadn't been to a book signing before, was interested in the phenomenon. He noted that some authors shook fans' hands heartily, some ignored the outstretched palms. Larry Sharp was a shaker, but he used antibacterial spray after each grip, which seemed a bit insulting. Some authors agreed to have pictures taken with the fans, others didn't. Some signed all the books that fans bought, while others limited the signing to five or ten, or only the hardcover.

The authors were, as a rule, friendly but reserved, even cautious, bordering on paranoid. Joe Devereux, for instance, firmly explained to a fan—a young man wearing a narrow-brimmed fedora—that he wasn't able to accept the unpublished manuscript offered him.

Tailor told him, "He wants Joe to give him a blurb—you know, a recommendation—so he can show it to publisher. But you can run into legal troubles doing that."

Handle watched the fan grimace and walk off unhappily.

And he noted that Joan Wilson turned down an offer by a husband and wife—clearly people she'd never met—to "come on back to our trailer with us and doing some soakin' in the hot tub."

Frederick James declined to sign a fan's breasts with the same Sharpie he'd just used to inscribe her book. Handle noted that he could have written a whole paragraph on the offered cleavage before telling himself to look away.

"Kind of a three-ring circus," he observed.

"Oh, it can be," Tailor said.

"Who's gonna win that ugly award, you think?"

"Oh, I know who it is. The committee chairs a friend of mine. But I'm not allowed to tell."

"I'm a cop."

"And you have the uniform to prove it."

"We're good a keeping secrets."

She debated, he noted. Then in whisper: "It's Devereux."

"Which, I sense, you're not too happy with."

"Not really."

"All that game playing of his?"

"Aw, he's not so bad. Just, I was rooting for Billingsley. It was a close call, the votes. But Joe nosed her out by just one or two."

"There's always next year," Handle said. He shook her hand and wandered off to the book room to make a purchase or two then he headed out to his car for his dinner break.

He returned an hour later and made the rounds. He conferred with the guards and checked video cameras. No al Qaeda cells seemed poised to punish infidels. No armed robbers were planning heists. No stalkers lurked.

Which wasn't to say that there were no issues that required his attention. How much trouble could they get into? Well, a fair amount, it seemed, especially now that the bar was open.

A screaming domestic erupted when a wife learned that her author husband had carelessly said he'd liked the escort he'd had recently on tour. After Handle separated them, it turned out he wasn't referring to a hooker; 'escort' was the term used to describe a media representative hired by publishing companies to accompany authors to and from book signings.

One author was nabbed sneaking into the closed book room to rearrange the displays, putting his own books on top of his fellow authors'. An embarrassing, if noncriminal, offense.

The most violent occurrence: A fist fight broke out when one author criticized another for referring in his book to a Glock pistol's safety catch—the gun doesn't have such a lever. The same thing happened ten minutes later with two other writers, this argument being about the proper use of "magazine" versus "clip" to hold ammunition in rifles. Handle reflected that the more essential argument about Second Amendment rights to keep and bear arms was positively tame compared with the uncompromising passion about getting the facts concerning deadly weapons right.

But these incidents and a half-dozen others were simply grist for every law enforcer, and Handle took care of them with stern humor, minimal intervention and no handcuffs.

It was the murder that truly complicated his weekend.

When the front desk clerk got a call near midnight, unintelligible but desperate gasps, she assumed the guest in room 305 needed a Heimlich intervention.

Two young members of the bell staff sped to the room, ready to expel the offending olive or grape. They also brought along a defib, just in case.

Opening the door with a master key, they stopped fast, looking down, both thinking: Damn good thing that resuscitation procedures no longer recommended mouth to mouth.

The volume of effluence and vomit that had erupted from the guest was quite astonishing.

A fast check, though, clearly revealed that no life-saving techniques should be employed.

Joe Devereux wasn't coming back from the dead.

Jim Handle strode into the room, accompanied by the night manager.

"My God..." the skinny, suited man gasped. "All that, from choking?"

Handle regarded the rictus on the face, the fierce grip of the fists, the pale residue on the writer's face, the cocoon posture. "Didn't choke. He was poisoned."

"Oh. My. Well." the manager said this while staring at the food cart on which sat half of the hamburger that the celebrity writer—soon to be more even famous, if considerably less productive—had been enjoying while he died.

Handle leaned down and smelled the air near the victim's mouth. Stood again. He said to the manager, "You can relax. Wasn't your kitchen killed him. Pretty sure he was poisoned intentionally."

"*What?*" the manager blurted.

"I could smell—"

One of the bellboys blurted, "The scent of almond. I saw that in *NCIS-LA.* Cyanide, right?"

"Nope," Handle replied. "The smell's pear. Chloral hydrate. Probably concentrated, to cause death so fast."

"How'd you know that?" the manager wondered.

"Research. The Jonestown massacre? The crazy cult leader, Jim Jones, used chloral hydrate, mixed with some other stuff, in the Kool-Aid to kill his whole village. Now, this room's a crime scene. I want everybody out now."

Handle called the office to report the incident and asked CSU to get here pronto. He stationed a security guard outside Devereux's room to seal it and then did some preliminary investigation. He returned back at the same time as the Sheriff's Department crime scene unit.

"Hey, Jim. You drew this one, hmm?" Scott Shreve, the lead forensic tech, and the deputy were good friends.

"Didn't so much draw it," Handle explained, "as it fell into my lap." He gave a synopsis of what he'd learned so far, and he and Shreve walked through the room, the tech photographing the scene from all angles. Shreve then leaned down and sniffed at the bottle of single-malt scotch on the desk. "Yep, like you said, chloral hydrate. Somebody spiked his whisky. And there, under the table, that glass? Looked like he dropped it after taking a slug or two."

Handle was looking around. "And that gift bag, the sort for bottles."

"So the killer brings the bottle over and gives him the present. The perp drinks something else, something safe, and Devereux downs the fatal whisky."

"I'd guess, more likely, the killer left it on the door handle and knocked and skedaddled."

Shreve added, "Bet he didn't knock. Probably called from a lobby phone and told him he'd left a present. Anonymous. Pretended to be the bellman."

"Makes more sense," Handle said. "And look at that. A gift card. Under the bag."

Shreve pulled on blue gloves and opened the gold-colored card, which had the words "You're the Best!!!" printed on the front.

"Blank inside."

"Never make it easy for us, do they?" Handle said. He'd learned the value of handwriting analysis in solving crimes.

"Whatta you got?" said a firm voice behind them.

Handle turned and found himself looking at chief of detectives Stan Mellers.

"Stan."

"Jim, Scott. So?"

Handle noted two TV reporters, lurking near the security guard holding back the crowd to the left. Cameras were pointed their way.

In low voices, he and Shreve told Mellers about the author, the likely poison, delivered via anonymous gift.

Mellers asked, "What about motive? He ruffle any feathers? Put his you know what where he shouldn't?"

"Nothing yet, Stan. Jumping out."

Mellers looked up and down the corridor, the guests, most dressed, some in bathrobes. Word had spread fast and it was crowded. He sent guards to keep them away from the scene.

Handle and Mellers found themselves staring down at the body.

"A shame about this," Handle offered. "He was going to get that big award tomorrow."

"Award?"

"That the conference gives out. Best book of the year, something like that."

After a moment: "Read one of his books," the chief of detectives said. "Was okay. Had a big twist at the end. So. Let's get to work."

The next morning, Jim Handle was back on security detail, though he found himself with little to do except tell the hundreds of attendees who asked that he didn't know anything about the murder.

This was Cop 101 about being reticent. He really didn't know anything.

He was amused at the number of people who came up to him with theories. Wouldn't happen at an accountants' or engineers' convention. But most of these people made their living, or a part of it, at crime, so to speak. He nodded studiously and listened. But didn't jot a single note.

The hours dragged by. A pall had settled over the convention, thanks to the death, and Handle didn't need to play schoolmarm, like he had the day before, with petulant or argumentative writers. Everybody was on good behavior.

Afternoon turned to evening and he was pleased that the agent, Deborah Tailor, tracked him down and offered him a ticket for the banquet and award ceremony. Together, they headed into the cocktail reception, he still in his uniform, Tailor in a classy black number with an uneven hemline. Handle thought his wife would like it. The banquet hall lights shot a dozen colors off the sequins.

"Don't worry," she said.

"Wasn't. Why?"

"I'm not going to ask you about the case."

"Wouldn't have anything to tell you anyway." He was struck by the truth of his comment.

The lights dimmed, announcing dinner, and they found their seats.

"Not many people've gone home," she noted. "You'd think after the murder, nobody would want to stay."

"No, that'd seem suspicious."

"You think the killer's here?" her eyes danced around the room. His, too.

"Wouldn't be surprised."

She sipped a martini—Handle was having an on-duty iced tea—and asked, "You think it was a one-time murder? Or part of a serial killing thing?"

"Happens I've made a study of serial killing. This isn't one. That's a very specific, and rare, psychosis and Devereux's death doesn't fit the profile. Besides, poison's rarely a serial killer murder weapon; ruins the chance you can chow down on your victim....Oh, sorry, shouldn't've brought up cannibalism at dinner."

Tailor creased her brow. "Don't worry about my appetite. I haven't eaten rubber chicken at a writers' conference for ten years, and I'm not going to start now."

Handle laughed. They greeted the other attendees at the table. Everybody wanted to ask about the case, but nobody did. Handle sipped his tea and enjoyed the banter. Although Tailor had told him about the jealousy among the nominees, these folk—working class authors, midlist, he'd heard they were called—were amiable and easy going. Smart too.

The food was as inedible as Tailor had predicted, though Handle was hungry and ate every last morsel of the chicken impersonator, along with the potatoes and the star of the event—the key lime pie. After, came some speeches and then the honoring of a lifetime achievement winner, whose comments would be a cure for insomniacs around the world.

The awards ceremony went on as planned. It seemed that the by-laws, the director of the program explained to the audience, did not provide for posthumous awards, so it would go to the first runner up.

The male and female presenters strode onto the stage and read from a sheet of paper—a writer's conference teleprompter—while the pictures of the nominated authors and the jackets of their books flashed on a screen behind them.

Finally the woman presenter tore open the envelope, paused with suitable drama and said, "And this year's winner of the Tombstone is.... Edith Billingsley."

Everyone on their feet. Applause, cheers.

The elderly woman walked to the stage, a picture of elegance in her long, layered deep-blue gown.

Handle glanced at the other nominees. Larry Sharp, Joan Wilson and Frederick James all shared the identical expression: a goddamn-it-I-have-to-seem-happy smile bolted onto their faces.

When the applause died down Billingsley gripped the award in one hand and pulled the microphone down to her mouth—she was only a little over five feet or so.

"My Goodness," she began, breathless. "My goodness. I hardly know what to say...." She gazed at the ceramic award. Then set it on the podium. She pulled off her pink, glittery reading glasses and said, "Before I thank those who have helped me along the way in my career as a writer, I must first give voice to the thoughts that are on all our minds at the moment. The tragic loss of Joseph Devereux. I was thinking about his death and his contribution to our profession all day and I'd like to share with you some of my reflections."

She never got started, though. At that moment Chief of Detectives Stan Mellers stepped briskly from the wings, accompanied by a burly detective nicknamed the Hulk, and arrested Edith Billingsley for the murder of the man she was about to eulogize.

A half hour later, after the author had been booked at headquarters, Stan Mellers was back, holding a press conference in a meeting room off the front hall of the convention center.

There were many more reporters than before. Edith

Billingsley's arrest had been picked up by everybody from TMZ to CNN to the *New York Times*; YouTube benefited the most: Hundreds of smart phones had recorded the stage of honor being turned into a perp walk.

Viral, big time.

Mellers and his boss, county Sheriff Joaquin Del Rio, took to the podium. Del Rio was broad as a tree trunk, part Anglo, part Mexican with mahogany skin. He didn't say much on the job and he didn't say much now, leaving communication to his chief of detectives.

Handle wasn't on stage, which was fine with him. He wouldn't have anything to say anyway. He sat beside Deborah Tailor. The room was packed. Handle noted the fire department rule, set forth on a wall sign, limiting occupancy to fifty. There had to be twice as many inside.

Mellers looked over the cameras and the microphones and then the audience. He read from a prepared statement. "The Santa Rosa Sheriff's Department today arrested Edith Billingsley, a resident of Ridgefield, Connecticut, for the murder of Joseph Devereux. We believe she removed the seal on a bottle of whisky, added poison, replaced the seal and then left it in a gift bag hanging from Devereux's hotel room door. The whiskey was Glenmorangie, which Devereux has said was his favorite Scotch. The bottle and bag and a gift card contained traces of Ms. Billingsley's cosmetics and hand cream, as well as strands of her hair and fibers from her clothes."

Scott Shreve's team was really, really good.

"We also discovered prints matching her shoes in the stairwell near Mr. Devereux's room on the third floor. And a fingerprint of hers on the ground floor doorknob to that stairwell. Miss Billingsley's room was on the tenth floor, and it's extremely unlikely that a woman of her age would take the stairs to get her room, unless the elevators were broken, which they were not.

"Internal phone records show that late last night someone placed a call from the house phone by the tenth floor elevator to Mr. Devereux's room. The call lasted just one minute. It wasn't recorded but we're sure it was Ms. Billingsley calling to tell her victim of the present on his door.

"I should add that from reading through her novels we've learned that the accused is familiar with poisons and administering them, including the substance that has been determined to be the cause of the victim's death. Chloral hydrate."

"Stan," a man called from the back, "What was the motive?"

"We believe Mrs. Billingsley learned that she was the runner up to the prestigious Tombstone award, given by the writers' conference. She knew that if the intended recipient died before the ceremony, the honor would go to the next highest vote winner."

"Detective Mellers," one woman reporter called, "has she made a statement?

"She denies the charge and claims she was by herself at the time of the killing, walking on the beach, thinking up ideas for her next book. No witnesses saw her, though. We know she's lying."

It was then that Handle cocked his head with a frown.

"What is it, Jim?" Deborah Tailor asked, noting his expression.

"I'll be back in a few minutes." He rose, and left the room, pulling his mobile out of the holster, where it sat next to his Glock 17.

Fifteen minutes later, Deborah Tailor was growing bored with the press conference. She looked around. Jim Handle, whose wry humor and easy-going nature had been one of the high points of the conference so far, still had still not returned. She'd give it a few minutes more and then head up to the room.

Standing out in the hoard of reporters, a blonde in a fiery red dress and clashing yellow scarf, asked stridently, "Stan, you actually think winning an award, especially one that has no cash prize, could be a motive for murder?"

"Guess it was, Tiffany. Lookit what happened. We got a dead author.... These creative sorts. Big egos. Easy to get rubbed the wrong way."

Noting they were in the world of CNN speculation at this point, Tailor decided to leave and return to her room for a Kahlua and a streamed episode of *House of Cards*. She got as far as the door when two gunshots from inside the hotel, not far away, shook the walls and sent most of the attendees diving for cover.

Del Rio, Mellers and the Hulk went into *COPS* mode. They drew their black weapons and headed out the door.

Hot on their heels were the journalists, ditching caution and hoping against hope that the gunfire wasn't over and that they could, for once, live up to the name plastered on their vans and videocams, "Eyewitness."

Jim Handle stood in the corridor outside the door to room 110 in the hotel attached to the convention center. He'd used a chair to wedge the self-closing door open.

His grim face turned toward the lawmen, approaching.

"I've cleared the room," he called, noting their drawn guns. "Nobody else inside."

"What happened, Jim?" the sheriff asked. The three slipped their weapons back into the holsters.

"Take a look."

Everyone stepped inside. A table was turned over and a man about thirty years of age lay on his back. He had two gunshot wounds—one in the chest and one in the middle of his forehead. A hipster fedora, spattered with blood, rested near the shattered head.

Mellers asked, "Who is he?"

"An attendee. A fan. His name's Josh Logan. He's from Portland."

The Hulk grunted, as if the man's city of origin explained the carnage. Handle himself thought Oregon was a pretty nice place. He'd gone up there on a fishing trip more than a few times.

"What's the story?" Sheriff Del Rio was looking around the room, squinting, trying to figure it out.

When Handle hesitated, Mellers said, "Well, Jim? Out

with it."

Another pause. Then: "Fact is, Stan, I'm sorry, but I had a bit of a problem with your case against Mrs. Billingsley."

"Problem?"

"I did."

"Go on, Jim," Del Rio said.

"Just didn't sit right."

"What're you talking about," Mellers snapped. "The evidence's all there. Hair, fingerprint, fibers, shoe print."

"He planted 'em." A nod at the body.

"But the print," Mellers said testily. "How could he plant that?"

Handle grimaced. "No, he didn't. But that was on the door that all the attendees used to walk upstairs to the book sales room, if they didn't want to wait for the elevators. Which sure take their time here."

Nodding, Del Rio asked, "He snuck into her room to steal the evidence. How?"

"Here." Handle used a tissue to lift a hotel room key card from the table. It was completely blank, unlike the ones issued to guests, which bore the hotel's logo. "Dollars to donuts, it's a master key. Stole it from the security office. There's one missing. I asked." Because there were guards nearby, he added in a whisper. "They're not the most buttoned-up folk in the world."

Mellers remained defiant: "But the poison? Chloral hydrate. It was in her books. She knows what it does. How to administer it."

"Which tells us," the sheriff snapped, "she *wouldn't* use it as a murder weapons. Too obvious. But somebody who wanted to frame her might. Jim, assuming you're right, how'd this boy come by it?"

"I talked to Narcotics. You can buy chloral hydrate on the street; it's not too strong, it'll give you a high. You concentrate it, you've got a deadly poison."

Handle pointed to a hotplate and a small pan on the floor in the closet. A whitish residue crusted the sides and bottom.

"I...uh," Mellers said and then stopped trying.

The Sheriff asked Handle, "Why'd you suspect him, Jim?"

He didn't look Mellers's way as he said, "I haven't been much included in the case, so it was a surprise when I heard Miss Billingsley didn't have an alibi because she was walking on the beach at the time the poison was delivered. I called our tech people and they got in touch with her cell phone provider. She didn't make any calls or sends texts around then, but her GPS showed she *was* on the beach.

"Sure, it was possible she gave the phone to somebody to carry, to make it look like she was on the beach. But that wasn't reason to give up looking for another suspect. I remembered yesterday this fan tried to give Devereux a manuscript. He got mad when he said no. I asked around and got his name."

"That's him?" Del Rio asked. Another glance at the body.

"Right. I came up here to talk to him. He didn't want to let me in but I told him I'd get a warrant and that'd look worse for him. He agreed finally, but closed the door—like he was unhooking the chain—but he didn't do it right away and I heard some noises inside. Like he was hiding something. When he let me in, first thing I did was open the closet door and saw the pan and hotplate and a copy of Mrs. Billingsley's book. And her hairbrush, too....He grabbed that." Handle gestured toward a steak knife, lying on the floor beside his hand. "He came for me." A shrug. "He wouldn't stop. I didn't have much choice, Sheriff."

"It's all right, Jim. You know the rules. Have to suspend you with pay for a couple days, while there's an inquest. It'll go fine."

"Sure, Sheriff."

Del Rio looked outside and noted that the reporters were hovering like frenzied baitfish. He said in a low voice, "You get to work on your statement now, Jim." His eyes swiveled to Stan Mellers, who was looking everywhere but back at his boss. "And Stan, you and me, we need to talk."

At eleven p.m., Jim Handle was sitting outside the convention center on a bench facing the beach. The tide was coming in gracefully, the ocean still friendly.

Handle had given up smoking years ago but he felt like a Marlboro at the moment. It had been that sort of day.

His phone dinged with a text. It was from Becky.

CONGRATS!!!!!!! Luv U!!!

She was generally a pretty laid-back person but she could go hog-wild when she texted, her joy or anger given voice through punctuation and case.

There was a reason for her enthusiasm at the moment. Her text was in response to one that he'd sent a few minutes ago. Handle had shared the subject of his most recent conversation with Sheriff Del Rio. Starting tomorrow, Jim Handle would be the new chief of the Detective Division of the Santa Rosa Sheriff's Department. He would also be taking charge of the Susan Bennett murder case. His salary wouldn't puff up very much, but that didn't matter. Money never did, when you were doing what you loved, what you were meant to do.

Good news all around.

Everything going as he planned.

So sorry, Stan, he thought to his former boss. You just weren't cut out for the game.

At least not playing against me.

Handle nearly—but not quite—felt guilty setting Mellers up to arrest poor Edith Billingsley in front of both the audience and the carnivorous media. He thought back over the past twenty-four hours. He'd come up with an improvised but workable plot.

He learned all about the writers' conference and the people involved—the manuscript-toting fan Josh Logan, the jealous nominee authors, how the judging for the Tombstone worked and who the winner and the runner-up were. Then he planned out the next steps.

On his dinner break last night he'd bought and read Billingsley's novel to find a suitable means of murdering Devereux, one she'd be familiar with.

Ah, perfect, chloral hydrate.

Handle had stopped in the barrio and scored some from a gangbanger, then reduced it down to lethal strength and added it to the bottle of Glenmorangie scotch—Devereux's favorite. He'd returned to the convention center to steal a master key from the laughably inept security staff. Then broke into Billingsley's room to pick up some physical evidence—hairs, cosmetics, a pair of her shoes—to plant in and on the gift bag and the whisky bottle.

Then, he'd left the bottle dangling from the author's door, taken the elevator to Billingsley's floor and called Devereux, saying he was the bell captain and had left a gift from the hotel on his door.

Next, one dead author.

Then, with a little guidance from Handle, even Stan Mellers could conclude Miss Billingsley was the culprit.

As soon as the chief of detectives announced the arrest, Handle went to Josh Logan's room, shot him, pressed a steak knife into his hand for the fingerprints and planted the hotplate and pan and the rest of the evidence.

Success! The chief of detectives was gone. Jim Handle had his job.

And, most important, he was at last safe.

Now his eyes took in the scene before him tonight: the cool yellow moon's fluttery reflection in the Pacific's surface. Ah, so beautiful.

Just like the night about a month ago, that moon nearly full, as well. The ocean, close to this calm.

A perfect night.

Handle recalled kneeling in the stern of his twenty-foot fishing boat.

Seeing that delicate moonlight on the teak deck.

On his bare arms.

On the blade of the knife he gripped.

On Sally Bennett's naked, white body, so smooth, so pure. She'd been bound hand and foot, duct tape. Thrashing in terror, but not going anywhere.

Handle had admired the light on her flesh for a few minutes more. Then he got to work. With her jaws taped shut, like Handle did with all his victims, Sally couldn't muster any significant volume of screaming. This method of taping was one of many facts he'd learned from all his research into serial killers—a subject he studied so diligently not to catch predators but to avoid being caught.

When this particular diversion was your hobby, you had to be just as informed as those who would pursue you.

Evading detection was also why he'd married Becky. The profile of serial killers is that they are loners, rarely with spouses. So he'd found somebody pleasant enough to seem a suitable mate, insecure enough not to ask too many questions about his whereabouts when he took his "fishing trips" and eager to have kids (being a father pushes you further into the "no" column when cops analyze serial suspects).

And if he wasn't much aroused by her, that was no problem. Every few months he'd spend a day or two with a victim like Sally Bennett, and that would satisfy the great need within him.

Then had come the close call—the inconsiderate school of fish gnawing through Sally's rope, her body floating heavenward. Handle had been careful, but having the woman's body was a terrible risk. He'd tried to get onto the case to destroy evidence and misdirect the leads, but Mellers wouldn't cooperate.

So Handle needed to destroy his career and replace him.

Thank God the writers' conference had come to town. It offered everything he needed.

"Detective?" a woman's voice cut through the night.

It took all of Handle's willpower not to jump. He turned slowly. His hand strayed to his Glock.

Deborah Tailor walked slowly down the street-lamp covered sidewalk. She carried her shoes. She would've been walking on the beach.

"Hi," he said, relaxing.

"Join you?"

"Sure."

"Nice tonight. The heat broke."

"Think the Santa Annas're gone for the year. And no wildfires. We were lucky. So. All these writers' conferences as exciting as this one?"

She laughed. "Usually it's mostly passive aggressive behavior we see. Not aggressive aggressive."

Handle noted her quick eyes, looking him over. She was

sharp, observant. He hoped there wasn't going to be a problem

"Got a question for you," she said after a moment.

"What'd that be?"

She asked, "You ever write anything?"

"Write anything? Police reports is about all."

Tailor said, "I heard how you figured out Edith wasn't the killer. And how you tracked down the real one."

"All in a day's job."

"Interesting you mention that. It's exactly what I'm thinking of."

"How's that?"

"Would you be interested in writing a series of first-person crime novels with somebody like you as the protagonist?"

"You're joking."

"Nope. Not at all. You've got a voice."

"Voice?"

"I don't mean speaking voice. I mean thinking voice. A personality voice. What about it?"

Handle laughed. "Oh, I don't know."

Though he was thinking: One of the aspects of serial killers—that research again, all those books—is that they avoid activities in which they're public personalities. If he were to become a published author, that'd tamp suspicion down a bit further, after he went on his next fishing trip, which he was already looking forward to.

Still, he had to be realistic. "I've got my college degree, but, fact is, I don't know much about style and grammar and all that. English wasn't my strong suit."

"You'd have copyeditors and proofreaders to handle that. The only thing they can't help you with is plots." Her eyes scanned his face once more. "But I have a feeling you'd be good at plotting, Detective Handle."

He considered this a moment, then said, "You know, I think I would, too."

"We have a deal?"

And Jim Handle firmly shook her outstretched hand.

ABOUT THE CONTRIBUTORS

Patricia Abbott is the author of the ebook collections MONKEY JUSTICE, and HOME INVASION. CONCRETE ANGEL will appear summer 2015 with Polis Books. @pattinaseabbott | pattinase.blogspot.com

Al Abramson is a man of few words; unfortunately you'll find them in this anthology. When he isn't abusing literature, he volunteers at Bouchercons.

Roger Angle lives in greater Los Angeles, where he writes novels and short fiction about criminals, liars, con-men, and cheaters. You know, old friends. rogerangle.com

Anthony Award nominee **Craig Faustus Buck** is an L.A.-based author/screenwriter. His noir novella PSYCHO LOGIC is at Bookxy.com and his novel, GO DOWN HARD, will be published by Brash Books in 2015. craigfaustusbuck.com | @CFBuck

A denizen of Oregon, **Bill Cameron** writes the Portland-based Skin Kadash mysteries, including the Spotted Owl Award winning COUNTY LINE. bill-cameron.com | @bcmystery

Award-winning author **Dana Cameron** writes crime fiction and urban fantasy. The third Fangborn novel, HELLBENDER, will be published by 47North in 2015. danacameron.com

Prize-winning short-story writer **Judith Cutler** has written forty novels, most featuring feisty female protagonists. Her work has been broadcast and widely anthologized. http://judithcutler.com/

Ray Daniel is the award-winning author of TERMINATED. Born in Boston, Ray graduated with honors from the UMass in computer engineering with a minor in English. raydanielmystery.com

A former journalist, folksinger and attorney, **Jeffery Deaver** is an international number-one bestselling author. His books are sold in 150 countries and translated into twenty-five languages. He's the author of thirty-five novels, three collections of short stories and a nonfiction law book, and the lyricist of a country-western album. jefferydeaver.com

Phillip DePoy author of the Flap Tucker mysteries, Fever Devilin novels, and upcoming Christopher Marlowe series, also won the Best Play EDGAR for EASY. phillipdepoy.com

Sharon Fiffer is the author of the Jane Wheel mysteries published by Minotaur and co-editor of three anthologies of literary memoirs, HOME, FAMILY and BODY. sharonfiffer.com | @janewheel

Delaney Green is the author of JEM, A GIRL OF LONDON. She lives under the Polar Vortex with four cats, one dog, and snow. delaneygreenwriter.com

Eldon Hughes lives in Southern Illinois with his wife and a menagerie of four legged freeloaders. Find more at ifoundaknife.com, and strange musings @williebee.

Tanis Mallow wrangles her dark and twisted imagination into short fiction found around the web or at Noir@theBar Toronto. Novels are in the works. facebook.com/tanismallow | @TanisMallow

Edward Marston. Prolific author of plays, short stories, historical mysteries, including Domesday books, Nicholas Bracewell series and Railway Detective mysteries set in Victorian England. edwardmarston.com

Krista Nave is a college-bound student. This is her first published story. She prefers fantasy and the supernatural, but sometimes surprises herself with a murder mystery.

Gigi Pandian is the *USA Today* bestselling author of ARTIFACT, PIRATE VISHNU, and THE ACCIDENTAL ALCHEMIST. She loves writing locked room mystery short stories. gigipandian.com

OTHER TITLES FROM DOWN AND OUT BOOKS

See www.DownAndOutBooks.com for complete list

By William Hastings (editor)
Stray Dogs: Writing from the Other
America (*)

By Matt Hilton
No Going Back (*)
Rules of Honor (*)
The Lawless Kind (*)

By Terry Holland
An Ice Cold Paradise
Chicago Shiver

By Darrel James,
Linda O. Johnston
& Tammy Kaehler (editors)
Last Exit to Murder

By David Housewright
& Renée Valois
The Devil and the Diva

By David Housewright
Finders Keepers
Full House

By Jon Jordan
Interrogations

By Jon & Ruth Jordan (editors)
Murder and Mayhem in Muskego

By Bill Moody
Czechmate
The Man in Red Square
Solo Hand (*)
The Death of a Tenor Man (*)
The Sound of the Trumpet (*)
Bird Lives! (*)

By Gary Phillips
The Perpetrators
Scoundrels (Editor)
Treacherous (*)

By Gary Phillips, Tony Chavira
& Manoel Maglhaes
Beat L.A. (Graphic Novel)

By Robert J. Randisi
Upon My Soul
Souls of the Dead (*)
Envy the Dead (*)

By Lono Waiwaiole
Wiley's Lament
Wiley's Shuffle
Wiley's Refrain
Dark Paradise

By Vincent Zandri
Moonlight Weeps (*)

(*)—Coming Soon

Made in the USA
San Bernardino, CA
19 October 2014